For the Love of Cooking

Kat Neil

LOWELL STREET
PUBLISHING, LLC

*This book is dedicated to those who carry a
burning passion in their hearts and have the courage to
chase it with unwavering love and determination.*

Author's Note

If you're like me, you enjoy a good meal. I also enjoy preparing comfort foods for my family. This story is a tribute to the art of cooking. Cooking is a labor of love and I love my family. I hope you enjoy the characters and their passion leaps right off the page.

This book contains sensitive topics such as a brief discussion of child death, emotions surrounding a hard breakup, mention of previous drug abuse, and challenges around parent/child relationships. There are also steamy explicit intimate scenes. Please read with care and prioritize your well-being.

Prologue

Aubrey

Sweat beaded on Aubrey's forehead as the pressure mounted. Each second grew heavier than the last. This dish had to be perfect. Her impeccable record was on the line. For the last month, Benson had trailed her in final marks. She couldn't let him win. Not this time. Not ever.

Aubrey dipped her spoon into the blueberry compote. It was flawless. Pastry was her strength. She poured the batter into the muffin pan and swirled in the compote. Her blueberry streusel muffin had to secure her top rank for the week. She glanced up, catching sight of Benson meticulously crafting his chocolate souffle. The intensity in his eyes and the precision of his movements were mesmerizing, almost as if the kitchen outside his bowl and whisk didn't exist. His relentless focus was nothing short of infuriating, like a laser beam that refused to waver, even when it made her want to scream.

"Focus, Aubrey," she whispered to herself. "Oh." Forgetting the most important ingredient for her streusel, she ran to the pantry to grab it, walking right into Benson.

"Hey, girl. Watch where you're going. I know you want to get close, but this isn't the time," he said, giving her a smirk, then a wink.

"Trust me, if I wanted to get close, you'd know it. Now, how about you watch where you're going? I have an assignment to outscore you on, again. So try to keep up," Aubrey barked back.

"Chefs, you have forty-five minutes," the head chef reminded his students.

Before she pulled her pastry from the oven to top it with streusel, Aubrey had to mix the items together. In a haste, she grabbed her ingredient to replace what she ran out of and jogged back to her station. She quickly mixed flour, brown sugar, sugar, salt and butter, topped the muffins and shoved them back into the oven.

With seconds to spare, Aubrey dressed her plate with the muffins and used a clean cloth to wipe the blueberry stained edges.

"Time!" the head chef yelled, just as Aubrey held up her hands.

Slightly out of breath, Aubrey looked at Benson's station, only to be met with the sight of a perfect chocolate souffle. It looked like the happy ending of a fairytale. Face darkening at his pristine dessert, she glared at him and found Benson staring at her. Their eyes shot daggers as they awaited judging.

The head chef and two pastry instructors approached Benson's station. Three sets of eyes narrowed in concentration as they examined his souffle. It gleamed under the light. With a gentle tap of the spoon, one chef carefully broke through the exterior, releasing the rich, velvety aroma of melted chocolate. They all then scooped up a spoonful. Aubrey noticed Benson's eyes closing. Why couldn't he witness the horror in their faces when they tasted his dessert? It was terrible. Pastry had not been his strength.

Instead of a look of distaste, the chefs exchanged quiet nods, evaluating his technique and the taste of the souffle.

"Perfect," the female chef muttered, kissing her fingertips. A chef's kiss? Was his souffle that good? All three of them turned to commemorate their marks. Nodding in unison, they moved to Aubrey's station. They gathered around her blueberry muffin topped with streusel, visually inspecting their appearance. One chef slowly broke a muffin open, her eyes scanning the crumbs for texture.

The pastry chef took a bite, and her expression immediately shifted. Her eyes narrowed, and she paused, taking another slow chew. "The muffin itself is light and tender, but the streusel..." she trailed off, raising an eyebrow. "It's too salty."

"I see what you're going for here. A savory, sweet twist," the other chef mused, "but the saltiness doesn't harmonize. Is it trying to take the spotlight from the muffin?"

Was Aubrey supposed to answer that? She didn't understand what was happening. All of her pastries had been perfect before today. The chefs marked their score cards and moved to the next station. She scanned her station in a panic for the betraying ingredient. Her eyes locked onto the container of salt—*not* sugar. Her heart skipped a beat as she realized her mistake. The dish she worked so hard on was about to take a very salty turn. And so were her marks.

"Benson," the head chef announced. "Your chocolate souffle was absolute perfection. You earn top marks."

Everyone erupted in applause, congratulating him.

Benson stood gloating, soaking in the praise, then took a bow. Who does that?

Aubrey dumped her muffins in the trash and began cleaning her station. She felt Benson's presence. The clean, citrusy scent of him drifted over, sharp and refreshing, making her pulse quicken despite herself.

Arms crossed across her chest, she turned to face him. "What do you want?"

Benson mirrored her, his arms crossed his chest. "I think you want to congratulate me, right?"

Laughing, Aubrey replied, "Oh, is that what you think? I was actually going to ask you if you tripped and fell into success."

"Don't be a sore loser. It's not my fault the better chef just happens to be me."

Aubrey glared up at Benson. "Oh, I don't think I'm better than you. I know it."

Benson stepped closer and knelt, placing his lips close to her ear. Then he whispered, his warm breath sending a shiver down her spine, "Looks like salt was your downfall today. Maybe next time, you'll remember sweetness wins, sugar."

Chapter 1

Aubrey

Clad in her favorite black chef's coat, hair in a neat tight bun, eyes staring at the speckled carpet, Aubrey inhaled a deep breath before pushing the elevator down button. The pinging sound alerted her of the elevator's arrival to her floor. The doors opened and two men greeted her, adorning crisp, white chef's coats, their names embroidered on their lapels. She nodded at the gentlemen and flashed a brief smile, then stood, watching the door shut. The elevator shook as it descended to the next floor. A pink haired woman, dressed in a pale pink chef's coat, entered the cabin.

"Hi, y'all. Y'all in the competition?"

No one said a word. Everyone just nodded their heads in unison. When the elevator door opened, the cheerful woman stepped out first. "Good luck!"

"Good luck to you." Aubrey didn't want to be rude.

Aubrey moved smoothly with the crowd, slipping through clusters of people around the competition area. The expansive room was a bustling, state-of-the-art kitchen as large as a football field. Long stainless steel workstations covered the expansive floor. Each chef's space was equipped with lustrous appliances, varying sizes of cutting boards, and neatly arranged utensils. Bright lights illuminated the entire room, casting a professional sheen over every surface. Chefs scuffled around, trying to locate their assigned posts. Massive screens dotted the room, each broadcasting a live feed that showed crew members darting around, carefully adding last-minute touches to each station. The close-up shots highlighted gloved hands arranging garnishes, wiping surfaces spotless, and making sure every detail was camera ready.

"This is pretty amazing, huh?" a tall, thin, gray-haired man asked as he and Aubrey walked toward the check-in table.

Cameras hung suspended from the ceiling like watchful eyes, while at least five men moved through the crowd, each balancing a hefty camera on their shoulder. The lenses glinted under the overhead lights, capturing every angle of the competition preparation with relentless focus. An immediate rush of butterflies fluttered wildly in Aubrey's stomach. "Is this competition being televised, live?"

The chef's brows shot up, eyes widening slightly as he looked at her. "You didn't know we're going to be on live TV?"

Aubrey pursed her lips together, frowning, but caught herself. She struggled to mask her surprise, keeping her expression neutral as her mind raced. She replied, "No. But you're right. This is pretty amazing." The words barely made it past her lips, soft and hesitant.

Recording the competition for a later broadcast was a logical choice, but live? A wave of fear washed over Aubrey. Her parents watched the network. They would see her. They would know she was in San Francisco and not at the local beach resort, attending a chefs convention. Pushing the images of her parents aside, she forced her mind to settle on the task in front of her.

The vastness of it all unfolded before her, each detail sharper than the last. Aubrey's senses swam with the energy around her. The sheer size of the space and the movement of everyone reminded her of a scene from *Ratatouille*. The crew worked in harmony among the chaos. Hands shaking, the surrounding air thickened. Her chest tightened. The pressure was mounting, each passing minute amplifying the weight of expectations ahead.

"Take a deep breath, Aubrey," she whispered. This competition could be life-changing. Winning, or even just standing out, could launch her career into another sphere. Years of her parents' doubt and caution they'd drilled into her mind could evaporate. She could take her next step, independent of Tara and Bill Carroll. This was her moment to forge ahead, free from the chains of their well-meaning but stifling apprehensions. The contemplation of being free from confinement was enough to bring her calm.

Aubrey's heart drummed like a rapid pulse. Competing for the big prize in front of a live viewing audience intensified her nervousness. The professional chefs competing were cooking in timed rounds. Each round would be judged by a panel of culinary superstar food critics and chefs. She hadn't cooked under this kind of pressure since culinary school. Her culinary skills and creativity needed to shine brighter than ever before. Being eliminated was not an option.

Passing the bustling crowd and the excitement that buzzed around her, Aubrey headed to the check-in table, its bright banner marking the start of her journey.

"Hello. What's your name?" the woman asked, pen in one hand, the stapled list resting on the table in front of her.

"Aubrey. Aubrey Carroll." Her name slipped out as though it were whispered by a child.

"I see your name here, Ms. Carroll. You'll be here." The woman circled her station on the map. "Here's your lanyard with your name tag. Please keep this on at all times. And here are the instructions for each cooking round. Good luck!"

"Thank you!" Aubrey gave the woman a warm smile and stepped aside.

She slowly walked over to an empty bench and began flipping through her packet. Aubrey was in section C, row two, station four. Her assigned space was in the middle of the room, a good place to be. She walked toward her section and turned down her aisle, focusing on the numbers placed at the corner of the rectangular tables. Aubrey passed table one, table two, table three, and then stood in front of table four. She tucked her tote bag under the station and began exploring the pots, pans, utensils, and seasonings placed for her use. Just as Aubrey categorized her supplies, she sensed someone standing next to her. The invigorating and fresh, crisp blend of citrus notes of his cologne tickled her nostrils. She recognized that scent. Heat rose to her cheeks, and her eyebrows drew together, forming the beginning of a frown. Her lips grew tight, recognizing it was him.

Standing directly next to her, he said, "Hey, sugar! Long time no see."

Chapter 2

Aubrey

"What the hell are you doing here?" Aubrey's blood boiled just at the sight of Benson Carter. His calling her sugar added to her fury. His tag for her was not endearing. It was a smug reminder of her past mistake she'd rather forget.

"Oh, I could ask you the same thing, but let's be real—we both know why we're here." His beaming smile grated on her nerves.

"Please tell me you're not competing *here*." Aubrey directed her index finger to the empty station next to hers.

"You've always been the brainiac of the bunch. Yes, I'm in this competition." Benson crossed his sculpted arms across his wide chest and glared down at her.

"I beat you before, and just for fun, I'll do it again," Aubrey snarled.

From the very first day of culinary school, they'd been rivals. Their disdain was immediate, sparking like oil on a hot pan. If her memory was correct, he was an excellent chef. But she was competitive. As one of the few women in her cohort in culinary school, she had a fierce drive to prove herself. Benson made it clear he too was ambitious and had a desire to outdo her. She learned to be blunt and critical of his food, and he bit right back with sharp criticism—words dripping with contempt.

"May the best man win," Benson breathed, a semblance of laughter.

"Oh, don't you worry. I'm sure you will have a front-row seat to my victory as the *best chef*." Aubrey spun her body to focus on getting ready for the first round.

The sound of someone tapping on a microphone caught the attention of everyone in the room.

"Good morning, chefs. The Recipe to Table Network is proud to sponsor this inaugural Chef Supreme competition. We'll bring you back in seven minutes to explain the first round. So get ready, chefs. And remember, we're going live."

Aubrey closed her eyes at the reminder the contest was live. After one deep breath, she faced Benson. He looked different—more refined and mature. His tightly trimmed mustache and beard suited him, and his tall physique had grown even more defined since culinary school. Much as she hated to admit it, he looked undeniably good.

She didn't want to invite any bad karma by getting into an argument with her nemesis. "I don't have time to argue. I have a competition to win. Good luck." With that, she turned to face her work area, hands gripping the edge of her station table, mentally preparing to get to work.

"Aww, you wished me luck. How precious. You're just a little ray of sunshine today, aren't you?" Benson snickered under his breath.

"Whatever." Aubrey truly despised him. She didn't want to engage with the man beside her anymore. She could hardly believe her luck. Of all places for him to be assigned, he ends up right next to her, a twist of fate that felt both serendipitous and torturous. What was he doing here? The last she heard, he was in New York, killing the restaurant game.

The announcer tapped on the microphone, then spoke. "Chefs. Get ready. We go live in one minute."

Aubrey kept her gaze straight ahead. She stared in horror as the cameras swept across the room, zooming in on each chef's face and capturing every flicker of her nerves. Maybe her parents would miss her face plastered on the television screen. She wouldn't be able to explain herself. Bill and Tory thrived on knowing every detail about her whereabouts. Her traveling to San Francisco would trigger concerns about potential dangers, like an accident or forced illness. She took a deep breath in, steadying herself, and let it out slowly, pushing thoughts of her parents aside, as she zeroed in on the competition. Regaining her composure, she was ready, her head now in the game.

"And we're live," the director announced.

"Hello. Welcome to our first Chef Supreme competition. My name is Jonathon Sneed, and I'm your host. The chefs competing today are all professionals. They've been vetted, and we believe top talent is among us. However, there is only one Chef Supreme. It's time to prove who has what it takes to rise above the rest. Over the next rounds of cooking, our competitors will face a series of intense challenges that will test their creativity, skills, and composure under pressure. Each dish they create could bring them one step closer to victory or send them home. So chefs, sharpen those knives, and let's talk about the first round."

Aubrey looked down at her feet, her well-worn cooking clogs grounded against the stained concrete floor. The dark gray with scattered red specks reminded her of embers in charcoal—a flicker of the fire she felt inside, ready to ignite for the competition.

"This first round is one you'll be most comfortable in competing in. However, it's the round that will reduce the fifty of you down to twenty-five. You have forty minutes to make your best dish. It can be an appetizer, a side dish, an entrée, or dessert. Whatever you make, it better be your very best. Twenty-five of you will be eliminated after this round. Now, at the end of each row, stations are stocked with top ingredients. You should find everything you need for this round. I hope you know what you are making because your time starts… now!"

Aubrey rushed to the end of the aisle to grab flour, granny smith apples, and the other ingredients she needed for her fried apple pies. Crispy apple turnovers, is what she would officially call her first plate. Could she make them in what was now less than forty minutes? It was ambitious, but she had to try. As she turned to go back to her station, Benson collided with her, rattling everything in her hands. Thank goodness nothing fell. If looks could kill, Benson would've dropped on the spot from Aubrey's deadly glare.

"Be sure to add sugar, not salt," Benson commented as he dropped his ingredients onto his station.

Aubrey had no time to give his comment any attention and was certainly not going to look in his direction. She hadn't forgotten the sugar. She was locked in.

Within a few minutes, her dough was ready to be rolled out. As she chopped apples, the camera moved past her row, panning in on her technique she used with her knife.

Aubrey separated the dough into small balls, setting them aside to mix the sugar and brown sugar to sprinkle over the apples after they came out of the pan. Tossed flour flew across the marble board as she grabbed a dough ball to roll out. She took a quick peek at Benson's station, then at him. He stood at the fryer, watching something cook. Based on the aroma, it was some kind of beef cooking. Maybe he was making meatballs? He was famous for his perfectly seasoned and mouth watering meats. Whatever he was cooking would be far from ordinary.

Their eyes met. He winked at her, and she quickly turned away, feeling a wave of heat warm her entire body. Since when did a look make her body react to him in this way? Feeling annoyed, she focused on rolling her dough. She loathed him even more with each movement, fueled by the memory of their constant rivalry and the smugness in his smile.

The big clock said Aubrey had twelve minutes to cook her dessert. Thankful she made her pies bite size, she placed a few in the pan to cook on one side. She quickly added the ingredients for caramel whipped cream and turned on the mixer to do the work for her.

"You might want to avoid burning those—unless you're looking for an early ticket home," Benson said with a smirk on his face.

"Mind your business." Aubrey didn't have time to dig into him with a sharp comeback.

She flipped her pies to find them golden brown.

"Chefs? You have five minutes," the host said.

Aubrey finished her second batch and plated her pies. She dropped dollops of the whipped cream next to the pie and sprinkled chopped mint leaves on top. She surveyed her work, taking a cloth to clean the edges of one plate.

"Time!" the host called.

Aubrey scrutinized her perfectly shaped rectangular, perfectly cooked fried apple pies. Her drops of the sweet, caramel-flavored whipped cream weren't as neat as she preferred, but she was certain the dessert tasted delicious. She peeked over to Benson's plate of amazing looking chunks of meat that was beautifully plated. They looked scrumptious. She was certain one bite of the delectable meat would melt in her mouth. Was his dish too basic? She wasn't the judge. She didn't want to think about him or his appetizer.

Three celebrity culinary icons stopped at each station, sampling each dish and scoring the chefs on taste, creativity, technique, and plating.

Benson's station was first in their row. One judge lifted the plate close to his nose and inhaled the yummy aroma. Another judge bit off a small bite and chewed with a slight smile adorning his face. He stood, hands behind his back, and nodded as the chefs marked his card. Aubrey was thankful his dish was savory. Her sweet pastry would be a retort to the judges' palates. Hands on her hips, she shifted her weight from one side to the other. She observed their faces, one closing his eyes as if to savor the taste, while the other nodded. A flicker of warmth and a brief smile broke through her focus as she watched them move to the next station.

The judge, tall in stature with a sharp gaze, passed the stack of scored cards to the host.

"Chefs," the host announced, pausing to let the tension build. "You've all shown incredible skill and creativity today. But only twenty-five of you will move on to the next round." The room fell silent as he began to read the names of the chefs moving onto round two. Aubrey put her head down, anxiety swirling in her stomach like a tempest as she anxiously awaited to hear her name called.

"And the last two chefs moving onto round two? Benson Carter and Aubrey Carroll."

Aubrey didn't know if she heard correctly. Did the host say her name? She let out a sigh of relief. Wait. Did she hear Benson's name, too? She could feel his gaze on her. Her jaw tightened, and her eyes stayed locked straight ahead, refusing to shift even a fraction. His presence next to her was palpable, like a heat on her back, but she didn't dare acknowledge it. She blinked hard, took a slow breath, and stayed rooted in place, determined not to let her focus waver.

Chapter 3

Benson

Benson exhaled slowly, clearing his mind to prepare for the next round. He wasn't surprised Aubrey made it to the next round. She was a master in the kitchen, especially with pastry. Clasping his hands together while awaiting the next set of directions, he scanned the floor. A once-bustling makeshift kitchen grew quieter as stations emptied. The absence of bodies was noticeable, like a sudden thinning of the air, making the room feel both larger and heavier. Chatter and hurried footsteps gradually faded, leaving only half the chefs anxiously waiting to get started with round two.

"Alright, chefs," the host uttered.

Everyone stood at attention, wanting to hear the next directive.

"In this next round, you will prepare an entrée using the ingredients in the mystery basket now placed at the end of your row. Each basket contains the exact same ingredients, so it doesn't matter which one you grab. You'll be judged on taste, creativity and plating. But you will be given an additional score based on how you incorporate the basket ingredients. You must use everything in the basket. You are free to use additional ingredients from the shelves. However, the basket ingredients must shine."

Benson shook off his nerves. He wasn't good at cooking mystery food without preparation. Previous experience proved this was not his strength. Aubrey, however, was a quick thinker. He had to sharpen his mental tools to move onto the next round. Her presence was quickly becoming a distraction, pulling his focus in ways he wasn't prepared for. Her smooth, slightly tanned skin and slim but shapely frame warmed his cheeks when she was close. He remembered her being cute, but now would he say she was beautiful?

The sound of the host's voice pulled him out of his head to center on the competition. "Inside your baskets are a duck breast, fennel, pomegranate, quinoa, and miso paste. You have forty-five minutes to prepare, cook, and plate your entrée." The host waves an arm, then says, "Time starts now."

Benson crossed his arms and closed his eyes, trying to envision what he was going to make. He didn't usually work with fruit. Was pomegranate a fruit? He could sear the duck. He knew that much. He wasn't a fan of quinoa, but people ate it as a rice substitute. The meal suddenly came to him, vivid and complete.

"Got it," he said, rushing to the end of the row to grab his ingredients.

He whizzed past Aubrey, surprised she had already grabbed her things and started preparing her dish.

"Only the truly *special* ones have full conversations with themselves, Benson."

With a chuckle, Benson whispers as he walks past Aubrey's station, "Who even talks during a food competition? Focus on the food, not your commentary!" Playtime was over. Aubrey was already cooking, and he still didn't know what to do with the rest of the basket ingredients.

Time seemed to evaporate, slipping through his fingers like grains of sand.

"Thirty seconds, chefs."

Benson drizzled the light vinaigrette over the pomegranate fennel salad. He wiped the three plates on their edges to beautify his presentation, inhaled and let out a deep breath as the host yelled time. Examining his plates, his chest inflated with pride. The seared duck breast was crispy and glazed with a savory-sweet miso sauce. The fluffy quinoa was accompanied by a refreshing salad of thinly sliced fennel, pomegranate seeds, and the dressing.

His eyes immediately darted to Aubrey's station. He cursed in his head. This woman made duck and quinoa-stuffed fennel with a miso-pomegranate reduction. He couldn't believe she had time to roast the fennel bulbs stuffed with a mixture of quinoa, diced duck breast, and pomegranate seeds. That's what she was dicing when he walked past her station earlier. He missed her standing at the stove, making the miso-pomegranate reduction. No doubt it was a burst of umami and sweetness. Benson truly despised this woman.

In what seemed like seconds, the judges were at Benson's station, one holding up his plate and turning it in different directions to inspect his plating technique. For a split second, he wondered if the mystery basket ingredients were at the center of flavor and taste. He didn't add too many additional ingredients. He couldn't watch as the judges tasted his food. Not this round. He didn't feel confident. Would he be sent home for a basic entrée?

Benson shifted his stance, subtly angling himself toward her station, eyes locked on every movement as the judges leaned in to inspect her dish. The corner of his mouth twitched slightly as he watched them take their first bite. His gaze never wavered, following their every reaction, trying to gauge their thoughts, each slow chew and glance exchanging more weight than words ever could. She wasn't going home. That was absolute.

After the judges left their row, Benson narrowed his eyes and said in a low tone, "Sure, you won this round, but let's be real—I'm not going anywhere."

Aubrey pivoted smoothly in his direction. As she moved closer, a soft, floral scent filled the air, lingering between them. His breath caught slightly, the perfume unmistakable and distracting, pulling his attention completely toward her. This is not what he wanted.

With a smirk, Aubrey whispered, "Giving up already? My skills are clearly on a whole different level."

Benson shook his head. "We'll see about that."

Chapter 4

Aubrey

Round two and three were successful rounds for Aubrey. They were now down to six chefs. One of the six being her archrival, Benson.

"Congratulations," the announcer praised. "You all have made it to the final round. You're competing for the big prize. Are you ready?"

In chorus, the word yes hummed in the sections of the remaining chefs.

"In this final round, you will be teamed up with the chef nearest to you."

The host wiggled his eyebrows, then said, "Instead of one Chef Supreme, two of you will be crowned today. In this final round, the prize is two-hundred-fifty thousand dollars each."

Chefs looked around their space. Aubrey's breath hitched, and for a brief moment, everything seemed to freeze. A heavy, sinking sensation spread through her chest, as if the ground had slipped away beneath her. Her hands trembled ever so slightly, and her grip tightened, trying to steady herself against the wave of dread that surged through her body.

She flew her head back in disbelief. Benson was the chef closest to her.

With a sly grin, Benson leaned in and said, "Looks like you and me, sugar."

Aubrey blinked several times before turning to Benson. "You'd better be on your A-game because I didn't show up to be given a participation trophy."

Benson faced Aubrey. "We've resorted to eye rolling now. I came here to win, too, sweetheart."

"You ready?" They chimed in together.

Aubrey narrowed her eyes. "I stay ready."

Benson nodded. "Let's do it."

The tension in the kitchen was suffocating. This was it. They were so close to the end. Aubrey could feel Benson standing too close, his presence a constant, irritating reminder of every smug comment and arrogant glance over the two years they spent at the Culinary Institute of America. They clashed over every assignment in culinary school, but this was different—they had to work together, and that made her blood simmer.

The host looked around the room, now all eyes on him. "In this final round, you have to create an entire meal. You have two hours to plan, cook, and plate. Three appetizers, two entrees with sides, and two desserts. Chefs, get cooking."

"So, what are you thinking?" Benson asked.

Aubrey glanced up at him, unexpectedly admiring his smooth brown skin and luxuriously long lashes. She didn't remember him being so handsome. She really hated him.

"I can make just about anything. Maybe some southern classics? What do you serve in your restaurant in New York?" Aubrey noticed the sudden shift in his eyes, transforming from bright enthusiasm to a frosty detachment at the mention of New York.

Benson's jaw appeared to tighten at the mention of his restaurant. With slight hesitation, he responded. "I serve elegant American cuisine." He cleared his throat. "Steaks, roasted duck, rack of lamb. That kind of stuff."

"Maybe we can give a little of both. I'll do a collard green spring roll to start. You prepare a cut of beef and two of your signature sides? I'll fry chicken, saute some green beans and make a quick mac and cheese." One thing Aubrey could do and do well was plan a menu.

Benson appeared to shift his mood, his voice solid and deep. "We need more freshness. I'll make a salad, and maybe a soup? I'll do a porkchop instead of beef. Some butternut squash puree with hints of nutmeg and butter for my entrée."

Aubrey wanted to lick her lips. Everything sounded delicious. "What about a vegetable?"

"Sauteed broccolini."

Their ideas gelled instantly. With the way they were getting along, she couldn't deny her growing attraction to Benson.

Getting her mind back on the competition, Aubrey offered, "Dessert is my speciality."

Benson tapped his finger on the side of his face, then asked, "Do you still make your lemon pound cake?"

"You remember that?" She thought he despised everything about her. "Yes, I still make it. I now add a lemon drizzle to the cake, so I'll do that." Aubrey glanced at Benson, waiting for his dessert contribution. Could he bake anything? Back in school, she always outscored him in the pastry rotations. Except that one time.

"What dessert do you want to contribute?"

"An ice cream sandwich?" His eyes sparkled with a mix of encouragement and sincerity at the suggestion, as if they were silently urging her to take the leap.

"Wow, a top chef like you? And all you've got is an ice cream sandwich? Guess we're all aiming high today." She couldn't believe him. They weren't serving eight-year-olds. "Can you make your infamous chocolate souffle?"

"I can whip up a chocolate souffle that'll melt in your mouth. You remember that, right?" Benson responded, smiling.

Aubrey lowered her eyes at him. "Make your chocolate souffle." If they wanted to win, his souffle could definitely put them in the running.

"We better win this. I mean, my food's obviously flawless—just hope you can keep up." With that, Aubrey folded her arms across her chest, waiting for Benson to respond. He only glared down at her, eyes raging.

"Are we set or what? We need to get cooking." Benson's shoulder rubbed Aubrey's when he walked past her to gather ingredients.

His touch sent a shiver through her body, leaving a tingling sensation. Where did that come from? She hated him—had always hated him. Yet, in that moment, the conflict between her sudden attraction to him and her literal hate left her bewildered, grappling with the strange chemistry that suddenly ignited every time he was near. It was infuriating. How could she feel this way about someone she swore to loathe? "Let's go!" she whispered to herself.

For them to be decent collaborators, their next moves were awkward. Every step they took was out of sync. Aubrey reached for the olive oil just as Benson snatched it up, barely sparing her a glance. When she went to drop her chopped collard greens into the salted boiling water, he muttered under his breath about her technique, as if she didn't already know what she was doing. She gritted her teeth, ignoring his critiques while trying to focus on her dish.

The worst part? She couldn't help but notice his skill. The way he flawlessly diced vegetables with perfect precision, the confidence in how he handled the grill—everything about him irritated her, and yet she couldn't deny that he was good. Too good.

Each time they brushed past each other, a subtle jab or snarky comment followed, adding fuel to the fire. It was like trying to cook with a lit match in a gas-filled room. She had to bite back a dozen insults just to get through the round without losing her focus, despite the pull she felt when he was close to her. Benson's presence could not throw her off.

The sweat beaded down Aubrey's back, a testament to the heat of the kitchen and the pressure of the moment. Or was the heat from Benson's allure?

The humidity wrapped around her like a heavy blanket, making her clothes cling uncomfortably to her skin. The sizzling sounds of pans and the sharp aroma of spices filled the air, but it was the relentless heat that threatened to distract her. It was the final seconds of the competition. She wiped her brow, her mind racing as she focused on drizzling the lemon glaze over the slices of lemon pound cake. She quickly glanced at Benson as he wiped the sweat off his forehead with the sleeve of his chef coat. His brow was furrowed in concentration, and despite their rivalry, she couldn't help but admire the way he handled the chaos.

"Time." A collective sigh and a few groans littered the air.

Brushing her own forehead on the sleeve of her chef coat, she surveyed her work, then Benson's. Everything looked picture worthy. Each plate of food was vibrant and elegantly plated. Aubrey scanned to her right and found one pair had prepared what looked to be gourmet burgers with fresh cut fries and apple pie. How American. To her left, the pair made pasta, pizza and tiramisu. Although everyone's food appeared very appetizing, a cold rush swept through her, settling deep in her gut. She and Benson had this in the bag.

The judges approached the tasting table with quiet anticipation, their eyes scanning the array of dishes before them. Aubrey and Benson were up first. They reached for the fried chicken. The crackle of the crispy skin echoed slightly as they cut into it, revealing tender juicy meat beneath. One bite and their faces lit up—Aubrey's seasoning was perfect, with just enough spice to tingle the taste buds. They exchanged quick, approving glances.

Next, the pork chop. The knife slid through the thick cut with ease, juices pooling on the plate. Each judge took a slice, their forks piercing the perfectly cooked meat. They nodded as they chewed—Benson caught Aubrey's attention and nodded with a grin. He then bent down to whisper in her ear, "The balance of my smoky flavor and subtle herbs are impeccable."

Aubrey's cheeks went flush with the sensation of his breath against her ear.

One judge dabbed at their lips with a napkin and murmured something about it being "unapologetically savory."

Digging into the chocolate souffle, the spoon cracked through the delicate top, revealing a molten center that oozed rich, velvety chocolate. Aubrey would give anything to taste it. As each judge tasted, there was a moment of silence. One judge couldn't help but close their eyes. Aubrey imagined they relished the way the souffle melted like silk across their tongues.

When the judges arrived at the lemon cake, a wave of nausea hit Aubrey's stomach, and it lurched, sinking like a stone. A moment of déjà vu had her thinking she forgot an important ingredient. Or maybe she added too much of something.

Aubrey's slices of cake were moist, with a glaze that shimmered under the lights. They took a bite. She was certain the brightness of the lemon hit first, followed by the sweet, buttery richness of the cake. A soft sigh escaped one of the judges, and they scribbled something quickly onto their notepad, clearly impressed with the perfect harmony of tart and sweet.

In sync, Aubrey and Benson crossed their arms across their chests and took in a deep sigh, relieved their judging was done. Rather than watch the scoring of the other dishes, they both leaned against the station table and put their heads down, silent in their own thoughts. They had a chance to actually win the competition. Would they both be Chef Supreme? First prize was a nice chunk of money Aubrey planned to put to good use.

In that moment, Aubrey could feel the weight of Benson's gaze on her. She couldn't turn to him. She couldn't look. Why was he staring? He could've been hurling flaming daggers at her with his eyes for all she knew. The intensity of his gaze was a challenge, igniting her competitive spirit. But she was feeling drawn to him in ways she couldn't explain. Was he daring her to acknowledge the tension simmering between them, to rise above the petty rivalries and step into the fray of what she was beginning to believe was seductiveness? She could feel the heat creeping up her neck, a mix of annoyance and adrenaline urging her to surrender whatever this was bubbling between them. Instead, she took a deep breath, straightened her shoulders, and focused on the final moments of the competition, determined not to let his smoldering look distract her from the prize that lay ahead.

"If we win, can we be friends, or at least call a truce?" he asked.

Why did he want to be friends now? Aubrey cleared her throat. "Us being friends is a stretch, don't you think?"

"Sugar. It's about time we be friends," Benson said with a smirk.

"Don't call me sugar. My name is Aubrey."

"Sugar, I know your name, but I like this one better." Benson flashed her a huge grin.

Just as Aubrey was going to reply, the host approached the microphone.

"Ladies and gentlemen. The judges had a great time tasting the amazing food put before them. But we know there can only be one winner. Or should I say, a winning pair. You all have been on a remarkable journey."

Aubrey could hear her heartbeat racing as the host paused for dramatic effect.

"The winning pair is," the sound of a drum roll thundered through the speakers. He looked down at his note card, then said, "Aubrey Carroll and Benson Carter."

Aubrey wasn't sure if she heard correctly. Did he say her name? Benson's name? Before she could realize what was happening, cameras were shoved into their faces. She moved to turn away. In what was obviously a burst of excitement, he scooped her up into a tight hug, spinning her around in a whirlwind of joy. As her feet touched the ground again, his grin faltered, and a flicker of realization crossed his face—his spontaneous gesture might have caught her off guard, perhaps even crossed a line.

Replacing the wide smile on his face, he cheerfully yelled, "We won! We won!"

Catching her breath, Aubrey tried to hold back her tears of joy. She was proud of herself and the work she did today. The work they did, together. She was speechless. All she could do was hold her hand up for Benson to give her a high five. The crowd erupted into a round of applause. She finally brought herself to look at the man that helped her to victory. He stepped forward, a smug grin on his face that sent an unexpected wave of gratitude through her. Despite their rivalry, she couldn't deny the thrill of winning this competition. And she did it with Benson Carter.

The host raised their hands to calm the crowd, a broad smile now plastered across their faces. "Congratulations to our winners! You are both two-hundred-fifty thousand dollars richer. Do you have any words for our audience?"

The host shoved the microphone in her face. All Aubrey could muster to say was, "Thank you all for an incredible competition!" She turned to Benson and flashed a tentative smile.

He grabbed her hand to pull her close and said, "Tonight, I'm buying you a drink."

Chapter 5

Benson

Benson checked behind him to make sure Aubrey was walking in his footsteps through the bustling crowd. She was so close, her body heat radiated through him, igniting an unexpected flutter of nerves as they navigated the sea of people. Women didn't make him nervous. Why did his culinary enemy push a boundary that he was tempted to cross? Her fineness was evident from the first day he laid eyes on Aubrey. It's been some years since they were face to face. Now, her beauty was an unexpected attraction he thought he would never feel for this woman. Her skin glowed, catching the light with a soft sheen, while her presence lit up the bar. He had the urge to twist strands of her now loosened hair around his finger and slightly pull to bring her closer to him. Her body, graceful and perfectly curved, seemed to fit the outline of his, as if they were two halves of a puzzle waiting to click into place.

Today was about the food, the flavors, and the artistry they were both so passionate about. He needed to remain professional. This moment was about victory, a victory that proved his talent in front of the judges and his peers, not about his growing attraction for Aubrey.

Forcing a smile, Benson channeled all of his energy into the excitement of celebrating their big win.

"Care to sit at the bar?" Benson gestured for Aubrey to sit on the stool a few feet ahead of her.

"Sure." He tried not to gawk at her as she pulled her stool up to the bar, the smooth motion a blend of grace and casual confidence. The bar itself was a long, rectangular piece of black marble, its surface sleek and polished, flecks of white shimmering like distant stars, embedded within the dark stone. The atmosphere was lively, with laughter and clinking glasses echoing around them.

Behind the counter, shelves towered with an impressive array of liquor, from the well-known basics to top-shelf selections that sparkled under the dim lighting. Groups clustered together, some sharing animated conversations, while others leaned in close, exchanging secrets and smiles.

As Aubrey settled in, a sudden rush of admiration came over him, her presence commanding attention amidst the hustle and bustle. He couldn't help but notice the way her dark brown, shoulder-length curls shimmered under the light, framing her face perfectly as she scanned the drink menu. There was something intoxicating about her, something that made it hard for him to look away.

"What are we drinking?" Aubrey asked.

"Champagne, of course. We just won a huge competition. Do you know what doors will open for us now?" Benson waved the bartender over to take their order.

The bartender nodded and set a napkin on the surface in front of each of them. "Good evening. What can I get you?"

"We'll have glasses of your best champagne," Benson said, beaming, and gave Aubrey a wink.

With an expression of curiosity, the bartender asked, "Are we celebrating? What's the occasion?"

"We're here to celebrate a big win," he said, both answering the bartender and reminding himself that desire didn't bring him to the bar.

Aubrey straightened her back and said, "We just won Chef Supreme."

"Congratulations. I guess that's a big deal, huh?" the bartender asked, totally clueless.

Benson paused for a moment. Was this guy living under a rock? The competition was in the very hotel this bar was in. He was pretty sure it was streamed on all the televisions mounted around the place.

"Yep." Benson sat on the stool next to Aubrey, turning his body to face her.

"Coming right up. The first glass is on me."

Benson turned to watch the guy gather glasses and rinse them. "Can you believe that guy?"

"He's busy attending the bar. I'm sure it was a lot to watch," Aubrey said as she adjusted herself onto the stool. "Tell me. What have you been up to, Benson? It's been a few years since we last saw each other."

Benson released a soft laugh. "I've been busy. You?"

"I opened a restaurant. I'll open a bakery soon." Aubrey rested her head in her hand and leaned on top of the bar.

"Oh yeah? Not bad for a beautiful woman like you. What's your favorite thing to cook?

"Believe it or not, I enjoy baking bread or biscuits. I like to get my hands in there, knead the dough." She licked her bottom lip. "Manipulating it the way I want."

Benson's eyebrow arched, a slow smirk on his lips. "You like to manipulate it, huh?"

They were silent, Benson watching her watch him. Were they having a moment?

Aubrey studied him for a few more seconds. "The last I heard, you were in New York, running a successful restaurant. Ranked one of the best in the city. Not bad for a young man of your age. What brought you to San Francisco to compete in this competition?"

And there went the moment. He tried not to make it obvious that the mention of New York was painful. His restaurant in New York was not going to be a topic of discussion. He wanted to put New York behind him. The future was enough to focus on. Benson pushed his regretful thoughts down and forced a grin. "You know I like to compete. It's one of the things I do best."

"What we do best. I'm just as competitive as you. Maybe more. This win was a joint effort. And now we have two-hundred-fifty thousand dollars more in our bank accounts. All in a day's work." Aubrey smiled up at Benson. They lingered in the moment, their smiles holding them captive. Their breaths quickened as she chewed on her upper lip.

"Here you are." The bartender set down two glasses of bubbly. "Congratulations again. Enjoy."

Benson picked up both glasses, handing one to Aubrey. "Let's make a toast. To good food always, and the love of competition. And can I dare say friendship?"

Aubrey held her glass up and grimaced. "Friendship? Maybe?"

Their glasses met with a soft chime, the sound lingering in the air as they lifted them to their lips. The cool liquid tasted slightly tart, finishing with a sweet note.

"This is good." Aubrey set her glass down, her fingers tracing small circles against her palm, restless and fidgeting, betraying the calm she tried to hold on to.

"I know we rarely have civilized conversations, but I'm hoping we can try tonight. Are you still in Los Angeles?"

Aubrey nodded.

"Do you sell your lemon pound cake at your restaurant? I remember it being the best I'd ever tasted."

Aubrey picked up her champagne glass and took a sip before responding. "Why? Are you looking to start a fan club? You can be the president."

Benson shook his head. "Are you always snarky?"

"Snarky? I was just stating a fact. But, yes, I sell my lemon pound cake at my restaurant. It's a bestseller." She took another sip of her drink, then asked, "You and Alan were good friends. Do you stay in touch with him?"

"As a matter of fact, I do. He's in Los Angeles, too. Alan owns a breakfast and lunch spot by the beach. He's married and has a young child. I'll give you the name of his place so you can stop by. I'm sure he'd love to see you. He didn't participate in our competitive shenanigans, but he would definitely remember you."

He leaned in slightly, his smile warm as they chatted about his favorite dishes to prepare. "You can't go wrong with a classic steak," he said, sipping his champagne. "Nothing beats the simplicity of it."

Aubrey laughed, shaking her head. "Oh, please, steak is so overrated. It's all about the seafood—delicate, full of flavor, and versatile. The fried catfish is one of my best sellers."

He raised an eyebrow, his smile fading into a teasing smirk. "Seafood? Sure, if you like eating something that smells like the ocean floor."

She shot him a playful glare, but there was a hint of challenge in her voice now. "You mean, unlike steak, which is just a slab of meat drowning in butter? Real creative."

He chuckled, but his tone sharpened. "It's not about being creative;

it's about perfecting the basics. You can't mess up a good steak. But seafood? One wrong move and it's rubbery. No thanks."

Her eyes narrowed, leaning forward. "At least seafood requires skill. Anyone can throw a steak on a grill and call it a day. Real cooking takes finesse."

He set his glass down with a bit more force than necessary, his grin fading. "Finesse? You mean hiding behind strong seasonings to mask the lack of flavor of a piece of fish? I'll take a juicy steak over a soggy piece of fish any day."

The playful banter had shifted, the tension rising between them as each defended their culinary preference with growing intensity. What had started as a pleasant exchange had quickly turned into a full-blown food debate. Voices rose, and what was once laughter turned into clipped, pointed comments.

"Steak is for people who don't know how to experiment," Aubrey snapped.

"Seafood is for people who don't understand real flavor," Benson shot back, his jaw tightening.

By now, their pleasant conversation and glass of champagne were not so celebratory. Flirting with Aubrey was not in the cards tonight. Their conversation soured and veered into a battle of stubborn wills. Neither was backing down, and the attempt at charm from earlier in the evening was long gone, replaced by a tension similar to a pot about to boil over.

Aubrey stood, drank the rest of her champagne in one gulp, and placed her hands on her hips. "I thought, just maybe, we could be nice to each other. It was a miracle we were able to work together and win the competition. But I see there is no use. You're impossible."

"I'm impossible? Wow." Now Benson was on his feet. He swallowed the rest of his drink and reached for his wallet, pulled out a twenty and laid the tip on the bar.

"I think we should call it a night. I want to be a gentleman and walk you to your room, if that's okay. Then, I may say goodbye. I might not. But after tonight, you don't have to worry about seeing me."

"I can walk myself to my hotel room, thank you very much." Aubrey turned to walk toward the door, Benson on her heels.

Their steps fell in unison, the space between them thick with unvoiced thoughts. The attempt at a civil conversation over drinks had long evaporated, leaving a quiet heaviness between them as they neared the elevator. He glanced over at her, hoping to catch her eye, but she kept her gaze fixed straight ahead.

They stepped into the elevator. She pushed her floor number. Benson nodded in her direction. He was on the same floor. He stood beside her, rubbed the back of his neck, irritation creeping into his tone. "Come on, I wasn't trying to make you feel bad. You're overreacting."

"Overreacting? Seriously?" She laughed, but it was a cold, sharp sound.

His jaw clenched, the patience in his expression fading. "You're taking things way too personally." Benson needed to turn this conversation. He didn't want to end the night angry. He didn't want her to be angry.

Benson turned his head to look at Aubrey. He softened his tone. "You're not wrong for having your own opinion." He took a deep breath. "Can we agree to disagree and move on?"

Aubrey's eyes flashed. She took a step closer to him, her words pointed. "It's not about the damn seafood! It's you. You get under my skin."

He exhaled sharply, now facing her, hovering. He twirled his tongue around in his mouth. "I get under your skin, huh?"

She stared at him, her frustration lowering from bubbling over to a low simmer. "Maybe if you actually listened to me, you'd appreciate a different perspective."

"I'm listening. I'm listening to every spoken and unspoken word."

They stood there, faces inches apart, the energy between them thickening as the seconds passed. Benson chuckled under his breath. She was cute when she was mad.

"What are you laughing at?" Aubrey asked.

The elevator door opened. Aubrey rolled her eyes and stepped out. Benson followed behind her.

They had a wordless exchange in the moments it took to be in front of Aubrey's hotel room door. Benson rested his left arm against the door frame. "I'm sorry for tonight. Will you accept my apology?"

Aubrey turned to face him. She glanced up at Benson. Their gazes locked, neither looking away. She shifted closer, their bodies only a few inches apart. "I can forgive you," she whispered.

Benson's chin slowly tilted toward hers. His lips parted. "This may be unexpected, but... I really want to kiss you."

Aubrey licked her lips, her gaze never leaving his. "We're not friends. But... you can kiss me."

Benson gave her a devilish smile. After this kiss, she would beg to be his friend. He reached down to grab her hands, lifting them above her head, pinning her arms to her hotel room door. She appeared taken aback, her expression full of surprise. The slight grin and lust on her face gave him permission to press against her heated body. He claimed her mouth, softly kissing her lips, playfully opening her mouth with his tongue.

The sound of Aubrey's moans made the bulge in his pants tighten. He deepened the kiss. She welcomed his tongue into her mouth. He grabbed her by the waist, pulling her closer. Her hands reached for his face, then her arms circled his neck, their kiss not breaking.

They must've made out in the hallway for several minutes, never coming up for air. As a set of footsteps drew closer, Benson ignored them, unwilling to let Aubrey go just yet.

"Oh my God. You two are a couple? How cute?" a young blonde woman, appearing to be in her early twenties, said, standing only a few feet from them.

Aubrey quickly pulled away. A sudden look of horror flashed across her face, her eyes widening and her breath catching in her throat.

Benson looked down, realizing they were still in their chef coats. He lightly tapped his head on the door frame, realizing the predicament they were in.

Benson turned to the woman to respond, but Aubrey spoke first. "Oh no. We are not a couple. You have this all wrong."

The young woman grinned. "You two competed against each other, only to be paired and win together." She clapped her hands together in excitement. "How romantic. And you couldn't even make it to the room. You were going hot and heavy there."

Benson glanced at Aubrey, pleading with his eyes to let him do the talking.

He turned to the woman. "Thank you. Yes, we won. Have a good night."

"You guys, too. And congratulations."

They both waited for the woman to walk down the hall and into her room.

Benson put his finger over his mouth to gesture to Aubrey to not say anything. "Before you go off, I had to say something. Otherwise, she would have stood here talking, having a whole conversation with us."

"This was a mistake. What if she's a reporter or something? This is not a good look. Professional chefs making out in the hotel hallway." Aubrey fished her room card out of her purse and swiped to open her door. "Benson, I need to say goodnight." She walked into her room and shut the door without a word or explanation.

Chapter 6

Benson

One month later

Benson stepped off the plane. A wave of anxiety, yet excitement, washed over him. His bank account was two-hundred-fifty thousand dollars richer. He was returning to the city of beautiful people. Los Angeles and its warm weather caught him in a comforting embrace. It had been years since he called L.A. home. The clear blue sky paved the way for the shining sun. Despite the beautiful day, the uneasiness in his stomach made it flip, butterflies suddenly soaring inside. His core aim was twofold. He wanted to please his mother, and most importantly, himself, with redemption as his target. He was beginning a new chapter. New home, new restaurant, new adventures, all in the city of angels.

Benson pulled up to the open space in front of his new space and cut the engine. His gaze drifted toward the cluster of people gathered a few doors down. They stood in an easy line, their postures relaxed, the low hum of conversation barely reaching him. Stretching his neck to read the sign through his car's front windshield, he only read the word restaurant. Great. Now there were going to be two restaurants in very close proximity. He shifted his stare to the structure in front of his car, taking in the worn facade and less than ideal location. With a resigned sigh, he stepped out of his silver BMW 540i, already imagining how he'd make it work. He walked up to his front window and peered inside, seeing a blank slate that he was determined to make his own. Lost in his imagination, Benson didn't notice his realtor approach.

"Hey, man. You okay?" Manuel said, softly resting his right hand on Benson's shoulder.

"I'm good, man. I was just imagining how I'll make this empty canvas into Stonewood and Ember."

"If I know you, it'll be like no other restaurant in the area. I got the keys." Manuel dangled the key ring in Benson's face. "You ready to go in?"

"Now or never, man. It's now or never."

Manuel unlocked the front door and gave his favorite client a big grin. "After you, L.A. restaurant owner."

The two men stepped into the enormous room with its concrete floors and white walls with peeling paint. Sunlight filtered through the floor to ceiling windows, casting long shadows that stretched across the dusty floor. The air was thick with the scent of damp and decay. How long had this place been vacant? He stood, arms folded across his chest, closing his eyes tightly, imagining the built out. He was starting from scratch, building the kitchen, an office, and a dining room. The highlight of the room, however, was the exposed brick wall, which extended the entire right wing. Its rustic charm brought a sense of warmth and character to the otherwise bare space. The wall, with its rich, earthy tones and occasional weathered imperfections, would go well with his planned anesthetics.

"Whatcha thinking?" Manuel asked as he circled the space.

"I'm thinking about how much work this will be," Benson sighed. He clapped his hands together, then said, "I'm ready, though."

"I'll be your first reservation."

Los Angeles was foreign, its streets unfamiliar under his feet, but that was the point. He needed to be unfamiliar—needed a place where the memories of his old life couldn't cling to him like smoke. Benson stepped out of his new space and onto the sidewalk breathed in deeply, letting the scents of the new city swirl in his lungs—the smell of fried chicken and something baked lingered in the air. The sharp bite of exhaust from a passing bus mixed with the sweet, earthy scent of incense, creating a strange fusion of city grit and calm in the air. This was home now.

His hands flexed at his sides, fingers tingling with the longing to be back in the kitchen, back in control. But the past had burned him—literally and figuratively. The restaurant he'd built from scratch in New York had collapsed, by his own doing. He had left it all behind, hoping to leave his old self behind, too.

Smokewood and Ember would give him his second chance. The neighborhood, the street, was deeply woven into the city's fabric, a cherished cornerstone of its historic charm. He was lucky to have purchased space on the block. The nerves would pass, he told himself. They always did. Getting the restaurant ready was just like preparing a meal: one step at a time. But starting from scratch wouldn't be easy. His mind wandered to the late nights ahead, the countless hours of perfecting a new menu, reinventing flavors, creating a new signature as a top chef. He was Chef Supreme, after all. Even with this new title, he would have to earn his way back, plate by plate. He had been the best once, and now, in this city, with no one to judge him for his past, he could be the best again.

The group of folks still stood patiently waiting to enter the spot that could be his competition. "Hey. Do you know anything about the restaurant a few doors down? And what's the name of it?" Ben asked Manuel.

"No. This is out of the area for me. I'm usually in Orange County. All I know is the owner of the restaurant bought the space you wanted. She paid top dollar. Her realtor said something about needing the new bakery to be next door to her restaurant."

"Did you learn the owner's name at least?" Benson was curious about his new neighbor.

"No. The bidding stopped once the price got above the amount you wanted to spend, so I stopped asking questions." Manuel played with a ring of keys in his hand.

Benson stood thinking until Manuel spoke again.

"Here are your keys. It's all yours, man. I have another appointment. I'll call you soon?"

"Sure. And thanks again for all of your work. This place is growing on me."

The two men shook hands. Then Benson watched Manuel walk to his car, get in, and pull off into the afternoon's traffic.

Benson lounged on the couch, one arm draped across its back, a beer in hand that he took slow sips from between glances at the game. His other hand rested on the baby, his fingers gently tracing circles on her tiny belly as she cooed, her tiny fist wrapping around his thumb. The sounds of the game faded into the background, blending with the quiet rhythm of his playful motions, a small smile tugging at his lips. Ryelee was the cutest baby ever. His friend was a lucky man to have such a beautiful family.

Alan Keller and Benson met in culinary school, struck up an immediate friendship and had been close since. With a stunning wife and a baby girl by his side, he stayed in L.A. and opened a now bustling beachfront restaurant that hummed with a loyal customer base. Alan had the perfect life. A family, something Benson wanted one day. He yearned for it. It was always something he pictured for himself, a quiet dream tucked away in the corners of his mind, waiting for the right time to become real. Despite his mother's view, romantic relationships interfered with success, he would reestablish his career, and most importantly, have love in his life. It was Alan's question that pulled Benson out of his thoughts.

"So, you got your space. What happens next?"

Benson's breath rushed out in a sigh. "I have to build the restaurant out, from scratch. I'm not sure how much this will cost me. The purchase wasn't cheap."

"If it wasn't for my wife's money, I don't know how I would have opened my place. It's always over budget, and you don't finish on time." Alan shook his head.

"Can you get the money from your mom?"

Benson barked a laugh. "I think you know the answer to that. Nope."

"I don't understand. She sold her restaurants for a pretty penny. She'll never have to work another day. She can't spot you a few hundred grand?"

"On principle, the answer is no. I did win a nice sum at the contest in San Francisco." And you would never guess who I competed with." Benson watched Alan's face morph from a questioning expression to one of wonder.

"So, I walk over to my assigned station. I glance over and see a woman bending down, surveying the cookware. She stands and before me was Aubrey Carroll. You remember her, right?"

Alan belted a laugh. "Yes, I remember Aubrey Carroll. You two hated each other in culinary school. How did you two end up in the same contest? And better yet, your stations were right next to each other? Fantastic!"

Benson covered his mouth for a brief moment. Then he said, "So, I plastered a huge smile on my face and greeted her with, 'Hey, sugar. Long time no see.' She scowled. It was hilarious." The look on her face when he greeted Aubrey was imprinted on his brain.

"Man, I know she was pissed. Sugar? Why, man? You couldn't greet her by her name? You're horrible." Alan threw his head back, a genuine burst of laughter spilling from him, deep and unrestrained.

"Anyway. We pretty much worked on our own until we had to be paired in the last round."

"And how did that go? You guys won."

"We did. We were getting along pretty well. She shared her ideas. I shared mine, and we compromised on our menu. We then pretty much just went to work." It was in those moments that he thought he and Aubrey could make amends. It was the reason he suggested they go out for a celebratory drink. It didn't take long for them to bicker like old times. Attraction pushed aside. She was too cute when she was pissed off. His mind drifted back to the kiss they shared, the memory persisting like a bee drawn to a flower.

"She asked about you," Ben told Alan.

"Yeah? We didn't talk much. I do remember how good she was. Especially with pastry. She's here in L.A., somewhere." Alan put his beer down and stroked his daughter's curls.

"In L.A.? Really? So, she didn't leave after culinary school?"

"No. She grew up in L.A. Remember?"

"I forgot about that. I may have to look her up just to irritate her." Benson laughed. He wanted to pick up where they left off, to continue that kiss.

"Honey? You two come eat," Jessica yelled from the kitchen. "I'll take Ryelee."

They settled at the table. As they dug into their delicious meal of roasted chicken, perfectly seasoned and crispy-skinned, the conversation flowed effortlessly between bites. The roasted potatoes were golden and crispy, each forkful a perfect complement to the tender chicken. The fresh salad, vibrant with greens and topped with a tangy vinaigrette, added a refreshing crunch that balanced the richness of the main dish. One of the benefits of being a chef and having friends who were chefs: the food was always good.

"So, Benson. Tell us what your concept is of Stonewood and Ember," Alan asked as he took a bite of chicken.

"I've been researching smoked meats. I didn't find an upscale restaurant with meat being a focal point other than your steak houses. I'm thinking of building a smoke room in the back of the space." Benson sipped his white wine, then filled his fork with potatoes, putting them in his mouth.

Jessica finished chewing her salad, then spoke. "That sounds really amazing, Benson. I think you have a unique niche."

"I hope so. I want this place to be one of the best spots in L.A." He bit into his chicken leg.

"We know New York didn't pan out the way you originally wanted. We're happy you're close, though." Alan relaxed into a smile.

The mention of New York stirred up memories he tried to bury, the fiasco gnawing at the edges of his mind. But as he glanced around, admiring Alan's house and family, he forced himself to let it go. There was no need to dredge up old regrets here. Surrounding himself with those who genuinely cared would help him focus on building a strong reputation.

For dessert, they savored the homemade strawberry ice cream, its creamy texture and sweet, fruity flavor. The evening buzzed with energy, filled with the simple joys of good food and great friends.

Instead of taking the freeway, Benson took the street route home. He navigated through the grid of city streets, passing storefronts and stop lights. All the businesses on the street of his new restaurant space were closed, their windows dark and lifeless. It was quiet and empty, barren of the usual hustle and bustle. Empty sidewalks created an eerie stillness, broken only by the occasional rustle of leaves or the distant hum of a passing car. He pulled along the curb, the tires crunching softly on the scattered pebbles that lined the side of the street. After turning his engine off, he got out of the car. Peeking into the window, he quickly imagined the restaurant build-out. He then walked down a few doors and stood in front of his restaurant neighbor. Its menu was posted on the glass window.

"Ooh. These are soul food classics," Benson said softly to himself. The menu listed mouthwatering favorites like smothered pork chops, meatloaf, fried catfish and chicken, peach cobbler and lemon pound cake. Lemon pound cake? He took a few steps back and peered up to the sign.

"Aubrey's Favorites? It couldn't be," Benson mumbled to himself. Pulling his phone out of his pocket, he searched for an article or review of the place.

"Five stars. The food and service are superior," one review read.

"The best lemon pound cake ever. Better than my momma's," another review said.

Underneath the reviews was a full spread on its owner. The headline read, "New Restaurant Opens on Main Street." Benson scrolled through the first few paragraphs. "Home cooking. Southern recipes, catering." "L.A.'s new culinary sweetheart." Mid scroll, he stopped on the featured photograph. He froze.

"Aubrey's Favorites? Aubrey's Favorites is owned by Aubrey Carroll?" Was this coincidence a curse or fate? He thought he had rid himself of her in San Francisco.

"Wait until she learns I'm opening a restaurant on her block."

Chapter 7

Aubrey

Aubrey's Favorites' kitchen was a whirlwind of controlled chaos. The air hummed with high stress energy as the lunch rush reached its peak. The sizzle of grilled burgers and chicken mingled with sharp scents of garlic and herbs. Steam poured from boiling pots of collard greens and gumbo. The clang of metal against metal was constant. Food orders were called out in rapid succession. Aubrey's face flushed from the heat as she barked commands, her voice cutting through the clamoring of swift movement and the hustling of plates going out. The tension was thick in the air, even though there was a rhythm to the madness. The rush, the challenge, and the satisfaction elated her when each plate left the kitchen with nothing short of perfection. This was all worth the pressure.

With the lunch crowd gone, Aubrey finally made it to her office to sit down and catch up on the stack of supply orders, catering contracts, and staff schedule requests, among other tasks that required her attention. She opened her laptop, tapped the power button, and snuggled into the most comfortable chair in the entire restaurant. Taking a long sigh, she reached up to the band that gathered her hair and released her curls from the tension of her usual ponytail. Aubrey removed her clogs, wiggled her toes, unbuttoned her black chef's coat, and scanned the white four walls surrounding her. The familiar sight of cluttered bookshelves filled with every cookbook imaginable, the bulletin board pinned with proposed menus and notes, and the aroma of fried chicken hung heavily in the air. She was drained, her energy long gone.

"Here you go, boss," Starr announced as she set a plate of smothered chicken, wild rice, and collard greens onto her desk. "And your lemonade. Can I get you anything else?"

"No, Starr. Thank you. This is what I need. Good food and a breather. Thank you for taking care of me." Even a smile was a struggle as Aubrey tried to give Starr her attempt at one.

"I'll get started prepping for dinner. Take all the time you need." Starr smiled and swung her long braids around to her other side. She turned to leave Aubrey's office. "You want your door closed?"

"Yes. I'll be out in a while to help." Aubrey grabbed her drink and downed a hefty gulp.

While reading a news article on soda sales and the regaining popularity of flavored sodas, a pop-up ad flashed across the screen, advertising San Francisco and its romantic charm. A lover's getaway. The night after the food competition replayed in vivid detail. Benson's intense gaze, his soft lips and how his kisses made her feel things she hadn't in... forever. Why did she succumb to his advance? They were both high on their win, but there was something else about him she didn't realize in culinary school. Benson Carter was a sexy man, and she couldn't resist his invisible force that drew her in.

Taking a sip of her lemonade to clear her head, Aubrey clicked open her email account to a long list of unread communications. A new message at the top, the subject line reading, "New Accountant" snagged her attention. She didn't have an accountant. She did all of her books herself. It must be a mistake. She hovered her mouse over the message and clicked to open it. Taking a bite of her food, her eyes drifted over the words.

Hello Ms. Carroll,

My name is Christy Young, Certified Public Accountant. I was hired by Tory and Bill Carroll to assist and oversee all monetary matters related to your businesses. Please call me at your earliest convenience to set up a meeting. I look forward to working with you.

Sincerely,

Christy Young, CPA

Young and Associates

The last name Young was familiar. Aubrey's parents worked with that accounting firm. Why did they hire an accountant for her? She was behind on her accounting, but didn't think it was necessary to have her own accountant. The realization hit her. A Christy Young went to college with her and Nicole. She lived on their floor in the dorms. Aubrey could've sworn she got her degree in accounting. She was certain it was the same person. The ringtone she gave her parents for incoming calls and messages interrupted her thoughts. Grabbing her phone, she tapped in the security code and opened the text message.

Mom: Hello, dear. Your father and I need you to come over after you close today. It's important.

All she wanted to do was get home and collapse into bed. Something she rarely did.

> **Aubrey**: I'm off in a few days. Can we talk then?

The three dots bounced on the screen as her mother responded to her question.

> **Mom**: We need to discuss business, and it can't wait.

She wasn't getting out of this one. Her parents were usually flexible people. Their demands left no room for an escape.

> **Aubrey**: I'll be there at about 10. I'll get Starr to close.

> **Mom**: See you then, dear.

For the next hour, Aubrey finished her meal, reduced her task list, and responded to emails. When she entered the kitchen, the clatter of pots and pans echoed and the smell of garlic and herbs greeted her. Dinner. Her sous chefs chopped vegetables and seasoned meats for made-to-order requests, concentrating on the upcoming influx of dinner guests. Aubrey lost herself as she stirred the creamy cheese sauce. She tenderly stirred the sauce into the pasta, then folded in shredded cheese. She topped the pan with more cheese, then placed it into the oven to bake. While one of the top menu items was baking in the oven, Aubrey went over the inventory for the night with Starr.

"Do we have all we need for the dessert selections?" Aubrey asked, checking the racks for items left over from lunch.

"Peach cobbler, chocolate chip bread pudding topped with a brandy sauce, and red velvet cake are our choices tonight, right?" Starr asked, checking the pantry for all the ingredients.

"Yes."

"Then we're all good. We'll have to order some things in the morning to restock, though." Starr always stayed on top of replenishing what they used.

"Can I ask you a favor, Starr?" The lingering weight of the night's meeting with her parents pushed down on her shoulders.

"Sure, boss. What is it?" She stood in front of Aubrey, hands on her hips, popping her gum.

"Can you close tonight? I have to meet with my parents. I'll close tomorrow if that works for you."

"I have to cancel my date for tonight, but I'm sure Jamaal will understand." As she said his name, her eyes sparkled.

Starr Grayson first walked into Aubrey's restaurant three years ago, eyes wide with a blend of hope and determination. Fresh out of community college and uncertain of her path, she nervously asked Aubrey for a job, her admiration evident. Starr had devoured the article on Aubrey's grand opening and couldn't help but gush about her inspiration. She admitted to a little kitchen experience but promised to learn whatever it took, even if it meant starting at the dish sink. Aubrey, caught off guard by her enthusiasm, hired her on the spot.

Starr was her protégé. A restaurateur in training. She was young, trendy, and full of energy. Her beautiful light honey brown skin and signature clear lip gloss reminded Aubrey of her younger years when she and Nicole tried to be the trendsetters at their school. Like Starr, they wore the latest shoes and outfits. Starr looked exceptional in her clothes, standing five feet eight inches tall and model thin. Even at her tender age of twenty-three, Starr was dependable, reliable, and someone Aubrey was happy to have working at Aubrey's Favorites. Her ability to handle things when Aubrey had to step away always came in handy. The bakery wasn't going to miraculously prepare itself for the opening.

In matters of love, Starr's heart seemed to leap from one romance to the next, always chasing that high, falling fast and replacing the last with the latest. She was in love with the idea of love, constantly swept away by it. She was the total opposite of Aubrey, dodging affection like it was a complication she couldn't afford. Aubrey steered clear of any man who even hinted at interest in her. These were reasons her kissing Benson was out of character for her.

"Jamaal, huh? He's been around for a while now, right?" Aubrey couldn't keep up with Starr's dates. But his name had been on repeat for a few weeks now.

"Yeah, Jamaal. It's fine. We can go to the movies tomorrow. I got you." Starr beamed a big grin.

"Thanks. I appreciate it," Aubrey said with dread.

The dinner crowd was steady, but not too busy. A few hours before closing, Aubrey bid her staff goodnight, grabbed her tote bag, and headed to her car.

As Aubrey drove up the driveway, the warm glow from every window of the house illuminated the night, casting soft beams of light onto the front lawn. She sat in the car a moment longer, hands gripping the steering wheel, and took in a deep, steadying breath. The conversation awaiting her would be anything but easy. An accountant? She needed every ounce of composure she could muster to get through this talk.

Before she could ring the doorbell, Bill Carroll stood in the open doorway, an expression of concern across his brows.

"Hi, Dad," Aubrey greeted, reaching out to hug her father.

"Aubrey." Bill gave her a tight but quick embrace before speaking. "Let's sit in the living room, shall we?"

Heavy unspoken words loitered in the living room. The silence of the space pressed against her like a thick fog. Aubrey shifted uneasily on the chenille, sand colored couch. The ticking grandfather clock amplified the tension, each second a reminder that sitting in that room rarely led to anything good.

Aubrey's fingers tightened around each other, knuckles turning pale as she gazed at the framed photo, eyes tracing the familiar smile she'd seen only in still images and never in real life. The face of the one she longed for—her silent partner in dreams and imaginary conversations. If only her sister had been here, her world would be different, freer somehow, with a kind of support that was more like strength rather than restraint. She wouldn't be bracing herself for another attempt to cage her in "for her own good". Another talk meant to remind her of limits she didn't feel but that her parents imposed.

"Hello, dear." Tory walked up to her daughter and kissed her cheek.

"Hi, Mom," Aubrey said softly, hoping to conceal the nervousness in her voice.

"We asked you here tonight to discuss the finances of your restaurant." Bill's tone carried an air of authority and seriousness.

Aubrey could only affirm her dad's statement with a nod. Tory settled beside her husband, nodding in agreement.

Bill sat, legs crossed, hands folded on his lap. "We hired an accountant to handle all of your finances for the restaurant. As your investors, we believe it prudent to transition this burgeoning empire you're constructing into a more corporate arena."

Aubrey's gaze darted between her dad and her mom. Was this it? Was this why they insisted she come in person to talk? This conversation could've been handled on the phone. They made all of her business decisions, anyway. God forbid she did something on her own. Their business success was admirable. She wanted to build her own empire. She was compelled to speak.

"Dad. I know the restaurant is increasing in profits. This is why we were thinking opening a bakery was a good idea. I guess you have a point about the need for an accountant. It'll be hard to manage the books for both."

"You decided to make the purchase. You took a huge risk without consulting us. Is opening a bakery at this time a good idea? And you thought it was okay to pay the excessive amount of money for the space next door to Aubrey's Favorites? Your mother and I wouldn't have said no. However, we would have consulted our accountants first. We would have seen if the budget could withstand such a big purchase. Budgets are important, Aubrey."

"Dad, I know. But this isn't the first of us discussing a bakery. When I learned the space became available, I couldn't wait. I had to move quickly, otherwise I was going to lose the space."

For the first time in her life, Aubrey made a compulsive business decision. For the first time, she didn't think about what could go wrong. For once, she took control of what she was sure was a good business decision.

"Aubrey, dear. You should have come to us. We're a team in all of this." Tory's words were always warm, and her intent was not to scold or hurt her child. "Your father and I would not have been able to build our string of Brewed Awakening coffee shops without being guarded in our decision making."

"So, how do you intend to finance the build out of your bakery? Do you have a plan? Do you have estimates?" Bill went straight to the point.

"I haven't made a plan yet. I just bought the property. Aubrey's Favorites has been really busy. We have a few big catering contracts to fill. I'll be able to make a plan in a few months." When the words came out of her mouth, Aubrey knew her father would not like her answer. She watched her father's face flush with anger.

"I suggest you use the money you won. Ms. Chef Supreme," Bill snapped.

Aubrey quickly smoothed her expression, forcing a neutral look as her eyes darted away, but the faint flush on her cheeks and the nervous twitch at the corner of her mouth betrayed her. She kept her gaze low, hoping her forced calm would mask the guilt twisting inside. They watched the competition. There was no hiding that fact. They waited for this very moment to tell her.

"Aubrey, you won two-hundred-fifty thousand dollars. Were you going to tell us? The fact that you lied to us about where you were is for another day." Fury radiated from her father's face, flushed with betrayal as he stood and began pacing the room. "How could you just leave without telling us?"

"I told you I was leaving. I just didn't tell you exactly where I was going." Aubrey flinched after her last word. Her tone was not making her case.

Disappointment laced Bill's voice. His eyes suddenly bore into hers, his accusing glance a reminder of the trust she broke. "You know how we worry."

Aubrey sat, twisting her fingers anxiously in her lap. The crease in her brow deepened as she glanced at the beige carpet. Worry. That word was in her ear her entire life. She understood their worry was rooted in Avery's death. Could she live her life without her parents worrying about her? Worrying about her safety? Her ability to run a business? Living life away from their coveted nest?

Bill cleared his throat. "Meet with Christy Young. She can help you figure out how you'll build out your bakery with your Chef Supreme winnings. Your mother and I aren't giving you a dime."

"Dad. You know it'll cost more than that to build out the bakery," Aubrey said, her voice trembling a little, the quiver betraying the calm facade she tried to maintain. She could feel the heat rising in her cheeks.

"You should have thought about that before you placed the outrageous bid on the property. You went way above market value."

Aubrey didn't think about market value. She had to have the property next door to her restaurant. The word around the culinary world was a few chefs were looking at that same space. At the last Los Angeles chefs collaborative, Aubrey's seatmate shared there was a big name chef looking to relocate from New York to the L.A. area. A text message from Kate, her realtor, said there was another bidder on the property—the property she had to have. Was Benson Carter the chef who was moving from New York to the west coast seeking a new restaurant space? The time spent in San Francisco was for another purpose. Her intuition told her he was the other bidder. No way was she going to mention the property she won. Her time to gloat would come later. She was determined to win. And she did. She couldn't bring herself to confess the truth to her parents. Their support for her business empire was dwindling. The truth would ruin her.

"Mom? Dad? You said that having a bakery next door to the restaurant was ideal." Aubrey hoped her parents would recall the practicality of having the restaurant and bakery side by side.

Bill sighed before responding. "Yes, we see the importance, and it makes good business sense. But was this the right time? Did you have permission to spend what you spent? The property purchase was your statement, a bold flex of your influence and ambition to be completely independent. Which is why we hired Christy. You and Christy can figure out how to build your bakery with your winnings from the televised food contest."

Aubrey needed to shift the conversation. "Is Christy related to the Youngs from Young and Associates?"

Tory smiled, then spoke. "She's Mr. Young's daughter. She went to college with you."

Aubrey's eyes lit up with this news. She could discuss finances with Christy and keep her parents out of it.

"I got an email from her today. I'll reach out to her next week and set up a time to meet with her."

"Good." Bill's expression softened with relief, knowing she now had a professional to handle all the business's finances.

For several moments, Aubrey sat silently simmering in anger at the person responsible for her property predicament. Damn Benson Carter.

Chapter 8

Aubrey

Aubrey stood in front of the glass building, taking a deep breath to steady herself. Her reflection stared back at her, mirroring mixed feelings of determination and apprehension. Gathering her nerves, she squared her shoulders and took the first step forward, the weight of the moment pressing heavily on her. She didn't understand why the idea of meeting with the accountant her parents hired for her was so challenging. She was usually assertive and embraced difficult tasks with grace. The sleek, modern facade loomed above, both intimidating and inviting as she moved closer to the entrance, ready to face whatever awaited inside. Mr. Young had been her father's accountant for as long as she could remember. The chain of coffee shops her parents owned in California, Nevada, and Arizona required financial oversight. Now her one restaurant and soon to be bakery required the same attention.

Aubrey's memories of her parents' Brewed Awakening coffee shop on Olive Street, downtown, went as far back as about age four. She stacked the empty cups near the coffee machine. Her small hands grabbed sugar packets to fill the empty clear plastic containers on the condiment station. She filled the napkin holders with fresh white napkins and added straws to the container for iced coffee drinks they sold. The older she became, her responsibilities grew to wiping down the tables and unloading the deliveries in the kitchen. A few years after that, her mom let her help with the baked goods. It was in the coffee shop kitchen where she learned to make her infamous lemon pound cake. By the time she was in high school, her parents opened ten more shops around California and were scouting spaces in Arizona. High school was supposed to be time for fun, dating, and going to football games. But the coffee shops were all Aubrey knew. They were all her parents allowed her to experience. She was always under their close watch.

Losing Avery changed their family dynamic. Avery's death sent shockwaves through her life, even though Aubrey was an infant when she was killed. When Avery died, a piece of her parents' world shattered in a way that could never fully be repaired. Grief gripped their lives, not just in sadness but as a fierce determination to keep their remaining daughter safe. Every small risk, every step outside their protective reach, sent a pang of fear into them, as though letting Aubrey go too far might result in another unbearable loss. Over the years, their love for her became layered with caution, as if by holding her close, they could shield her from every harm. What began as a quiet watchfulness evolved into constant check-ins, gentle but firm boundaries, and subtle reminders of all the things she should avoid. Their protectiveness, born from love and loss, wrapped around her like a cocoon—meant to keep her safe, yet stifling in its weight.

Business school was the plan her parents prepared for. Taking over the family business was the safe plan. By the time she was a junior in college, though, Aubrey was certain she had to blaze her own path.

"Hello. I have an appointment with Christy Young," Aubrey said to the man sitting at the security check-in desk.

"Name?"

"Aubrey Carroll."

"Ah, yes. Ms. Young is expecting you. You can head up to the fifth floor. The receptionist will direct you from there," the man said, handing her a visitor's sticker to place on her person.

"Thank you." Aubrey headed to the elevators. The one on the right opened immediately. She entered and pressed five. As the door closed and the elevator moved upward, she lowered her head, took in a deep breath and exhaled all her fears. She would face this with no apprehension. With renewed resolve, she stepped forward, exited the elevator, and walked in with her head held high.

"Aubrey. It's so nice to see you again," Christy greeted, with her extended hand waiting to make Aubrey's acquaintance.

"Christy. It's so good to see you. How have you been?"

Christy led them into her office, waving for Aubrey to sit in the chair opposite her desk.

"I've been good. After graduation, I passed the CPA exam and jumped right into my parents' practice. I hear you are doing big things. And what about Seth? You two tied the knot, right?"

Seth was Aubrey's first serious relationship. Like her, Seth had a passion for food. They experimented with recipes and cooked for their college friends. He, too, wanted to go to culinary school after college graduation. Together, they researched the best cooking institutions and applied. They dreamed of owning a restaurant together. After graduation, they would begin their lives, not just as a married couple, but as partners in business.

The scene from that day played in Aubrey's head like an old movie. In the dim light of the dressing room, she sat wrapped in the cool soft pink slip robe, the fabric slipping through her fingers as she recognized the look on her father's face the second he walked into the room. The mirror reflected her wide eyes, still glistening with remnants of excitement, now clouded with hurt and disbelief. His look was one she was familiar with. Her father was coming to share bad news.

"Baby girl. I'm so sorry. Seth isn't coming."

Her phone buzzed against the vanity, shattering her stillness as her dad's words momentarily paralyzed her. She picked it up at the sight of Seth's name plastered across her screen. In a text message, he confirmed why her heart was shattering.

Seth: I'm sorry Aubrey. I can't marry you.

Tears rolled down her makeup-covered cheeks.

In a low, saddened whisper, Aubrey spoke, her words barely audible, heavy with the weight of unspoken emotion. "Seth isn't coming."

"He's not coming. The wedding is off." Bill walked toward his daughter, lowering himself to catch her in an embrace. Aubrey's breath caught in her throat as the gravity of this news settled over her. She was isolated in a sea of silence, her dreams unraveling like the delicate lace of her wedding dress.

In a low tone, Aubrey spoke. "Seth and I broke up right after graduation." To shift the conversation away from herself, Aubrey said with a bright smile, "But you know who is getting married? Nicole Graham."

"Really? Congratulations to her. How exciting," Christy said, opening a drawer, pulling out a brown folder with Aubrey's name spelled across the front.

"I'm catering it. As a gift to her."

Christy placed her folded hands on the desk, signaling she was ready to begin their meeting. "So, tell me about Aubrey's Favorites."

"After college, I went to culinary school. I wanted to ground myself in my career, instead of taking over my parents' string of Brewed Awakening shops. I perfected family recipes and created my own. My parents wanted an investment. I convinced them to invest in me." Aubrey was proud of her culinary story. It was one aspect of her life she owned and succeeded in, for the most part.

"Well, I see you have a lot of passion for what you do." Christy gave Aubrey a warm smile, then went straight for the jugular. "Your parents turned over all of your financials, and I have reviewed them. You just bought the property next door to expand your business and open a bakery, right? How do you plan to finance the build out?"

Aubrey was hoping there was some money to start the planning for Aubrey's Sweets. "Am I broke, Christy?"

"As of today, you can maybe pay the architect to draw up plans. But that's it."

This news was a shock to Aubrey's gut. What would she do now? No wonder her parents were so upset. She had to get back into their good graces. She glanced at her accountant, her eyebrows slightly raised and her lips pursed in a confused frown. The uncertainty in her eyes conveyed an unmistakably lost expression.

Christy stared into Aubrey's unsettled eyes for a moment, then spoke. "Your parents shared that you recently won a nice sum in a cooking contest?"

Aubrey gave Christy a jovial grin. "I won two-hundred-fifty thousand dollars in San Francisco. I'm the Chef Supreme." She was confident coming off that big win.

Christy flipped to Aubrey's file. "I'm not sure how much it'll cost to build out the bakery, but I'm almost certain that's not enough."

"What am I supposed to do?" Aubrey didn't know what to say.

"You can sell the property," Christy suggested.

At the mere thought of selling her property, heat crept up Aubrey's neck, her cheeks flushing with embarrassment. She wouldn't think of regretting her purchase. "I won't sell. You're the accountant. You have to help me figure it out."

Christy looked up from the file, an inquisitive look blasted across her face. "You get me three sets of plans and the estimated costs for the build out, and we'll come up with a plan."

If Aubrey was going to prove to her parents that she was ready and capable of breaking free of their hold, she had to do this on her own—no safety nets, no second chances.

Chapter 9

Benson

Smokewood and Ember renovations were well under way. The restaurant space was a chaotic symphony of hammers, saws, and voices. Dust floated in the air, illuminated by beams of sunlight streaming through the large, uncovered windows. Half-finished walls framed the dining area, where exposed wooden beams stretched overhead, giving a glimpse of the modern-rustic aesthetic Benson was aiming for.

In the back, the kitchen was slowly taking shape. Stainless steel appliances were being installed, the ovens gleaming under construction lights. Electricians worked on the wiring for the overhead exhaust fans, while plumbers checked the new lines leading to the sinks and dishwashers. Stacks of tiles lay near the bar, waiting to be placed, their rich, deep colors promising to transform the raw space into something warm and inviting. The back room was lined with massive, industrial sized steel charcoal smokers, their bulky frames dominating the space.

The contractor turned to see Benson inspecting the space. "Hey, boss. The screens will go in tomorrow. They'll give you the ventilation you need without letting in the bugs and critters that come with smoking meats."

Benson nodded in agreement. "Good. This is all good."

Benson moved from the back room into the kitchen to direct where to position the ovens when a woman's voice from the front of the restaurant caught his attention.

"Yes, I'm Piper Ramsey. And you are?" the woman said, condescension dripping from her voice.

"Ma'am, I'm with the crew. Are you here to see Mr. Carter?" the worker asked, wiping his paint covered hands on his company t-shirt.

"Please. Tell him I'm here." The man nodded and walked toward the back of the space.

Benson peeked around the corner to see his mother eyeing every inch of the front of the restaurant. Piper Ramsey, his forever discerning expert. Three-time Michelin awarded chef and restaurateur, she wore her signature salt-and-pepper pixie cut that framed her smooth brown skinned face perfectly, excluding elegance and confidence. She was decorated in her usual tailor-fitted suit and white button-up blouse. On this day, the heather gray tone of her slacks and blazer gave her an all about business look that he knew all too well.

"Mom! It's so good to see you," Benson said, arms open to greet Piper with a hug.

"Son. I like the exposed brick. That's a nice touch." Returning the embrace, she gave her son a peck on his cheek.

"Take a look around. I think it's coming along nicely," Benson said with confidence, knowing her critique was coming. No matter how well he was doing, she always had commentary.

"Well, I see the potential. Although, you had a beautiful restaurant in New York." Piper then glanced directly into Benson's eyes, no emotion on her face.

"Aww, New York. Well, Los Angeles is my home now, Mom." He couldn't let her bring his emotions down with her scrutiny.

"At least you are in a good location. I know a few restaurants in the area. You'll be in good company. Or not." Piper turned her body to face her son, giving her full attention to him. "So, tell me what your menu will be like."

Benson perfected his New York restaurant menu to be one of the best in the city. His one misstep crushed the hard work and dedication he poured into building New York's top food destination. It came crashing down and shattered within seconds. This new location and menu offered a fresh start.

"I'm installing a few charcoal smokers in the back. I thought it would add a new dimension to my signature meats."

"A smoker? Go on." Piper nodded.

"I'll take advantage of the fresh produce you can't get on the east coast. Salads, grilled vegetables, and the sides I'm best known for will be staples on this menu." Benson crossed his arms across his chest, waiting for the rebuttal.

"I like it. Do you think this place will provide the platform you need to repair your reputation in the industry?" Piper now stood directly in front of her son.

"Mom, I don't know. I hope so. I want to put New York behind me. This is a new beginning."

Piper was silent for a few moments, taking in her son's face. Her lips were set in a stern line, not a hint of a smile to be found. "Your top priorities are to open your new restaurant successfully. You can even earn the recognition you were on the path to earn in New York."

"Mom. I already know. I get it." Benson's irritation was written in his eyes.

Piper snapped him a look. "As I've always said, you must be mindful of the company you keep. Know their background, really who they are. You're back in L.A. Things are different from the last time you lived here. You have a reputation to rebuild. Dating should be the least of your worries. Relationships are the worst distraction. If you're to rebuild your status in this industry, you must adhere to this fact. I didn't get to where I am without that constant indication. A woman and your misjudgments put you here. I hope you've learned your lesson. I don't know if you truly know how much damage control I had to do to ensure that the blowup in New York didn't follow you here."

The lyrics to this song were well known. No time for a relationship. No time for a girlfriend. Business first. The song had played in Benson's ear since he was a teenager. Like his mother, he dreamed of being a chef. Piper Ramsey was the darling of the self-made, award winning, restaurant conglomerate chef and business woman. He watched his mother work tirelessly to make a name for herself, at the cost of her family. These days, Piper was a little more relaxed, mentoring up-and-coming chefs, consulting restaurant groups and taking on special projects. Most of her culinary criticisms were reserved for her son, including her unrealistic views on his personal life.

A weight of guilt sat on Benson's shoulders. In a low voice, Benson responded to Piper's statement. "I'm grateful to you. I know I made a mess of things in New York. I failed to do my homework—learning who she was and her status in the industry. Now I'm paying the price for the slipup. I owe you more than I can ever repay for giving me space to start new here in Los Angeles."

Piper Ramsey was so driven, to a point which executed her own marriage to his father. The wall around her heart was made of stone. He didn't think anything or anyone could blast through that encasing. Not even him. Benson couldn't relinquish what he was certain his mother was thinking. Failure was not an option.

With a quick shift in his tone, Benson spoke again. "My name will shine, two-point-oh. I'm talented. I'm a great chef." Benson was now on the defensive. He didn't know if his mother worked to protect his reputation or hers.

"Son, I know you are. If I didn't know your talents, I wouldn't have put my own neck on the line to conduct crisis management."

"And I appreciate it. My food and new restaurant will rehab the mess I made in New York." Benson had to believe his words to be true.

"When your name is restored, I am, too." Piper peaked behind her son, up to the ceiling, then back on him.

Benson thought his mother's eyes softened, if only for a second. Removing his work apron, he went to the counter to grab his wallet and car keys. "How about we get some lunch? I know a great place about ten minutes from here. I can share more details about Smokewood and Ember."

"Smokewood and Ember? Is that the name you settled on?"

Benson had to admit he liked the sound of it coming from his mother. "Yes. Do you like it?"

"I do." A quick smile flickered across Piper's face.

This was all he was going to get from the acclaimed chef he called Mom.

Chapter 10

Aubrey

Aubrey moved through the dining area of her restaurant, clearing tables that held traces of the bustling breakfast rush. Crumb filled plates, coffee mugs, and used silverware were carried from now empty tables into the kitchen for cleaning. Crumbled napkins from satisfied diners went into the trash bin. She wiped down each table with a damp cloth, the faint scent of pine cleaner mingled with the aroma of her cooking staff preparing lunch stables. With a hot cup of coffee in hand, she headed to the booth where Nicole sat, laptop open, culinary books, and a notepad spread out next to her.

"So, what's the best food stylist, writer, critic working on today?" Aubrey asked, sliding into the opposite side of the booth.

Nicole tapped on a few more computer keys before looking up. "Today, I'm wearing my food stylist hat. I'm finishing the menu layouts for the renovated hotel restaurant in Santa Barbara. Carol and I will shoot photos of the food next week. Can I get more coffee?"

Without a word, Aubrey took Nicole's mug, went into the kitchen to refill it and returned with a slice of her lemon pound cake.

"Is that for me? You know I come in here every chance I get to get lunch and a piece of your delicious cake." Jim Stone stood at the counter, dressed in his police uniform, joy radiating in his grin.

"Hey, Jim. How's it going? Do you want to order something?" Aubrey set the coffee and cake in front of Nicole and called for Starr to take his order. "Come join us while you wait."

"Hey, Jim." Nicole waved in his direction. She shot Aubrey a narrowed look. "Now you know I shouldn't eat that. I have to fit in my dress in a couple of months."

Aubrey smiled at Nicole, giddy for her upcoming wedding to Cameron. "I know. But a few bites won't hurt. You're working. I didn't see you eat any breakfast."

"I had some toast and fruit at home. I needed a change in scenery to finish this project. Cameron is there, and he's a distraction." Nicole took a sip of her fresh coffee and winked at her friend.

Jim walked toward Aubrey and Nicole. "Mind if I sit?"

"Please." Both spoke at the same time.

"How are you, Nicole? How are the wedding plans?" Jim asked.

"Yeah. I figured you'd be working on wedding stuff. Is everything all set? I know your menu is." The wedding menu was Aubrey's creation, something she carefully crafted the moment Nicole announced her engagement. Each dish, chosen with intention, reflected a blend of flavors and memories they shared growing up, making the food as personal as the day itself.

"I'm good, Jim. Really good." She flashed a wide grin. "Do you want to hear wedding details?"

"Been there, done that. I'm so glad Tara and I planned a small one."

"It was a beautiful wedding. I'm so happy for you two. Finding each other after dating in middle school."

"Being stranded on the freeway that day was a true blessing." Jim's eyes softened. "I'm happy you found Cameron."

"Me, too." Nicole's eyes glimmered with happiness. "Anyway, the venue coordinator will take care of everything from this point."

"What's left to do?" Aubrey catered weddings, but she never planned one.

"The flowers are picked out. You, Levi, and Carol have your outfits. Cameron's groomsmen have ordered their tuxedos. My dress will be ready next month. We'll come for food tasting soon. I think that's it." Nicole let out a deep sigh, hearts now dancing in her eyes. "You and Tara are coming, right?"

"We already requested that day off. We won't be patrolling the streets and highways that day."

At that moment, Jim's radio went off. "Suspect in custody, requesting transport."

He stood. "That's my cue." He turned to see his order waiting on the counter. "I'll take my lunch and eat it in the car."

"You eat while you have a suspect in the car?" Aubrey questioned.

"I'm not in handcuffs. Besides, I don't want my burger to get cold."

They all shared a laugh.

Slowly walking to grab his food, Jim said, "I'll see you at the wedding, Nicole. I can't wait to see you become Mrs. Cameron Davis. He's a good dude."

Nicole formed a heart with her hands and held them to her chest.

"I know I'll see you or Tara soon."

Jim jogged toward the door. "For sure. Bye, ladies."

Aubrey and Nicole watched Jim get into his squad car and pull off, fries dangling from his mouth.

Nicole released a swoosh of air. "I can't wait to be Mrs. Cameron

Davis."

"You two. Finally," Aubrey said with a smirk.

"I know. We had a great beginning, a rocky middle, but our ending is happily ever after." Nicole's eyes danced with happiness. "If you hadn't talked to Cameron that day, I don't know where we would be."

"I think he would have missed you too much and eventually talked to you. Or you would have gone to him." Aubrey was there when Nicole lost Tyler. Losing Tyler was hard for Jim, too. No one wants to lose their best friend. It was devastating for Nicole to lose the man she thought she would spend the rest of her life with. She wasn't sure if Nicole was ever going to love again. Cameron entered her life and showed her how to be loved in ways she didn't think possible. He rescued her.

Nicole pushed her back against the seat cushion and sighed. "I think I would've gone to Cameron. I know his love for me is unwavering, just as my love for him is unbreakable."

"Spoken like a woman in love." Aubrey was happy for Nicole. Love was not on her agenda. Lately, the mention of love takes her back to San Francisco and the hotel hallway. Benson's kisses.

"Aubrey, you didn't tell me how San Francisco was. I mean, you told me you won, but no details. Spill." Nicole closed her laptop and gave Aubrey her full attention.

Aubrey closed her eyes for a moment. Were her rosy cheeks telling on her? In an instant, a big ear to ear grin spread across her face. It radiated pure joy. "I won a huge sum of money."

"Really? What are you going to do with your winnings?"

Aubrey's bright smile faltered, the light in her eyes dimming. "I need to build out the bakery. My parents are upset with what I spent purchasing the space next door. I went way over market value. They think I don't value money. They're not helping me."

"What? What do you mean?" Nicole was confused. "I've always known your parents to invest in your business, no matter the cost."

"Well, I pushed it this time around. I didn't tell them about me buying the space next door. I just did it. We talked about it, but there was no immediate plan. I took a huge risk. I really stepped out of their shadow. I wanted to make my own decision. It may be a mistake, Nicole. I needed them to see me as capable and self-sufficient without being in their tight, overprotective hold. They refuse to fund the bakery build out now. They said I need to use the money I won in San Francisco."

"They found out about that, too? Oh, boy. What are you going to do?"

"Thanks to my parents and their unwavering support of my restaurant, plus the fact that they think I can't manage money, I now have an accountant that's overseeing my finances. My accountant said I may have enough for plans and some of the build out. I have to get three estimates and meet with her again to create a plan."

Aubrey's expression brightened. "You actually know my accountant. She went to college with us. Christy Young?"

"Christy Young?" Nicole held a perplexed expression until recognition showed in her appearance. "I remember her now. She's your accountant?"

"Little did I know her parents own the accounting firm my parents use."

"Oh. Small world. How's that going?"

Aubrey took a deep breath. "It's going. She's sweet. She'll keep me on my toes. I guess if I'm building an empire, I need an accountant."

"That's true. But how will you raise the money to open the bakery?"

Aubrey could finally come clean, the weight of the secret pressing heavily on her chest. Telling her best friend would mean unveiling her secret. It was the only way to lift the burden she was carrying.

"You know how overprotective my parents are. I wanted to do something on my own for once. I wanted to make my own decision. When the property became available, I jumped at the chance to bid. My competitive side got the best of me when I learned there was a second bidder."

"I know you're competitive. But spending that kind of money is really reckless. Did you assume your parents would foot the bill?" Nicole took a sip of her coffee and bit into her lemon pound cake.

"My parents have no problem building their investment portfolio. Real estate is one of the best ways to do that. I figured they would be upset initially. I just didn't know how upset they would be."

Nicole opened her mouth, then closed it before speaking. "Did you research the market? Did you even know how much you were spending?"

Aubrey shook her head. "See, that's the thing. When I learned who was bidding on the property, I needed to win. I had to have the building, no matter the cost."

"And the bidder was the guy you showed us when we were dress shopping? Why did you feel the need to compete with that guy?"

"I had to beat him. We were rivals in culinary school, pushing each other to the limit. Just hearing his name puts me on edge, like the crack of the starter pistol in a race. I'm ready to win."

"Aubrey. I'm shocked. When was the last time you saw him?" Nicole held Aubrey's gaze, waiting for her response.

Aubrey chuckled, then shrugged her shoulders. A wave of nostalgia crashed in front of her as she inhaled, breathing in the fragrance only one person wore. One she never smelt on anyone else. She turned her head to see Benson Carter standing in front of her booth, arms crossed over his chest. He nodded. Then he said, "Why are you lying to your friend?

We were just in San Francisco together, sugar."

Chapter 11

Benson

At the sound of his voice, Benson could see Aubrey's face marked with furrowed brows. Her sharp intake of breath, followed by a subtle clenching of her jaw, made him grin. She glanced up at him, her eyes slowly tracing his features as if recollecting every detail from their shared kiss. He was certain she was checking him out, admiring the look of his blue jeans and white t-shirt that clung to his upper body, perfectly hugging the contours of his muscles. Irritation showed on her face. He was certain his effortless swagger affected her, grating on her nerves. The smugness of his grin was sure to drive her crazy.

With her nostrils flaring ever so slightly, she asked, "What are *you* doing in my restaurant? Why are you in Los Angeles? Why aren't you in New York?"

Benson let out a low chuckle. "Well, sugar, I just couldn't resist trading freezing temperatures for flip-flops and sunsets by the beach."

"You live back in L.A. now?" Aubrey asked in a slow drawl.

Benson flashed his killer smile. "Yep! Can I order something?"

"Well, if you're feeling brave, there are plenty of other venues to test your luck with a meal. Why here?"

"I've done my homework. Let's hope you live up to the hype." Benson gave Aubrey a curt smile and walked over to the counter to order. Aubrey whispered to the woman sitting across from her. He took a certain pleasure in getting under her skin. He found amusement in every subtle reaction he provoked out of Aubrey. Since their kiss, she was in his head.

Benson walked back to the booth holding a tall glass of lemonade. "Mind if I sit?" He didn't wait for an answer. He sat next to Aubrey, forcing her to move further into the booth.

"Hello. I'm sorry for Aubrey's rudeness. I'm Benson Carter. And you are?" He held out his hand to greet Aubrey's booth companion.

"I'm Nicole. Nicole Graham. Aubrey and I are the closest of friends and sometimes business partners." They shook on their introduction.

"Aubrey and I go way back as well. We went to culinary school together. Lost touch and actually competed together in San Francisco recently." Benson could feel the heat radiate off of Aubrey's body. She was fuming.

"So, you were in San Francisco, huh?" Nicole asked, her gaze now focused on Aubrey.

"Yes, yes, I was."

"Did you win a prize, too?"

Benson guessed by Nicole's question, Aubrey neglected to mention him and their joint victory. "Yes, yes, I did. You see, there was a partner challenge that upped the competition, increasing the winnings. We're a pretty great team in the kitchen. Our cooking chemistry is spot on." Benson glanced over at Aubrey, giving her a wink.

"Really?" Nicole had an amused look on her face as her gaze moved from his face back to Aubrey's.

"Your burger and fries," a young woman said as she placed a full plate in front of him.

"Thank you, sweetie." Benson turned to Aubrey to watch her slump in the very spot she sat?

"So, Benson? You're a chef. Do you own a restaurant?" Nicole asked with heightened curiosity.

"I do. I'm opening my spot down the street." He shoved a few fries in his mouth.

He sensed Aubrey's body stiffen. "Down the street? What street?" she asked.

Benson swallowed his fries and raised his burger to take a bite. His first bite of the ground beef molded into the perfect thickness of a succulent patty cooked to juicy perfection. The cheese melted to create a luscious, gooey layer added to the burger's depth. Fresh, crisp lettuce and a slice of a ripe, thick tomato gave him a satisfied crunch and a burst of freshness. It was a damned good burger. Aubrey had talent. There wasn't a question in that. But he couldn't tell her these thoughts. "My restaurant will be on this street. We're neighbors." Out of the corner of his eye, he caught Aubrey's eyes rolling.

The delight that registered on Nicole's face was priceless. She followed up by asking, "What's the name? What kind of food will you be serving?"

"Smokewood and Ember. I'll be serving smoked high end cuts of meat, grilled vegetables. All fresh ingredients, of course, with signature sides."

"I'm a food stylist and critic. Let me know if you need marketing services or a good write up in the local publications. I have connections everywhere." Nicole glanced at Aubrey, then widened her eyes slightly. This was making her so mad.

Aubrey then spoke. "Oh, I'm sure you'll frame the write up right next to your 'humble chef' award. You're so full of yourself."

Benson took a sip of his lemonade, then barked back, "Well, someone's got to keep your ego in check, and clearly, I'm the perfect person, up for the challenge."

"Hey, baby," a tall man said as he bent down to kiss Nicole, then moved into the booth next to her.

Benson immediately recognized him. "Cameron? Is that you?"

The man glanced over at Benson. "Man? Benson Carter. How the hell are you?"

Both men stood up and greeted one another with a brief hug, slap on the back, and a handshake.

"I'm good, man. I'm opening a spot down the street. You?"

Cameron flashed a big smile, gazed at Nicole, then said, "I'm great. You met my fiancé, Nicole, it looks like."

"Your fiancé? Man, congratulations. I'm so happy for you. It's been a while. How's your mom?"

"She's well. So, you met Aubrey recently? She makes really good food," Cameron remarked.

"Aubrey and I go way back. Great friends. From culinary school." Benson looked at Aubrey and gave her another wink.

Aubrey sat up in the booth and asked, "How do you two know each other?"

"Well, Cameron's mom and my mom were childhood friends. When my mom had a free moment, they would connect, and I always tagged along. We haven't seen each other in a few years."

Cameron sat back down. "It's good to see you. We're getting married soon. You should come to our wedding."

"Why are you inviting him to your wedding?" Aubrey barked.

"I'd be honored to come to your wedding." Benson took another sip of his lemonade and popped another handful of fries into his mouth.

He examined Aubrey and said, "This burger is pretty good."

She glared at him. "Coming from you, that almost sounds like high praise. I'll take it."

"So, Benson, are you building out your restaurant from scratch?" Nicole asked. Her bright smile quickly shifted into a tight-lipped one, forced and strained the moment the dull thud echoed from beneath the table. Her eyes flickered, but she kept her composure, trying not to let the tension in her jaw give her away. Aubrey could be mean, but kick her friend? That was on a new level.

"Yes, I am. It's almost done. I'll be open in a month."

"And is that really expensive? To build up a restaurant from scratch?"

Nicole was asking more intrusive questions than Benson would normally answer, but since she was with Cameron, he opted to respond.

"It can be. It depends on the space. I wanted the space next door to this one, but I was outbid. It worked out, though. The space down the street has exposed brick, and it goes with the aesthetic I'm looking for in my restaurant." Benson took the last bite of his burger and polished off his fries.

"I'm asking for an article I'm writing." Nicole repositioned herself in the booth. "Do you have investors? Did you take out a loan? You don't have to answer if this is too personal."

"No, it's fine. I had some cash. Plus, with the winnings from the contest, I'm coming just under budget."

"Did you know Aubrey's opening her bakery next door?"

With this confession, Benson marked the moment Aubrey's forehead hit the table.

"You good, Aubrey?" he asked.

"Kill me now. Just kill me now," Aubrey said, keeping her face down.

"I did not know she bought the space next door. Now I know who

I lost to." Benson turned to Aubrey. "You didn't tell me that. When will you start the build out? I have a great contractor. I can give you his information."

Aubrey lifted her head and turned to face Benson. "Why are you back in L.A.? The last I heard, you were the man in New York. Lost your touch?"

Benson struggled to mask the ghostly expression that washed over his face at the mention of New York. He gathered his thoughts. With a devilish grin, he responded, saying, "I told you. I'm here for the sunshine and to open L.A.'s new favorite restaurant. By the look on your face, Aubrey, now I see I'm also here to give you a little extra annoyance. Unless you want to pick up where we left off in San Francisco?"

Before dropping her head in her hands, her icy stare blew a chill over Benson.

"What happened in San Francisco?" Cameron and Nicole asked at the same time.

"Nothing!" Aubrey snapped.

"I forgot you were in New York, man. It's good to have you back." Cameron put his hand out for a high five.

To avoid the chance of Aubrey, Cameron, or Nicole asking questions about New York, Benson stood, took in the rest of his drink, then said his goodbyes. "It was great to see you, Cameron. Let's get together soon. And congratulations to you and Nicole." He held out his hand to Nicole and shook it. He slapped hands with Cameron and turned to Aubrey. "And you—don't worry, we'll cross paths again real soon."

Chapter 12

Aubrey

Aubrey's hands clenched into tight fists at her sides, nails digging into her palms as she worked to calm her nerves. The heat crept up her neck, her pulse quickening in her temples. Her skin began crawling the moment Benson sat down next to her. His words echoed in her mind, adding flames to her boiling anger. Was she back in culinary school? Since then, he's been making her angry every time they're in the same room. Why did she let him get to her like this? With Cameron and Nicole now gone, she sat alone in the booth, simmering with emotion. He mentioned San Francisco, and not just the competition. He was thinking about the kiss, too. Despite the best kiss she's ever had, Benson was an enemy.

"Boss lady? You good?" Starr asked as she slowly approached the table.

Aubrey tried to slow her breathing. "That man makes me so angry. I can't stand him."

"He's kinda cute. For you, not me. Jamaal is winning my heart." Starr tried to give Aubrey a smile.

"Benson Carter is far from cute. He's the Antichrist in human form.

He brings darkness wherever he goes."

Starr laughed under her breath. "That's mean. From where I stood, it looked like flirting."

"Flirting? You've got to be kidding me? I was not flirting. We can't stand each other."

"Well, it looked like intense sexual tension to me."

"Starr! You can't be serious. You were far away. I wouldn't date him if he was the last man on earth." The memory of Benson holding her close against her hotel room door flashed through her mind. His lips on hers. Without notice, heat blazed through her entire body.

"If you say so. How do you know him again?" Starr asked, now sitting across from Aubrey.

"We went to culinary school together. On the first day, the first assignment, he turned it into a personal battle I couldn't ignore."

Aubrey caught sight of Benson from the moment he walked into the classroom. His six-feet-two-inch frame caught her attention first. His chef's coat fit snug across his chest, the imprint of pecs shone slightly. When he walked past her, a breeze carried the unmistakable scent of his cologne. The same one he wore today. He smelled of sharp bursts of citrus complemented by warm undertones of earthy notes and a touch of an ocean breeze.

In close proximity to her, she couldn't help but steal a few glances in his direction. Those glances made her feel a faint flutter in her stomach. With that initial introduction to Benson Carter, she found herself swallowing more frequently than usual as she tried to push down the slowly rising nervousness. He caught her staring. She immediately frowned and studied their instructor, pretending to focus on what he was saying. Aubrey learned all the basic kitchen hygiene and safety practices from her father. She could practically name all the rules by heart. Her dad made sure that was the first thing she mastered as a teen working in his coffee shops. The knife techniques were new. She needed to make notes on each step she needed to take to master Cutting 101. Before she wrote another word, she glanced at Benson to find him intently listening to the instructions. He wasn't taking notes, though. He looked bored.

When it came time to practice, he peered up at her as he slowly sliced the red bell pepper to accompany the onion he just sliced. His knife skills were very impressive. He gave her a wink, and in that moment, a surge of anger shot through her. Aubrey wanted no attention from anyone, let alone a man. Especially a man she had to see every day.

Fresh off her break up with Seth, she was ruined. Another man was the last thing on her mind. The words Seth sent in his text message on their wedding day played on a loop in her head.

He'd written, "You know, I get that your parents were always hovering, trying to shield you from everything. I empathize with the fact that your sister died. But I think it's made you put up walls in our relationship, like you're scared to let go or trust fully. It's like you're always waiting for something to go wrong, and it's hard to feel close when you're so guarded." Seth was supposed to be her forever. It was better to be alone and not entertain even a friendship with the cute male classmate.

"Competing with you?" Starr said, pulling Aubrey out of her memories.

"Our instructor had given us a lesson on the proper way to cut an onion, among other vegetables. He announced he was coming around to critique our work. He said my cuts were good but could be a little thinner. When he got to Benson's station, he praised his knife skills with a smugness that made it clear he was the chosen one in the kitchen."

"Then what? What did you do?"

"From that moment on, I vowed to be the best in the kitchen, determined to master every technique and outshine everyone. Especially Benson Carter." Aubrey could hear the snarl in her tone. She was becoming angry all over again.

Her phone buzzed in her pocket. She pulled it out to see Nicole video calling her. After a deep sigh, she ran her finger across her screen to answer the call.

"I already know why you're calling." Aubrey could sometimes read her friend like an open book.

"What? Cameron and I just had a few questions," Nicole said, smiling at Aubrey.

"Questions? What do you want to know?"

Cameron appeared next to Nicole and asked, "So, you two went to culinary school together?"

"How many times do I have to tell this story? Yes. We met in culinary school. Competitors since day one. We can't stand each other."

"But didn't you both just win a competition together? And what happened after the competition?" Cameron wondered.

"During the final round, we played nice because there was money on the line. Trust! We argued after the competition." Aubrey still couldn't believe the audacity of Benson. His mention of San Francisco insinuated there was more between them. Well, there was, but that was their business. The simple fact that he mentioned it made her hate him more.

"Then what happened after you argued?" Nicole gave her the look. The one look that could get her to spill and give her all the information. Aubrey turned her face away from the screen.

"It looked like chemistry to me," Cameron said with a chuckle.

"Not you, too. Starr said the same thing. He drives me up a wall." Aubrey pushed down the fact that even though she claimed to hate him, she did find him attractive. Always had.

"Aubrey. I know Benson. How he grew up. He's a good guy. If the two of you can get past your hatred for one another, you two could be a good match." Nicole nodded at Cameron's statement.

"In case you both forgot, I'm not dating. I'm too busy, and I surely wouldn't date him." Aubrey couldn't remember the last date she went on.

Aubrey looked up from her phone at the sound of Starr letting out a shriek in excitement. Starr leaped out of the booth to greet the tall lanky delivery man holding the largest bouquet of red roses she'd ever seen.

"Nicole, will you look at this?" Aubrey turned her phone around, so the huge vase filled with the beautiful flowers was on display.

"Oh my gosh, Aubrey. Whose flowers are those?" Nicole asked.

"Mine!" Starr responded. "They're from Jamaal." She leaned in, taking a soft inhale of the flower's delicate scent, her eyes shining with admiration as she admired the bouquet.

Nicole and Cameron said in unison, "Who's Jamaal?"

"Her latest boo thang," Aubrey said, tone full of sarcasm.

Aubrey turned her phone around so she was now looking at Nicole.

"Don't be sour. I bet Benson would send you flowers," Cameron teased.

"I don't want anything from that man." Aubrey really hoped her friends would not make Benson a big deal.

"Based on what Cameron told me, he really could be a good match for you, Aubrey. And. I'll likely do a write up on his restaurant when it opens. Can you play nice, please?" Nicole pleaded.

"I'm not looking for a match. And I'll think about being nice." Aubrey needed her friends to understand she was not interested in dating. "But didn't you see? He was mean to me, too. Why were you asking him all those questions about money? What was your angle for that?"

"I thought maybe based on his answers, it would jog thoughts for how you can get your hands on more money for the bakery."

Aubrey needed someone on her side. "Nice try. But his restaurant could be competing with mine. He could take my customers."

"You're L.A.'s culinary darling. No one will take your customers."

Nicole was right. She knew the writers that covered her restaurant.

"Fine." Aubrey gave her friend a tight-lipped smile. She had a feeling she would regret Benson being in close proximity to her, her life, and her business.

Chapter 13

Benson

The drill dove into the strip of wood, sawdust spraying into the air, just as Benson walked past the counter the worker was building. A ladder scraped across the floor, drawing his attention to the lighting guy as he climbed it to add bulbs to the empty light sockets. In about a week, he could begin adding the finishing bells and whistles to the space, his favorite part about opening a restaurant. To complete the kitchen, the countertops needed to be installed which would be in a few days. Today, Benson wanted to set up his office. He needed to finish his menu and get it to the graphic designer by the end of the week. In a matter of days, he would begin interviewing staff. He was thankful the agency he used in New York had a Los Angeles office. A good staff's dedication could elevate the dining experience, or their missteps could cave in the roof, sending everything crashing down.

Benson walked into his office and sat in his black leather chair. Stacks of cardboard boxes lined the wall across from his desk, each labeled with bold black letters. A few boxes sat half-open, revealing glints of polished knives and the wooden sheen of cutting boards peeking through the packaging. He opened his laptop, the screen casting a soft glow over his focused expression as it booted up. With a few clicks, his drafted menu filled the screen. Rows of meticulously listed appetizers, entrées, and sides appeared, each item carefully chosen and organized. What desserts would he serve?

At that precise moment, Aubrey came to mind. In culinary school, baking had been her strength. What desserts would she suggest? It was in school she perfected her lemon pound cake. He read it was a crowd favorite. One might think anyone can make a pound cake and add lemon flavor to it. But her recipe was different. The cake's dense, yet buttery crumbs gave way to a tender texture that melted in your mouth, tasting the tangy zest of lemon, with citrus brightness that balanced the cake's sweetness. It was the subtle crunch of the sugar glaze that added a layer of absolute indulgence, making it the best cake he ever tasted. Would she stock his restaurant with it? Could he add it to his menu and add homemade vanilla ice cream with a lemon drizzle to make it complete? What if he smeared that same glaze across her smart ass mouth and kissed it off until her lips were swollen from his intense nibbling of her mouth?

There Aubrey was, drifting into his mind, leaving him wondering what it was about her that had crept under his skin. Was it the way she laughed, or the way she never backed down in an argument? Whatever it was, it had him questioning himself—questioning why he was thinking of her that way at all. It was their kiss.

The sound of his name being called sliced through his daydream. The deep baritone voice got closer. David Carter now stood in his office doorway.

"Dad? I didn't know you were coming by." Benson stood and closed the distance between them. He threw his arms around his dad, giving him a tight squeeze.

"Son. It's so good to see you." David took Benson in. "I haven't seen you in a while. Has it been a year?"

"I think so. But you know what? I'm back. We can have lunch every week, if you want." David Carter had to be one of Benson's favorite people.

"Have a seat. Let me just finish up a few things and then we can get out of here and really catch up."

Benson would not be in L.A. had it not been for the incident. He would still be in New York running the restaurant he painfully built with his own sweat and tears. Being back in Los Angeles was an opportunity. He had goals to make this new restaurant bigger than New York. He hoped no one would recognize him or bring up the incident. If that was so, he had a fighting chance.

"What do you feel like eating, Dad? Burgers, salad, Chinese? There's a good restaurant a few doors down, but I already don't get along with the owner," Benson admitted.

David sat in the folding chair positioned in front of Benson's desk. It was silent for several moments, twirling the thin gold band on his index finger.

"You don't get along with the owner? You just got here." David stood. "Do you mind if I take a look around this place? How much longer before you open?"

"About a month. Please. Take a look. I'll be out in a few minutes." Benson watched his dad walk out and turn the corner into the main room of the restaurant. David Carter was still tall, fit, with smooth, Hershey brown skin. As a child, he had imitated his dad when he would shave or comb his hair. He wanted to be just like him. There were days he wandered through his dad's meat warehouse, the air thick with rich, savory scents of fresh cuts hanging from the rafters. He watched in awe as the butchers sliced through tender steaks. The vibrant colors of marbled beef and slabs of pork filled the room. It was the sizzling sounds of meat being seared and the gleaming steel of the kitchen that gave him the reason he was called into the culinary arts.

Benson pulled up his menu and stared at the empty space where the dessert selection was supposed to go. The more he thought about it, the more he liked the idea of contracting Aubrey to supply his restaurant with at least her lemon pound cake. It carried the subtle, refreshing tang of a lemon drop. The cake would go well with the smoked meats on his menu. The sweetness balanced perfectly with a zesty kick that danced on the tongue. Like her lips. Like a lemon drop. Her lips tasted like lemon drops.

He slammed his laptop closed, to shake her memory, and stood, put his computer into his worn brown leather messenger bag, and walked out to meet his father. He had to get out of his office and get Aubrey out of his head.

"This place reminds me of your mother's first restaurant," David said in a low voice.

"Really? She didn't say anything to me. She's been here. She circled the room, then started drilling me about rebuilding my reputation." A pit formed in his gut every time he thought about the pile of mess he left in New York.

"Son. Los Angeles is your permanent home now. You're not hiding here, waiting for it to be safe to go back to New York. Let all of that go."

Benson caught sight of his dad's furrowed brow and the tight line of his lips, the worry etched into his features. His father's gaze flickered toward him, searching for resolution.

"I'll be fine, Dad. Don't worry. This city is my permanent home."

David shook his head, searched in his son's direction, then said, "I know what your mother preaches. But I disagree. A woman can make your life better. Not be a distraction and detriment to your career. You can't let the incident in New York define you or convince you to swear off relationships. Every experience is a lesson, son. Not a reason to build walls around your heart."

Benson nodded. "I'm not thinking about a relationship right now. I want to get my restaurant open and make a name for myself on this coast."

He did want to find someone to at least hang out with. No attachments. If he got into a relationship, it would have to be with someone who understood him, his line of work, schedule, and how busy he stayed. If he were going to be in a relationship, he wanted a partner in business and life. He wanted someone who would complement him—make him a better chef and business owner. He wanted her to be just as driven as him, if not more. He stood in the middle of the restaurant dining room, eyes closed, trying to envision his perfect woman. Slowly, as if a sweep of air blew in front of him, a vision of Aubrey appeared, curly hair hanging wild, over her face. She flashed him a sly grin, walking toward him with her lips perched for a kiss. He quickly opened his eyes, cleared his throat and shuck his shoulders. Why was she creeping back into his thoughts again? He shook his head, frustration simmering beneath the surface. This had to be a sign of something wrong—he must be sick, losing his mind if he couldn't stop replaying the idea of her.

Voices came from the kitchen. The contractor and his dad were having a conversation. Just as he was turning to walk toward them, his phone rang. Alan's phone number flashed across the screen. He pushed the accept button and answered the call.

"Hey, Alan. What's up?"

"Hey. Have you got a wine vendor yet? A well-dressed young woman came by my place. She has a pretty extensive wine list. She ordered some breakfast, asked about businesses in the area, and I told her about you since I don't sell alcohol. You interested?"

"What did she look like?" Just as Benson asked that question, a chill raced up his spine, prickling his skin as if an unseen presence lingered behind him. The sensation sent a wave of unease through him, a cold reminder to not get involved with someone in the business. History could not repeat itself.

"Benson, you know you shouldn't date a vendor," Alan scolded.

"Dude. I just want someone to hang out with." Benson knew not to ask anymore about the woman, but he had to play it off. He did want to go on a date soon, to get Aubrey out of his head.

"I'll text you her information. You can arrange your own date. I'm staying out of it. Bye, man."

Alan hung up before Benson could say anything. Just as he placed his phone in his pocket, his stomach rumbled, signaling it was time for lunch.

"Dad! Let's go eat."

Chapter 14

Benson

Sitting on his couch, the glow of Benson's phone screen flickered in the dim room as he absentmindedly scrolled through a dating app. The same dating app he often perused in New York. Now, in L.A., he didn't really want to be doing this, but if thoughts of her kept invading his mind, he'd need a distraction. Something—or maybe someone—to pull him back to reality.

His thumb paused over a few profiles, not out of interest, but more out of distraction. Each swipe was mechanical, detached, like he was going through the motions. He wasn't looking for anything serious, just someone to take out, to occupy the little free time he had. He needed to silence the lingering thoughts of the woman who had a knack for getting under his skin, like an itch he couldn't scratch with just a glance or a well-timed remark. Yet, somehow, in the same breath, she'd captivated him—whether it was the fire in her eyes when they argued or the way she could turn a sharp comment into a challenge he couldn't resist. Aubrey frustrated him, but she fascinated him even more, leaving him torn between exasperation and intrigue. He could never let her in on the thoughts swirling in his mind.

Benson shook his head, determined to shove Aubrey out of his mind. Then he swiped right on a woman whose profile seemed like just the kind of distraction he needed.

Benson's fork sliced through layers of tender pasta, rich meat sauce and creamy ricotta. Lifting the bite toward him, the gooey mozzarella stretched from the plate and into his mouth. He savored each flavor of tangy tomato sauce and garlic and herbs that mingled with the ground meat.

"Alan? Tell me why you don't sell your grandmother's lasagna at your restaurant?" If Alan didn't sell it, he would at his new restaurant.

"Lasagna is too heavy for a breakfast and lunch restaurant. And it's too time consuming to make. I make it here at home where I can enjoy it."

"I get that, but it's so good." Benson knew Alan wouldn't share the recipe. It had been in his family for generations.

Alan grabbed his glass of wine and motioned for Benson to follow him. "Honey? Benson and I are going to sit outside for a bit."

"Sure thing. I'll bathe the baby," Darcy called out.

Benson took in the scenery in Alan's back yard. The backyard stretched out like an entertainer's dream, with a full outdoor kitchen tucked neatly under a pergola, its sleek granite countertops gleaming in the soft afternoon light. A stainless steel grill large enough to handle any summer barbecue stood proudly beside a mini-fridge and sink, all ready for action. The smell of herbs from the nearby garden wafted through the air, mixing with the faintest hint of fresh-cut grass. Beyond the kitchen, the yard opened up to a breathtaking view—rolling hills, lush and green, stretching out toward the horizon.

"Being back here reminds me I need to get out of my duplex. Well, my mother's duplex. I want to buy a house," Benson said, taking a sip of his wine, now seated in the stretched lounge chair next to Alan.

"Do you want to buy one by yourself or with someone?" Alan asked.

Ideally, Benson wanted a wife. Since arriving in L.A., he thought of his whole life as being rushed and a little out of control. He was ready for a slower pace. He wanted companionship, despite his mother's advice. Running into Cameron was a nice surprise. He was getting married. He never thought he would see that day. At thirty-one, it was time. He stole a glance, finding Alan gazing up at the vast blue sky. The sunlight played across his features, illuminating a moment of peace. He yearned to experience that same sense of peace, an escape from the relentless chaos that had become his life. The noise of his troubles clamored for attention while he desperately sought a moment of stillness to breathe and reflect. He wanted New York to be a long distant memory, one that no one could resurface.

"I'd like to buy a house with someone." Benson didn't know who. But when he thought of someone steady, although uninvited and seemingly impossible to ignore, Aubrey popped into his vision. They never dated. Why was she on his mind?

Alan took a sip of wine, then turned to Benson. "Were you serious about her?"

"Serious about who?" Benson had no clue what Alan was asking.

"The woman in New York. Were you two at least a couple?"

Benson dropped his head and shook it. "We dated. Our first few dates had been smooth. She was charming, funny. She made me laugh. The spark felt promising."

"Go on." Alan took another sip of wine.

Benson sat, his hands tightly clasped together. "One night, though, she suggested we go out to a new bar she'd been excited to try. After a few drinks, things got a little crazy. Too much PDA and one click of a pic. Within an hour, we were trending. It wasn't a good look. Especially when you are one of the chosen few."

"Everything goes viral these days. Was that so bad?"

Benson chuckled. "Like the next day, I told her we couldn't date anymore. I told her I needed to focus. I had that big showing, remember?" He grabbed and rubbed the back of his neck. "It's really hard to talk about."

Alan sighed. "Enough about New York. It's a beautiful afternoon, man. And I have something for you," Alan said, turning to face Benson.

"What? It's not my birthday. It's not Christmas."

Alan lifted his legs and moved them to the side of the lounge chair, facing Benson. "I can't get my best friend, who I haven't seen in a few years, a gift for his new restaurant?"

Benson eyed Alan suspiciously before shifting to face him. "What is it?"

"If I told you, it wouldn't be a surprise. I'll go get it." Alan sprung up from his seat and ran into the house. A few minutes later, he returned with a large rectangular white box tied with a black ribbon.

"Alan. What's the occasion? Seriously."

"It's not every day my best friend moves to my city and opens a restaurant. I wanted to get you something to commemorate the occasion."

"Can I open it now?" Benson looked up from the box to find Alan smiling from ear to ear.

"Please do."

Benson took in a breath, then slowly untied the ribbon that held the box closed. He carefully lifted the lid to find neatly folded tissue paper being held together by a circular sticker that read, "chef." He painstakingly pulled the folded tissue apart to find a black jacket resting inside.

"Man, what is this?"

Alan didn't respond. He kept his huge grin while Benson pulled the jacket out of the box. Benson unfolded the jacket to realize it was a chef's coat. Embroidered on the lapel was his restaurant. Smokewood and Ember. Underneath it read Executive Chef.

"Oh, wow. This is gorgeous. I'm speechless."

"Welcome home, man. I know New York was the original plan, but things happen for a reason. I believe you're home now. Smokewood and Ember is just the beginning."

Benson stood and held the chef's coat to his chest, looking down at the beauty and sentiment of the gift.

"Thank you, Alan. Really." Benson carefully folded the chef's coat back into the box and reached to give his friend a heartfelt hug.

Chapter 15

Aubrey

Aubrey emerged from the kitchen, balancing a tray of vibrant red velvet cupcakes, their creamy white frosting glistening under the soft light. With a practiced hand, she lifted each one, placing it gently onto the riser. A satisfied smile crept across her face, feeling a sense of pride at her work. Just as she set down the last one, a woman approached her.

"Hello. I'm looking for Benson Carter? He owns this restaurant."

Did Aubrey hear her correctly? She looked up to find a woman of medium height, maybe five-feet-six, wearing fitted light blue jeans, black booties and a white blouse, her hair in a high ponytail. Her large silver hoop earrings were a nice touch to her look. "You're looking for Benson Carter?" Aubrey asked.

"Yes, he owns this place, right?"

Aubrey wanted to be polite. It wasn't the woman's fault she was in the wrong place. Was his address even above his door? He didn't have any signage up. She likely saw a restaurant and assumed it was his. "This restaurant is mine. The one you're looking for is a few doors down."

"Oh. I'm sorry. Thank you. Sorry to bother you." The woman gave Aubrey a short smile and walked out. She caught a whiff of her rich, heady perfume—a little strong for so early in the afternoon.

"Who was that?" Starr asked as she brought out a lemon pound cake to place in the display case.

"Who knows? She asked for Benson." Aubrey stood and watched the woman walk out her door, turn left and sashay down the street toward Benson's place.

Starr gazed out the restaurant windows. "A girlfriend, you think?"

"I don't know and don't care." Aubrey couldn't be worried about Benson, what he did with his time, or who he spent time with.

Starr glanced over to the doorway, then back at Aubrey. "Didn't you say he just moved back to L.A.? Dating already? He moves fast."

"Most men do." Aubrey could feel the irritation bubbling up at the mere thought of dating. It was as if the idea triggered a knot of frustration she couldn't shake. Dating had not been something he wanted to do until recently. At what point did she even think of a man? Maybe it was San Francisco. The kiss. She hadn't been that close to a man in a very long while. His life seemed like a closed book. She didn't know much about him. Now a flicker of curiosity ignited within her. His recent presence sparked questions in her mind, a desire to peel back the layers and discover who Benson Carter really was. With New York being the major capital of the food scene, why would he leave to open a restaurant here in Los Angeles?

"You know?" Starr had a look of mischief in her eye, hinting at a scheming plot. "You could go on a date with Benson."

Aubrey's eyes grew big. "No, thank you," she said as she brushed past Starr. "Can you finish filling the display case? I have some orders to place. I'll be in my office."

"I can set it up for you, boss lady!" Starr yelled as Aubrey walked out of sight.

Aubrey could set up her own dates if she really wanted to. She just didn't have time to date. She was at her restaurant every day. She loved it there. She was comfortable there. However, she was beginning to feel a need or want for more. Was it because Nicole and Cameron's wedding was soon? Did she and Benson really have chemistry? She experienced it in San Francisco. Her mental list of reasons he might actually be a good guy to date was growing. He was a chef, after all—he understood the long hours and the pressure of running a restaurant inside out. Not to mention, he was easy on the eyes, with that killer smile that always seemed to sneak up on her. And, of course, he always smelled absolutely divine. Benson was not interested in her, so she needed to not think about what it would be like to date him.

Sitting at her desk, Aubrey put her head down. "Focus, Aubrey Carroll. You have a bakery to open," she whispered to herself. How was she going to open her bakery? With what money? She got the estimates Christy requested. Her budget was dwindling. Especially after the purchase of her top of the line commercial ovens.

Her phone buzzed, vibrating on her desk's surface. She glanced over in its direction, noticing an incoming text message.

Dad: Aubrey. You bought ovens for the bakery yet have no plans for the build out?

The ovens. How did her dad find out about that? She paid with her business credit card. Did the payment not post before the billing cycle? "He's on the account!" she said aloud. How could she forget that?

> **Aubrey**: I paid that off, Dad.

> **Dad**: With what money?

Aubrey didn't want to tell him she was spending some of her prize money. She wanted something to keep to herself. Sure, her parents were her investors, but she made her business a success. It was her talent and good food that filled her tables and catering orders. She was going to apply the rest of the money to the bakery build out.

> **Aubrey**: I had money saved.

> **Dad**: And you didn't tell me and your mom about these savings?

Did she have to share all of her finances with her parents? She didn't like being put on the spot.

> **Aubrey**: Can we talk about this later? I have to get ready for the dinner crowd.

> **Dad**: We'll talk later.

It became exhausting, feeling like Aubrey needed permission to make her own decisions. She longed for a chance to explore her life on her terms, free from their constant oversight. Yet she felt trapped, bound by their love and the loyalty for their financial support. In moments of frustration, she did things like go to San Francisco, or purchase top of the line ovens, to flex the independence she craved. But each time she exercised her desire for more independence, they seemed to tighten their grip, reminding her of what they'd lost once and how they couldn't bear to lose again.

Living under her parents' watchful eyes was something she wouldn't be able to get over. But as their only surviving child, they worried in ways that never seemed to fade, even as she grew into adulthood.

Aubrey imagined if she was dating, they would be involved in her dating life. She was certain her parents were happy she was single and not dating. Especially after Seth. Her parents had always been skeptical of him. His charm was too smooth, his promises too easy, and his intentions, in their eyes, too self-serving. Her mother said things like, "I knew he wasn't good enough," and, "I should have stopped this before it got too far."

Aubrey didn't know her father tried to stop the wedding from happening. Seth convinced everyone around her that he was the perfect man. Everyone but her parents. As she sat, with her heart in shreds, she had to listen to her parents' words laced with not only anger, but also the kind of fear only overprotective parents know. The fear of having been right but powerless to shield their daughter from the hurt they had foreseen. Tara and Bill Carroll took her heartbreak as a personal failure to keep her safe. And as they watched her sit silently, clutching the veil she hadn't worn, they realized their greatest struggle wasn't hating the man who left. It was figuring out how to help their daughter heal. And so, they jumped into investments in their daughter and her restaurant.

At her restaurant, they micromanaged everything, eyeing everything from her staffing choices to the menu changes with an apprehensive look, often questioning if she needed more support or security. It wasn't just about the business for them; it was a constant reassurance that their daughter was safe, financially stable, and, most importantly, nearby.

Aubrey had to push her conversation with her dad to the back burner. When they talked again, she needed a plan. A clear concrete plan that would show her parents she could raise the money and build out her restaurant with no help from them.

Aubrey parked in front of the restaurant so she could easily carry in her farmer's market purchases. She exited her car, pulled bags of fresh produce, fruits, and other goodies out of the back of her SUV, and shut the hood. She walked into her restaurant to find Starr talking with an unfamiliar woman.

"Hey, boss lady. This is Erin. She's waiting for Benson."

Aubrey looked from Starr to Erin, then back at Starr. "What? Waiting for Benson? Here?" Aubrey didn't know what was going on, but her place of business was not a pickup joint for his dates.

"Yeah. She stopped by his restaurant, but it was locked. She sent him a text. He said he was running a little late. She told him she would wait for him here, since she's a customer." Starr smiled at the woman, then Aubrey.

Aubrey couldn't believe what she was hearing. "Well, thank you. For being a regular customer." She couldn't be rude. She didn't want to lose business. "Can we get you anything while you wait?"

The woman tapped the corner of her mouth with her long red fingernail. "I'm good. But I was wondering. Can you tell me if Benson is as handsome in person as this photo?" She tapped on her phone and turned it to face Starr and Aubrey. There was Benson, dressed in casual slacks and a white button up with the sleeves rolled to above his elbow. The logo for the dating app sat in the upper left corner of her phone.

Aubrey chuckled. "So, you've never met Benson in person?"

"We've only exchanged text messages." Erin put her phone back into her purse.

Aubrey examined the woman before her. Her light brown hair was cut in short layers with blond streaks. Her freckled nose and cheeks were adorned with little makeup, enough to enhance her natural beauty without masking the sun-kissed speckles that told a story of days spent in the sun. She was cute. Although she was seated, Aubrey could see her trendy fitted crop top and baggy pants. She was a little young for him. Who was she to judge?

"Well, if you like his type, you're in for a treat," Aubrey said through gritted teeth. Just as Aubrey turned to walk back to the kitchen, his familiar voice rang in her ear, sending a jolt of recognition through her that was impossible to ignore.

"Hey. Erin, right?" he said as he approached where Erin and Starr sat.

"Benson?" Erin stood to greet him. She was at least a foot shorter than him.

"I apologize for my tardiness. I had some business to handle. Are you ready to go?" he asked, giving Erin his most handsome smile.

A pang hit her chest as Aubrey watched his warm, effortless smile light up his face—only it was directed at someone else. That easy, charming grin that usually seemed so reserved was now given freely, without a second thought. Her stomach twisted, a flicker of heat rushing to her cheeks. Benson never looked at her that way. He did once. In San Francisco. The realization settled uncomfortably, and she quickly tore her eyes away, hoping no one caught the flash of jealousy she could feel tightening her chest.

"Yes. I'm ready to go. Thank you." She looked up at him, then turned to Starr. "Thank you for sitting with me." She peered around Benson and said, "And thank you for everything. I'll be in soon to get some of your amazing smothered pork chops."

Aubrey forced a smile, then said, "Looking forward to it." Benson glanced her way, and glared into her eyes before giving her a nod. She couldn't believe his gull. Who did he think he was, having dates wait for him in her restaurant? Two dates with two different women in two days was excessive. What was he trying to do? There was no way she would let this go without saying something.

It was after the dinner crowd, and Aubrey was helping her staff clean up. There was a knock at her window. A woman, dressed in a beautiful print wrap dress and high heels, waved, prompting her to come to the door.

"Can I help you?" Aubrey asked, after unlocking her door and cracking it open.

"Yes, I'm sorry to bother you. I see you're closing. I was looking for Benson Carter? He asked me to meet him at his restaurant."

Another date? Benson had another date with a different woman in less than five hours from his last date? "His restaurant is down the street, hun." She was beginning to lose her patience.

"I didn't see another restaurant," the woman said politely.

"His restaurant isn't open yet. If you walk a few doors down, you will see it," Aubrey directed.

Just as she waited to see if the woman understood, Benson pulled up in front of her restaurant. He rolled down the window of his car and called out, "Hey, Renee. I'm sorry I'm late. Hop in. We have reservations."

"Thank you," the woman said and turned toward Benson's car.

Aubrey just stood there, mouth agape, not believing what she just experienced. Benson looked in her direction and narrowed his eyes before letting out a chuckle. She was so angry she couldn't think straight. She slammed her door shut, locked it, and went straight into her office to look for his phone number. What she had to say couldn't wait until tomorrow.

Aubrey: So, let me get this straight. You managed to fit in two dates today? And what a coincidence. Both of them stopped by my restaurant.

Aubrey tossed her phone onto her desk and leaned back into her chair. Was sending the text message a mistake? She didn't want him to think she cared. It was just rude to do what he was doing. She opened her laptop to prepare for the next day. Five minutes later, her phone buzzed.

Benson: Hey. I like to keep things interesting. You know, variety is the spice of life.

Aubrey: I'm curious. Did they both enjoy the same experience or did you change the recipe between dates?

Benson: I have to keep my options open, right? You know how it is. You can't settle for just one flavor.

Aubrey: I bet it's all about variety. Just don't expect me to be your personal cleanup crew when your 'flavors' collide.

Benson: What's wrong? I can practically feel the hostility radiating off of you. Did I accidentally step on your culinary dreams, sugar?

Aubrey: Hostility? Nah, that's just the aroma of my ambition wafting your way. You might want to take a deep breath and appreciate it, Mr. Carter.

Benson: Ambition smells more like jealousy from where I'm standing. Maybe you should try a little less cooking and a bit more fun.

Aubrey: Jealous? Please. I'm too busy enjoying the show of you parading around with those women you call dates. Desperation must really suit you.

Benson: Desperate? Hardly! But if you're looking for a night of fun, I'd gladly take you out on a date. Just do me a favor, sugar. Try to keep that sharp tongue of yours on mute.

> **Aubrey:** A night of fun with you? Tempting, but I think I'll pass. You're about as fun as a soggy crouton. Why don't you tell your dates to meet you where you came from? L.A. is my playground. You might want to get a map and find your way back to New York, where you belong.

Fifteen minutes passed. Did Aubrey silence the beast named Benson Carter? Game on.

Chapter 16

Aubrey

The rain outside couldn't dampen her spirits as Aubrey pressed on. With extreme focus, she continued preparing the most mouthwatering bites for her best friend and her fiancé, determined to make every round of their tasting perfect as their big day deserved. Before her were small plates filled with varying dishes, all for Nicole and Cameron to choose for their wedding meal. She wanted them to be happy and, most of all, enjoy their food. Many couples ate very little at their weddings. They get back to their hotel room to find it's too late to order room service. They call down to the front desk and learn their only options for food are Cup of Noodles, microwave popcorn, or candy. She didn't want that for her best friend and soon to be husband. As a personal touch, she had specially designed "Mr. and Mrs." food bags, each adorned with delicate calligraphy. She would fill them with a few of their favorite food items. She couldn't bear thinking about her best friend and her new husband going hungry.

"Starr, can you bring the selections out? You may need help from one of the guys." Aubrey took off her chef's coat, smoothed down her black cotton v-neck and black pants and walked over to the table where Nicole and Cameron sat.

"Hey guys. Are you ready to taste some food?" Aubrey slid into the booth and placed her folded hands on the table. She caught the sparkle of excited anticipation in Nicole's eyes, her expression lighting up with a barely contained thrill. Starr set an array of small, artfully arranged plates of food onto the table.

Tiny roasted fig crostinis drizzled with honey glistened under the light, while miniature crab cakes sat atop vibrant dollops of aioli, their crisp edges begging to be tasted. Warm, creamy macaroni and cheese, with its golden crackling, waited for a fork to cut through the layers of gooey, rich cheddar. The collard greens, tender and fragrant, simmered with smoky hints of turkey and spices, sat beside juicy, perfectly grilled chicken breasts, resting on a bed of fresh herbs.

"Everything looks fantastic," Cameron said, eyes wide, waiting to devour into the tasting.

"Can we start?" Nicole asked, placing a napkin on her lap.

"Dig in. There are more samples to try. I wanted to give you a selection to choose from." Aubrey waved her hand to signal Starr to bring everything out.

Nicole and Cameron sampled each dish. Starr placed fried shrimp, seared scallops, nestled on a bed of micro greens, and filet mignon, cooked to a flawless medium-rare in front of the couple. Cameron glided his knife effortlessly through the buttery pink center, its juices pooling on the plate.

With a chuckle, Cameron said, "Ugh, this meat needs to cook a little longer."

"Honey, the meat is cooked to be at its most tender. If you cook it any longer, it will be overcooked." Nicole gave him a warm smile.

"Well, I know some people won't care if the meat is cooked to be its most tender. They see red and think the meat isn't done. Aubrey, can we select a different red meat?"

"I can make strips of steak and cover the meat in a mushroom gravy. How does that sound?" Aubrey held her laugh. She didn't want to upset Cameron.

"Add mashed potatoes, and we have a deal."

"Try these. Envision these pairing with the beef." Aubrey spooned the creamy, smooth butter and garlic infused potatoes onto their plates.

The couple lifted their forks, filled with the wonderfulness of the potatoes.

"Oh, Aubrey. These are delicious," Cameron said in delight.

"Only the best for my favorite couple."

Nicole and Cameron simultaneously leaned to rest their backs against the cushioned leather booth seats, closed their eyes, and smiled.

"Aubrey? You outdid yourself," Cameron said, eyes still shut.

"I loved everything. The food was beautiful. I don't know how we'll choose," Nicole said, tilting her head in Aubrey's direction.

Aubrey set a sheet of paper that appeared to be a checklist. "I've listed each dish under their category on this itemized list. Think about what you ate and make your decision. You can give this back to me tomorrow."

"We can do that," Cameron said, grabbing Nicole's hand and bringing it to his mouth for a kiss on her knuckles.

Nicole sat up slowly, her movements soft and deliberate, before sliding her arm around Cameron's neck. Pulling him closer, she pressed her lips gently against his, the kiss tender and filled with warmth, lingering just long enough to make Aubrey feel a pang in her stomach, a sharp twist of emotion she couldn't quite name. Was it jealousy? A yearning to have a special someone in her life?

"You two are just sickening in love. I'm happy I can be a part of everything." Aubrey was truly happy for her best friend.

Loneliness settled in like a heavy fog, dulling everything around Aubrey. Lately, the hollow ache in her chest, a longing that no distraction could fill. She went through the motions of the day, but everything felt quieter without that special someone to share it with. The silence in her home was loud, more oppressive. She imagined the comfort of a masculine hand to hold or the sound of his laughter beside you. The emptiness was heavier today, being left with the echo of her own thoughts. Watching her favorite couple made her feel the emptiness inside.

"We parked in front of Benson's place. There's a sign up now. He'll open in a few weeks," Cameron revealed.

The mention of his name shook her out of her musing. Aubrey understood how busy Benson must be, building out his restaurant from scratch, but opening in a few weeks was soon. What would his opening do to her customer base? His menu was different, right? Before her mind did a two hundred yard dash, she immediately stood up. "I'm going down there to see what's going on. Starr?" Aubrey said loudly.

Starr came out of the kitchen, wiping her hands on a kitchen towel. "What's up, boss lady?"

"We're going to Benson's restaurant. See what's going on."

"We? I wanted to finish the list for our next big order."

"Let's go. We can do that later," Aubrey said, tilting her head toward the door. "Do you guys want to come?"

Nicole glanced at Cameron and smirked before she spoke. "No. We have some errands to run. We'll catch up with you later. Tell Benson we said hello."

"Nope. We are not cool like that," Aubrey spit out.

Aubrey pulled Starr by her wrist, rushing her out the door. She glanced over and saw Starr winking at Nicole and Cameron, mouthing something. Suddenly, they were all nodding their heads. She didn't have time to think about them or what they said.

Aubrey and Starr stood at the restaurant's entrance, eyes widening as they took in the transformation of the once empty space. The previously bare, unfinished area was now alive with warmth, charm, and a touch of elegance. The walls were painted a warm rust color. Dark brown wood stained tables and chairs occupied the center of the restaurant. To the right, a handmade mahogany wood hostess desk stood, ready to greet guests and direct them to their tables. Along the walls were brown leather booths with wood tables stained a brownish burgundy color. Gold, orange and warm red toned lighting hung from the ceiling, casting the room in a golden glow. Large pictures of iconic L.A. locations hung on walls.

"I'm speechless," Aubrey whispered to Starr.

Starr spun in a slow circle to admire the new restaurant on the block. "I didn't think this place would look like this," she whispered back.

Just as Aubrey was going to announce their presence, Benson came from around the corner. "Well, well, well. If it isn't the lovely Starr and her boss lady. To what do I owe this honor?"

"We heard you were opening soon, so we wanted to see how things were coming along." Aubrey couldn't believe she was playing nice. Especially after their text message exchange.

"Do you want to see the kitchen?" Benson asked, holding his arm up to direct them to walk toward him.

Aubrey and Starr nodded and followed Benson into the commercial kitchen. Entering the space, the stainless steel surfaces gleamed with newness. Everything was in perfect order and designed for top efficiency. The massive, professional-grade range was the heart of the space with its multiple burners, double convection oven with glass doors, and a walk-in refrigerator packed with fresh ingredients likely for practicing preparing menu items. Rows of knives hung on magnetic strips along the wall, each blade polished to a mirror-like finish.

"Let me show you the room with all the smokers." Just as Benson moved toward the next room, Levi, Nicole's brother, walked out of his office.

"Hey, Benson? The ordering system is ready to be tested." Levi stood in surprise at the sight of Aubrey.

"Levi? What are you doing here?" Aubrey asked in shock.

Levi gave Aubrey an obvious stare. "I'm installing Benson's technology. You know. Like I did in your restaurant. Like I will do when you open your bakery?"

"When did you two meet?" Aubrey was taken aback to discover they had already been introduced.

"Nicole brought me in when she interviewed Benson for his media introduction." Levi chuckled, recognizing the irritation in Aubrey's tone. "You alright?"

"Yeah. I'm fine. Just surprised." Aubrey walked to Levi and gave him a brief hug.

"I'll check out the system in a sec. Let me show Aubrey and Starr the smoke room." Benson grinned with proudness. He led them into the vast back room, lined with three commercial sized smokers.

"What are you doing with the smokers?" Aubrey asked, eyes wide with amazement.

"Sugar, I know you're smart. What do you think? I'm smoking meat." Benson chuckled.

"Smoked meat, huh?" Aubrey was glad he wouldn't be competition for her place. His vision was the total opposite of hers.

"All the meats we'll serve with our entrées will be smoked."

"Did you learn that in New York? All kidding aside, this is a new concept for L.A." Aubrey couldn't believe his vision. The man had taste and innovation.

"I did my research." Benson stood, arms crossed his chest, admiring the room.

Aubrey scanned the room again, then turned to walk toward the front of the restaurant.

"Well. You did good. We just came to check out what you had going on down here." Aubrey forced a smile, her voice steady, though a twinge of envy threaded through her words. She focused on maintaining an even expression, but inside, dark clouds were gathering on the horizon. Thunder was beginning to rumble and soon the water would pour out, creating a flood in Benson's pretty new restaurant. Her words were on the tip of her tongue, ready to run out.

"Starr? Let's go." Aubrey abruptly reached for her wrist and pulled her toward the door.

"Everything looks amazing, Benson," Starr said loudly.

"Aubrey? What's the rush?" Levi asked as he pushed keys on his computer at the hostess station.

"I'll see you later, Levi," she yelled as she rushed out the door.

Benson laughed out loud as they quickly left the space.

Once they were out of earshot, Starr pulled Aubrey to face her. "Boss lady? His place is fabulous. What are we going to do?"

Aubrey stared into Starr's eyes. With determination in her tone, she said, "We're going to keep being one of the top spots to eat in Los Angeles *and* open the best bakery right next door."

Chapter 17

Benson

Three weeks later

A six o'clock alarm on a Thursday was not unusual for Benson. He preferred to hit the gym before beginning his day. This day, however, was unlike any other day. On this day, he would welcome customers to his new restaurant, Stonewood and Ember. Thanks to Nicole's write up in the newspaper, he had reservations for the afternoon. His mother invited a few of her friends who she was sure would spread the word. Her son was back in business, stronger than ever. Everything at the restaurant was ready. This wasn't his first restaurant opening. However, it was the most important opening of his career. New city, new restaurant concept, new opportunity to start over. It was high stakes for him.

Benson's phone vibrated on the nightstand. Incoming text messages from Piper Ramsey flashed on his screen.

Mom: I hope you're ready for today. Or are you still sleeping, nursing a hangover?

Mom: Today has to be perfect, son.

Mom: We both have a lot riding on your opening.

Mom: Are you ready?

All Benson could do was respond with a thumbs up. Piper Ramsey could not get in his head today.

To Benson's surprise and happiness, the gym wasn't crowded. He didn't have to wait to use the free weights he needed to burn off his anxiety. After a twenty-minute run on the treadmill, Benson walked toward the free weights. He grabbed the dumbbells and went to work. With each lift of the weight, the strain in his arms and shoulders was a welcomed sensation. Sweat began to bead on his forehead as he focused on his movements, but also his new restaurant, the mess in New York, his growing attraction to Aubrey, his reputation, his mother. His breath came in sharp, steady blows of air, as he timed each exhale with the lift. His body protested each movement, but his mind pushed him to keep going until he cleared his head. He went from bicep curls to lunges to shoulder presses, engaging his entire body. Although feeling fatigue, he set his jaw, eyes narrowed with a fierce resolve. He pushed on, ignoring the aches in his muscles and the doubts whispering at the edges of his mind. The final rep came with a grunt of effort. His body was now spent and exhausted. He took in a steadying breath, feeling a new wave of strength settle over him. With renewed resolve, he stood taller, ready to face this momentous day.

Benson walked into Aubrey's Favorites. "Hey, Starr. Is Aubrey here?"

Starr looked up from the clipboard she held. "Oh, hey, Benson. Boss lady isn't here. She'll be back shortly. Do you have a message?"

"Here's an invitation to my restaurant opening. I know you guys are open for business, but I hope you both can pop by. Even for a minute." Benson sat the envelope on the counter.

"I'm not sure if we can sneak away, but we'll try. Thank you." Starr gave him a smile, watching his expression.

Benson forced a polite smile, swallowing the disappointment that threatened to surface at the news Aubrey might not make it.

"Thanks, Starr. Oh, give Aubrey this exact message. She's welcome to swing by if she needs a masterclass on how a restaurant opening is actually done. You know, for the bakery opening?" Benson chuckled.

"I'll give her that exact message," Starr said, giving him a puzzled smile.

"See you around." He walked out and down to his restaurant.

Aubrey and Starr's visit a few weeks back surprised him. Was Aubrey Carroll trying to be nice? Probably not. They couldn't be in the same room for more than five minutes without arguing. But this time, he felt it. Seeing the look on her face when he picked up his date from her restaurant, the chemistry was there, the attraction. Many nights, he lay restless, the quiet darkness doing nothing to shutter his thoughts of her and their kiss in the hotel hallway. It played on a loop in his mind.

By noon, Benson and his staff were in the thick of prepping the food and smoking the meats. Thanks to his dad, he had top quality meats to supply his menu for the next six months. It was just like David Carter to give his son top cuts of poultry, beef, pork, and lamb that would have cost him thousands. He was that kind of generous. Growing up, after a long day at his meat factory, they would sit down and enjoy the best smoked turkey sandwiches he still had tasted to date. He enjoyed his dad's stories of his youth and how he dreamed of following in his family's footsteps. He would often be seen twisting the ring on his index finger, an absent gesture when his dad was lost in thought, maybe thinking about the weight of responsibility of owning a business.

The staff hustled around the room, straightening tablecloths, aligning chairs, and polishing every glass until it sparkled. Each detail was carefully checked and double-checked. Everything had to be ready for his mother's discerning inspection. Piper Ramsey arrived one hour before the doors opened. Dressed in her navy pants suit and setting her critical gaze on each corner of the restaurant, she prepared for her own inspection.

"Hello, son. Are you ready for today?" Piper said, as she greeted him with a kiss on his cheek.

"Yes. I'm ready," Benson replied with confidence.

"I'm going to look around, if you don't mind," Piper said, as she took in the finished look of the place. "The decor is very on brand with what you want to represent."

"Thank you." Benson thought better of giving her too much commentary. Piper asked the questions, and he answered.

Benson had prepared his staff for her interrogations. They were professionals, so he wasn't worried. He took a step back and watched Piper go through his restaurant with her invisible white gloves. Her gaze began in alignment with the glistening of the freshly cleaned floors. She surveyed each table, straightening a crooked tablecloth, positioning a chair until it perfectly aligned with the others at the table.

Satisfied with the front of the restaurant, Benson waited for what was next.

"I'll now move to the kitchen," Piper announced.

Piper inspected each station, scrutinizing the cleanliness of the countertops, the placement of the dishes, and the shininess of the silverware. She realigned the containers of seasonings so their labels could be clearly on display. The refrigerator doors were opened to check the temperature so nothing was at risk of spoiling. Nothing escaped her.

Her stare suddenly fixed on the pastry chef Benson reluctantly hired.

"I see you hired a pastry chef. I thought you were going to contract out your desserts?" Piper observed with a critical eye as the young gentleman took what would be the restaurant's signature cheddar and herb biscuits out of the oven.

"I wanted to create unique tastes for the cuisine. Chad came recommended by Alan. You remember my friend Alan, right? From culinary school?"

"Yes, I remember Alan. He owns that charming breakfast and lunch restaurant by the beach, yes?" Piper nodded in recognition.

"Chad worked part time with him. He was too talented to waste away in his place, so he sent him my way." Benson was thankful.

"Good decision." Piper did one full slow turn around the kitchen, then faced Benson. "Son? This place is absolute perfection. You can cook, so I'm not concerned about the food. Did you invite the press?"

"Yes." Benson gnawed on his lower lip.

"Son. Don't you worry about the press. I'm here and I know how to answer the tough questions. You focus on pleasing your new customers. Bringing out good food and ensuring service is excellent."

His mother was right. She would handle the press and he would focus on the food.

"Is your father coming?" Piper asked with a note of hesitation in her voice.

"Dad will be here. Of course." Benson was certain his parents could be in the same room together. They didn't argue. Their support in everything he did was invaluable. They could play nice for company.

"Did I hear my name? Only the world's best son calls me Dad." David Carter walked toward his ex-wife and son. "Are you ready for today? The place looks amazing," David said as he patted Benson on his back.

"Hello, David. I hope you're well." Piper looked at him, eyes narrowing, a stern expression settling on her face.

"Piper. It's good to see you." David smiled, grabbed his right hand and began twirling the thin gold band resting on his index finger.

"Now, if you'll excuse me, I'm going to freshen up and put on my chef's coat. I need to look like I own this place." Benson walked away, leaving his parents locked in a silent glare-off. He had more pressing matters—food to prepare, patrons to greet.

Forty-five minutes later, there was only standing room. Every inch of floor space filled with people standing shoulder to shoulder, eager for a taste of the new menu. Excited conversations mingled with the clinking of glasses and the occasional burst of laughter. Patrons leaned into one another, eyes widening with presumed delight after each bite of savory, tender smoked meats and perfectly charred seasoned vegetables. Benson stood in the entryway of the kitchen, admiring the scene. His eyes were locked on a woman who broke a piece of biscuit in half, her eyes lightening up as she tasted the flaky, buttery layers, then nudged her friend with an approving nod. The only remnants of the nearly spotless plates were the whispers of praise for each unforgettable flavor.

Stonewood and Ember had already captivated its audience.

Benson's attention turned to the entrance to his restaurant. His skin suddenly tingled as Aubrey's icy gaze panned the landscape of the space. She looked adorable in her white chef's coat and clogs, hair pulled back in a tight bun, very telling of her running out of her restaurant kitchen to check him out. Or was she checking out the block's newest dining option? From her face's expression, she's surprised to see this place full of patrons. Their eyes suddenly locked. The shackle of her stare drained his legs of strength to walk toward her. For a millisecond, his eyelids dropped. And just like that, he watched her walk out as quickly as she had walked in.

Benson shook his head, then turned to walk back into the kitchen. Someone called his name.

"Benson?" Nicole walked toward the back of the restaurant, with Levi directly behind her. "Benson. This is so amazing. You must be so proud."

"Hey!" Benson gave Nicole a brief hug. "I'm glad you came. Be sure to help yourself to anything. On me."

"Benson, how's everything working with the system?" Levi asked.

"Hey, man. Thank you for coming." Benson shook Levi's hand. "It's all working like a dream. You really know what you're doing."

"I try, I try." Levi stood proudly, looking around at the crowded space.

Nicole reached into her tote bag and pulled out her phone. "Cameron hates that he can't be here. He's at the fire station. He wanted me to FaceTime you. Hold on."

"So, Levi. I want you to add the data analytics feature to the system. Can we do that?" Benson asked. "My accountant would appreciate the reports that can come from that."

"Sure. Let's check in next week. That's an easy add on," Levi said, nodding.

"Say hi, y'all. Honey, can you see this place?" Nicole scanned the room with her phone.

"Man, Benson. I see you! I can't wait to come in and eat," Cameron said, grinning into the phone.

"It'll be my pleasure. Bring your mom, too." Benson smiled back at his long-time friend. "Hey, guys. I gotta go back to the kitchen. Enjoy yourselves. We can catch up later."

Just as Benson turned to walk back to the kitchen, a voice stopped him in his tracks.

"Mr. Carter. Steven Niles, from the New York Daily News. Can you explain what happened in New York? How is that affecting your new restaurant?"

Benson turned and yelled, "Get out of my restaurant!"

"Mr. Carter? What would you say to your customers who question your illicit behavior back in New York? Do you think your past will affect your work here in Los Angeles?" The reporter walked backward, facing Benson, phone in the air, ready to record a response.

Through gritted teeth, Benson sternly said, "Leave my establishment."

"What's going on here?" David Carter asked, stepping in front of his son.

"Do you think you can succeed here, given what happened in New York?" The reporter would not stop with the questions.

By this time, the restaurant was silent, customers glaring in wonderment.

"Mr. Niles?" Piper Ramsey called out. Can we step outside and have a conversation?"

"Oh, Ms. Ramsey? How will your son build trust with this community after such a high-profile crash in New York?"

Piper Ramsey had enough. She grabbed the reporter by the arm and rushed him outside and away from the windows of the restaurant. Chest heaving, Benson clenched his fists at his sides.

Nicole surveyed the room and then asked the people in the place, "Can we get a group photo for the Los Angeles Times?"

Nicole turned to Benson. "Nothing like a photo op to rally folks away from a distraction," she said and gave him a wink.

Piper re-entered the restaurant and headed straight toward her son. "Benson. In your office. Now, please."

With a roll of his eyes, he briskly walked into his cluttered office and sat behind his desk. David and Piper filed in, shutting the door behind them.

"I can talk to my son alone, David," Piper snapped.

"Yes, you can, but you won't. He's my son, too. What you say to him, you can say to me." David did not back down.

"Fine." Piper turned to Benson, her fists resting on her hips. "I did what I could to prevent the disaster that was New York to follow you here to L.A. But this is your fault. You didn't take my advice. If you had done your job, we wouldn't be in this situation."

Benson's nostrils flared as he tried to calm down before responding to his mother.

"Blaming him won't solve anything, Piper, and you know it. We need to focus on how we can fix this and not attack Benson." David moved to stand next to his son, facing his ex-wife, twisting his ring. "You know better than anyone, this takes time and support. You got your support when it was you."

Piper's eyes lit up like a moth to a flame. "Now is not the time for this, David. The focus is on Benson. Not me." She turned to Benson. "The press will come back. How will you handle them? And remember, perfection is the only option."

Benson was so caught up in the opening, he didn't take precautions or prepare for negative press. Nicole did such a wonderful job in her article welcoming him to L.A., he forgot the possibility of someone from the East Coast tracking him down in the West. The thought of the dumpster fire popping up in his new life didn't occur to him. Piper said she fixed it. He cursed himself for underestimating how connected everything could be, especially when secrets had a way of surfacing at the worst moments.

Benson slumped back into his chair. With a heavy sigh, he could feel the last flickers of hope dim within him. Understanding that his failures would forever be a part of him, and that his mother wouldn't let him forget his defeat, he responded. "I'll fix it."

Chapter 18

Benson

Just a month ago, Benson had been sure he was ruined all over again. When he returned to the restaurant floor on his opening day, he was surprised to see business as he left it prior to the exchange with the reporter. The scene was as if nothing happened. Patrons were drinking, enjoying their food, and smiling. Nicole was a true saint. She went from table to table, interviewing happy customers, gathering quotes in favor of the newest hot spot in Los Angeles. At the suggestion of his mother, Benson had Nicole sign a nondisclosure agreement before finally revealing the truth behind the disaster in New York. She then got to work and helped write press releases that went out to every major news outlet in the country.

In the last few days, the shine of Benson's new spot seemed dull. At first it was small things like a missed order, a delayed dish. The waitstaff, overwhelmed by the growing crowd, struggled to keep up. Orders were wrong, drinks were forgotten, and customers were receiving lukewarm food at best. Diners were showing frustration. Within a very short period, once crowded tables began to thin. Despite Nicole's press, some of his glowing reviews declined. This was not part of his desired introduction to the L.A. dining scene.

It was after hours, and Levi had just finished installing the last phases of his deluxe software applications when Benson pulled up the chair across from him and sat down. "I appreciate you coming after the restaurant closed to finish up this work. I know it's late."

Levi shut his laptop and put it in his messenger bag. "No problem. I have some clients with deep pockets, so I make myself available around the clock."

"Do you check the reports your system generates? There's been a decline in my business." Benson looked a little worried.

Levi gave Benson an investigative look. "I usually don't look. Do you notice a decline in business?"

"Within the last few days. It's something I'll keep an eye on."

"Nicole always says this can happen with new businesses. I've learned, listening to her and Aubrey, it may be a few things. Food, service, location, hype."

"Well, now that you've given me the state-of-the-art software, finding a reason for this is the first thing I do tomorrow. Can I get you some food? Are you hungry?" Benson was starving, but he wanted to leave his place of business for a change of scenery.

"Man, I'm good. I ate at Aubrey's before I came here. I had to reinstall some software at her place, so she fed me."

Benson nodded. "She is a great cook."

Levi nodded. "Nicole told me you two have known each other for a long time.

"Yes. We went to culinary school together. We were never friends, though. We were more like enemies, or rivals, to put it nicely."

"Aubrey has always been a part of my family. She and Nicole met in high school. They've basically been inseparable since."

Benson nodded. "Can I ask you a question?"

"Sure." Levi now sat across from Benson.

"What's Aubrey like?"

Levi sat in silence for a few moments. "What do you mean? What type of person is she?"

"Yeah."

"I've known her as long as Nicole has. They helped me out a lot. You know. With the ladies. She's been my sister's rock, always. Helped her through tough times. Helped her and Cameron get their shit together." Levi lowered his head, a shy grin spreading across his face. "She's like a big sister to me."

"Really?" Benson didn't know that side of Aubrey. He only experienced her angry side. The competitive side. He wanted to get to know her more. They were working on the same block. They had to get along, right? His sudden restless energy bubbled within him, a burning curiosity that made his hand twitch. "Is she dating anyone?"

Levi chuckled before responding. "No! She swore off men after her big breakup."

Benson's brows drew together with concern. "Big breakup?"

"Yeah. Just before she went to culinary school, she was supposed to get married. He broke it off. As far as I know, she hasn't dated since."

"Oh, yeah?" Why was Benson asking these questions?

"You checkin' for her?" Levi asked, one brow raised.

"Naw. Just curious." Maybe this explained her hostile behavior toward him. Was Aubrey jilted? That made his jaw slam shut and tighten. "So, what's the dating scene like here in L.A.? Are you in a relationship?"

Levi took in a deep sigh. "I'm what you call a serial dater. I'm on a few dating apps. I meet someone, we go on a few dates. I get bored and move on. There is one I keep close, though."

"A serial dater? You don't want a relationship with the one you keep close?" The term serial dater was new to Benson. Maybe he could be a serial dater. He had met a few women on dating apps. The last few dates he went on drew a quiet chuckle from him. All three women showing up at Aubrey's restaurant was classic. Getting her angry text messages from her spoke volumes. Deep down, he could sense her jealousy.

In a low tone, Levi replied, "Naw. Not now. I don't want a relationship. Not sure if I will ever get serious."

Did Benson have time to date? No. "Relationships are a distraction. That's what my mother has told me for my entire life. She said I won't be serious about my business if I have a partner."

"Naw. My mom wants me to be in a relationship. Ever since my ex and I broke up, she's been praying and hoping I find someone new."

"And what do you want?" Benson could ask Levi this question, but he couldn't bring himself to ask the same question of himself.

Levi's jaw clenched. "Real talk? I want my girl back."

"Your girl? How long has it been since you two broke up? You still love her, huh?" Benson had never gotten close enough to love someone. He was always too busy with work.

"I'll always love her." Benson noted Levi's eyes were turning cold. "Her father didn't like us together. We were sophomores in college when he stepped into our relationship, but we'd been together since high school."

Benson rubbed his chin. "That's tough, man. It sounds like it's a crazy story. I guess you two don't keep in touch?"

"Nope. It's a very deep story." Levi then stood.

"Okay." It was the look on Levi's face that told him it was best to not pry. "It's getting late. I'm going to lock up."

"I'm headed out. Let me know if you need anything else. Oh, and when Cameron and I go ball, you wanna come?" Levi asked.

"I'm not much of a baller, but I can play some defense. Why not?"

Benson shook Levi's hand and pulled him into a man hug. "I appreciate everything you've done here."

"No problem. My bill is in the mail," Levi said with a laugh.

"I got you. No worries. And thanks for the talk."

Levi gave Benson a thumbs up, and he was out the door.

Benson turned out the lights of his restaurant, walked out, shut the door and locked it. He glanced to his left, and there Aubrey stood. They hadn't spoken in weeks. She didn't come to the opening. She only sent Starr down to order a meal or two.

"Hey!" Benson said, slowly walking toward Aubrey, who just locked her restaurant door.

"Hello, Mr. Carter." Aubrey shifted her weight from one side to the other.

"Long time no see." Benson wasn't sure if this was the right greeting. He had to start somewhere.

"I can say the same about you. How's business?" Aubrey asked.

Benson stopped in front of Aubrey. "It's good. How are you?"

Aubrey gave him a searching look. "Are you being nice?"

"Can we call a truce? I'm going out for a drink and a light dinner. Do you wanna join me?" Benson was metaphorically holding out his olive branch.

"A drink? Light dinner?" Aubrey tapped the side of her mouth with her pointer finger. "A truce?"

Benson smiled and nodded.

"Sure. I'll go with you to get a drink."

Benson put his left hand on the small of Aubrey's back and led her into the bar.

The small tavern had an intimate charm. With the faint buzz of music playing in the background, the warm amber glow from the overhead lights cast a welcoming aura, dancing off polished wood surfaces and old copper bar stools. Behind the bar, bottles of spirits lined the shelves like old friends, their labels faded from years of use.

In the farthest corner, tucked away from the bustle of the bar, was a small table, sitting in the low lit space, its surface weathered, the wooden chairs pushed in, waiting for two people. It was almost inviting, as if the table held secrets of quiet conversations and moments shared. That table was the ideal spot for Benson to get to know Aubrey.

"Do you want a table or to sit at the bar?" Benson hoped she wanted to sit at a table.

"A table works for me." Aubrey peered up at Benson and gave him a warm smile.

Without waiting for the server to greet them, Benson told the server, "We'll take the table in the far back corner."

"Of course. I'll send someone to take your drink orders," the server said.

Benson pulled the chair out for Aubrey to sit. He then sat opposite of her, settling in and placing his arms on the table.

"Have you been here before?" Aubrey asked.

"One time. I came here one night after work. A lite dinner and a beer is a good way to wind down from the day." Benson studied Aubrey's face. His breath caught for a moment, captivated by the delicate curve of her jaw and the way her hair, free from the usual ponytail, framed her face. Her eyes sparkled in the soft-lit room, drawing him in with an almost magnetic pull. How was he going to pull back the layers of her facade, to discover the real Aubrey Carroll? He wanted to learn what made her smile, laugh, discover her passions.

"Hey, folks. What can I get you?" the server asked, tapping on her device to input their order.

"Aubrey? What would you like?" Benson could tell her mind was working, weighing her decision.

"I'll take an amber ale and a grilled chicken sandwich with fries."

Her order sounded pretty good. "I'll have the same. Thank you."

Taking the menus, the server said, "I'll be back with your beers."

Aubrey sat back and took a deep breath. They sat in silence for a few moments. "What's on your mind?"

With a slight chuckle, Aubrey responded. "Well. I can't believe we're sitting across from one another, and we aren't arguing or trying to kill each other."

"We did agree to a truce. Did you forget that fast?" Benson hoped they could really get to know each other now. They had restaurants on the same block. They could be friends.

"Yes, we did. Didn't we?"

Benson let out a soft laugh. "How was your day?"

"I should be asking you that. You've been open for, what? A month?

How are things going?" Just as Aubrey asked that question, she leaned in, placing her elbows on the table. She caught her face in her hands, giving Benson all of her attention.

"It's going great. Really. It was good to be in the kitchen again. It's been a while. I've been answering questions from the press." Just as Benson mentioned the press, the one reporter that asked him about New York came to mind. He didn't think anyone would know him in Los Angeles. His mother's public relations team wiped out all press related to New York. Or so he was told. He didn't want to dwell on that thought. He was more curious about Aubrey.

"Nicole and her brother Levi came by. Levi's a cool dude." Benson wanted to ease into the question that was top of mind.

"Nicole and Levi are good people. They're my people. My family," Aubrey said.

A few beats went by. The server arrived with their beers.

"Let's make a toast." Benson raised his bottle and prompted Aubrey to do the same.

"What are we toasting?" Aubrey's bottle was now in the air, hovering near Benson's bottle.

"Here's to our restaurants. May they both be successful. And here's to new found friendship." Benson clinked his bottle with Aubrey's, and they both took a slow sip from their drinks.

"New found friendship? Benson. Are you trying to be my friend?" Aubrey's eyes danced as she grinned.

"Can we be friends?" The more Benson sat with this woman, the more he wanted to learn about her.

"We've known each other for a long time. How many years has it been since we graduated culinary school?" Benson chuckled as he watched Aubrey try to do the math in her head.

"Six or seven years, I think."

"And we've been harboring hatred for that long?" Aubrey wondered out loud.

Benson never really hated Aubrey. In culinary school, she was his competition. Someone who had something to prove. He had to push aside her attractiveness and go to work. It was required that he graduate top of his class. Piper wouldn't have it any other way.

"We've known each other but haven't been around each other. We didn't speak at all after culinary school. We spent much of school bickering back and forth."

"Did we even speak during school? Or did we bark at each other?" Aubrey took a big gulp of her beer. Benson sensed a nervousness about her. Was she going to finish her beer sooner than later, for liquid courage?

"San Francisco was our reunion. Within five minutes, we were fighting like a cat and a dog. I tried to be nice to you, walked you to your hotel room, but that pretty mouth of yours wouldn't stop spurring digs at me."

"You always seem to get under my skin." Aubrey admitted.

Benson and Aubrey peered into each other's eyes. Their gaze was interrupted by the server setting their food on the table.

"Here you go. I hope you enjoy it." The server gave both of them a wink and left the table.

They sat in silence as they glanced at their food. Aubrey picked up a French fry, put it in her mouth, and began to chew. Benson picked up one half of his sandwich and took a large bite.

Benson broke the silence by asking, "Why didn't you come to my opening?" Aubrey finished chewing a bite of her sandwich, then she took the last sip of her beer before speaking.

"I have a restaurant to run. You know that."

"Yeah. And?" Did Benson sound bitter? He had to change his tone.

Aubrey signaled the server over and ordered them another beer. Then she tilted her head and asked, "Three dates in two days, huh?"

Benson shook his head and chuckled. "That was ages ago."

Aubrey giggled. "All of that was a train wreck waiting to happen. Your dating disasters are like reality TV—who wouldn't be curious?"

Benson wiped his mouth with a napkin, then smiled. "I'm glad to know my love life is your favorite form of entertainment. Maybe I should start charging for access!"

With that response, they both laughed.

Aubrey gazed into Benson's eyes. "I didn't come because I knew you would have a strong crowd. Especially after Nicole's article. And I will admit, I was jealous."

"Why are you jealous? You're the darling of Los Angeles. Aubrey's Favorites, and soon you'll open Aubrey's Treats, right?" Benson couldn't believe it. The confident woman he had grown to know would never be jealous. She was ambitious and fierce. Not jealous.

"I'm a little competitive."

Benson almost choked on his sip of beer with that statement. "A little is putting it mildly."

"I didn't want to intrude," Aubrey said in a whisper.

Benson studied her for a few moments. She was definitely nervous. Did he make her nervous? "I'm a busy man. I don't have time to date. And lately, the casual dating scene is whack."

"I don't have time for casual dating, let alone a relationship," Aubrey said. She took a big swig from her beer bottle.

Benson wanted to continue their conversation about dating and relationships, but he figured it was best to change the subject. "Tell me about your vision for your bakery?"

Chapter 19

Benson

Benson couldn't help but admire Aubrey as she talked about her bakery dream, eyes gleaming with excitement. There was something irresistibly captivating about the way her whole face brightened, making her even more alluring in that moment.

Aubrey's hands danced in the air as she spoke. "I'll take a page from my parents' coffee shops and serve high-quality brews, as well as pastries. What do you think?"

Benson was mesmerized by her. "What?"

"Did you hear anything I just said?" Aubrey tightened her glare, then took a sip of her beer.

"What you said was, you are very excited and have an amazing outlook for Aubrey's Treats." Benson did not take his eyes off of her as he took a gulp of his beer.

They sat in silence for several beats, staring into each other's eyes.

Aubrey was the first to speak. "What are you thinking about?"

Benson hesitated, then asked, "Do you want the truth?"

"Always the truth. I don't like to be lied to." Aubrey licked her lips.

"I'm thinking about kissing you again. Like San Francisco times ten." Benson admitted.

Aubrey took another sip of her beer, chuckled and said, "Oh, really? Like San Francisco?" Her breath caught. "Well, don't think too hard. You might sprain something." Aubrey chewed on her lower lip. It was maybe out of nervousness or being uncomfortable with his admission. He then said, "I'm not joking, Aubrey."

Aubrey took a deep swallow of her beer. She then replied, "Good to know. I'd hate to think that was your idea of humor."

Aubrey began laying with her beer bottle, peeling off its label. She was anxious.

"I'm not going to bite, lemon drop. You asked me what I was thinking about. I gave you an honest answer. It doesn't mean I'll act on it. That is, unless you want me to."

Aubrey's doubled in size. "Lemon drop? Is that my new name?"

In a hushed voice, Benson said, "Your kisses remind me of lemon drops. My favorite flavor. Like your renowned lemon pound cake. Delicious."

Aubrey inhaled, then exhaled before speaking.

"I didn't think you liked me very much. We've said some mean things to each other."

Benson dropped his head, flashed a slight smile, then said, "You do push my buttons. It's a natural response for me to snap back." He paused. Then peeled the label off his beer bottle. They were silent for a few seconds. "I think you're sexy. A fierce, captivating spark. If I touched you, would I singe my fingers?"

Aubrey gave him a daring gaze. "Only if you're not fireproof."

Benson shot back. "Guess I'll have to find out the hard way."

In a low whisper, Aubrey asked, "If I let you kiss me again. Then what?"

He let out a low laugh. "Then you'll be left wondering what took you so long."

"You're very sure of yourself, Benson."

"You can't blame a guy for shooting his shot, can you?"

"No. Not at all. Now what?"

"Up to you. I can be a gentleman and take you to your car and we go our separate ways. Or we can surrender to what I believe is a mutual attraction to one another." Benson stood and held his hand out for Aubrey to take it.

She stood and slowly walked away from the table, with Benson behind her.

Without saying a word, Benson opened the passenger door for Aubrey. She stepped into the car, and he shut the door behind her. When he got into the driver's seat, he turned to her. "I don't want this night to end."

With her head resting on the headrest, Aubrey tilted it toward Benson. He could see her eyes turning dark with desire. She then asked, "Do you think our bickering is a buffer for chemistry?"

Benson shrugged his shoulders. "Maybe. But there is no denying I'm attracted to you, Aubrey. No jokes."

Her hooded eyes searched his eyes. "Kiss me."

Benson leaned over, hovering over Aubrey's face. Her breathing was slightly shaky, with nervousness, he was certain. He slowly brought his lips to the edge of her lips. He planted a soft kiss, then kissed the edges of her lips. He then cupped a hand behind her ear and pulled her closer. Hesitant at first, making sure Aubrey didn't push him away. Benson tilted his head slightly to the left and brushed his lips over hers. As their lips met, a spark jolted between them, halting him from taking the kiss further. The sudden surge of energy left them both breathless, as if the connection itself held them in a moment of suspended intensity.

"Kiss me, Benson," Aubrey whispered.

Benson locked his mouth to hers like he would breathe her into himself. He let out a groan. She took his groan into her mouth, savoring it, savoring him. He opened his mouth to deepen the kiss, urging her lips apart and swept into her mouth, shifting the kiss from persuasive to demanding. She reciprocated, their tongues meeting, each movement slow and deliberate. The kiss was heated, passionate, and slick.

Benson pulled away first, leaning back, smiling. Aubrey covered her mouth with her hand, lightly touching her lips.

"Wow!" they both said at the same time.

He then brushed a thumb over the soft pillow of her bottom lip. "You are beautiful. You know that?"

The car was lit only by the street lamp a few feet away. Benson revealed the flush of her cheeks at his compliment.

Aubrey stared into Benson's eyes. "No one has called me beautiful in a very long time."

"Shame on them." He then leaned back and smiled. Seeking her hand with his own, he tangled their fingers together. "Are you ready to go back to your car?"

They sat in silence for a beat or two. She turned to him, paused and chewed on her lip. Aubrey then grabbed Benson's face, pulled it into her, her kisses featherlight and sweet at first. He was caught off guard. Was Aubrey this bold or was this the beers she drank, giving her liquid courage? She then lifted herself out of her seat, stretched her leg over the console and straddled him, then claimed his lips again, giving him a hot tongue-thrusting kiss that made him instantly hard.

Chapter 20

Aubrey

Aubrey stirred, eyes still closed, instinctively shifting toward the warmth beside her. Her hand grazed soft skin as she nestled closer, feeling the steady rise and fall of the chest of the man she shared a bed with. With a contented sigh, she tucked herself into the curve of the heat radiating off of Benson, moving to rest her head against his chest. He moved to smother her in an embrace, then used the strength of his arms to lift her onto him. Within an instant, her haze of sleep instantly evaporated. Heart racing, she shot her eyes wide open, the sudden realization jolting her off of him and onto her feet.

"Oh my god! What the hell?" Realizing she was completely naked, Aubrey used one hand to cover her breasts, the other covering her lower extremities. "What happened? Where are my clothes?"

In horror, she watched as Benson sat up, bare chest exposed, the white sheet pooled at his waist, tented, revealing his readiness to get active.

"Benson! Please don't tell me we..." Aubrey moved her pointer finger from her to him and back again.

"Babe. Calm down," Benson said, eyes pleading with her to relax.

"Don't call me babe. I'm not your babe." Her eyes scanned the room, settling on the nightstand on Benson's side of the bed. Her startled gaze zeroed in on the three opened condom wrappers. Aubrey gasped, her breath catching in her throat, eyes widening in disbelief.

In a frantic tone, Aubrey asked, "Where are my clothes?"

"Aubrey, I need you to calm down," Benson demanded.

She stood still, body unable to move as he reached for his boxer briefs and quickly slipped them on.

He took a few steps toward Aubrey. With a look of horror, she said, "We slept together."

"Yes. But it was," he took an inhale of breath, then said, "amazing."

Hearing those words, Aubrey sprung into action, turning on her heels to head into the living room. She would not stand and listen to Benson talk about what they did. Sprawled out all over the carpeted floor were her bra and panties. Her jeans and blouse were balled up, sitting in the corner of the couch.

She scooped up her clothes and rushed into the bathroom, closing and locking the door behind her, declaring, "This was a huge mistake. I don't do casual sex. I don't do sex. Period."

"Can you just stop for a minute?" Benson knocked on the bathroom door. "We should talk about this."

Hands gripping the counter, Aubrey leaned to get a closer look at herself. The raccoon eyes staring back at her were unrecognizable. Who was she? She hadn't had sex in years. How much did she have to drink last night? She turned on the faucet. The icy splash jarred her awake. She blinked rapidly. Droplets clung to her eyelashes as she mentally recounted the events of the previous night. It had been far too long since the warmth of another body was against hers, the spark of intimacy that was obviously last night. Sex with Benson was the best sex she had ever had.

After practically stripping in the car, Aubrey and Benson raced up his stairs. He fumbled with his keys. After several seconds, the door swung open, and they stumbled inside, tangled together in a rush of laughter and lust. Their hands found each other instinctively, steadying one another as they caught their breath. He pulled her closer by the waist so fast she couldn't even shake her face free. They reached for faces, pushing lips together in a frenzy of kisses, playful at first. Then kisses turned deep, passionate.

Aubrey grabbed his shirt, lifting it over Benson's head, exposing his sculpted chest.

"Wow! You are beautiful under there." Aubrey began giggling. "Can I lick you?"

Benson burst into laughter. "Can I lick you?" He lifted her shirt over her head, throwing it across the room. He signaled for her to follow him into his bedroom.

Aubrey threw her hands up in surrender and fell onto the bed. He followed, kicking his shoes off. She did the same. She then threw him back and straddled him.

Benson caressed her bare shoulder, down her arm, until her fingers tangled with his.

"Are you tipsy?" he asked.

"A little. You?"

"I'm aware of you. This." He waved his hand around their near nudeness. "What next?"

Aubrey bent down, kissing up Benson's neck and behind his ear. He flipped her, so he was on top. He cupped her breasts, kissing her soft skin between them. He moved up to her neck. "You smell so good."

"You always smell good. I can always tell when you're in the room."

"Really?"

They stared into each other's eyes. "I don't want us to do anything if you don't want to."

"Benson. I want to."

"Are you sure?"

"Yes." She then pulled down to kiss him, nipping and tugging at his mouth with a boldness that surprised him.

Without saying a word, he removed her bra, exposing her breasts.

"You are so beautiful." He kissed her deeply as his hands explored her body.

Aubrey's hands floated to his pants. She wrestled with his belt buckle.

"I'll take off my pants if you take yours off?" he playfully taunted.

Within seconds, they lay naked, finger tips stroking bare skin.

Unable to stand it, Benson leaned down to capture a breast in his mouth. He licked her nipple, rolling it with his tongue. She let out a moan.

His hands roamed to the outside of her thigh. He planted kisses between her breasts and moved to kiss a path down her stomach. He then kissed the inside of her thigh, slowly moving up to her center. He stroked her, sinking his finger deep inside of her.

"You are so wet," he said.

"Benson," Aubrey whispered. He inserted another finger, massaging her clit.

"Benson, please." The first touch of his tongue between her legs made her gasp. He licked her in long, sure strokes.

Against all logic, she melted against him.

"I need you inside me," she demanded.

Benson reached into his nightstand drawer, pulled out a condom, and put it on. His gaze held her captive as he slowly slid into her, inch by inch. She was tight and wet around him.

"You okay?" he asked.

Aubrey smiled, nodding.

He then drove into her, sinking deep with one strong thrust.

"Oh, God. Benson. Yes," Aubrey whispered.

He grabbed her hips and thrusted into her with deep, long strokes.

She tightened beneath him. "Let go, baby," he whispered.

Aubrey gasped as he pressed right against the spot guaranteed to ignite her.

With one long stroke, she broke, shivering under him. He kissed her softly as she shuttered.

"You feel so good," he said against her ear.

"I want you to cum."

And with that request, he softly pumped into her. She could feel him strain. His thrusts got faster."

"Aubrey," he whispered.

And with that, he let loose, slowly rocking side to side, coming down from his release.

"That was..."

"Magic," they said at the same time.

In a mad panic, Aubrey pushed her thoughts of last night aside and quickly dressed. She flung the door open. "Where's my phone? What time is it?"

In her cloud of haste, Benson grabbed Aubrey's wrist. "Stop. Aubrey. We need to talk."

She huffed air out of her lungs and said, "I have to get home and get ready to open the restaurant. I don't have time to talk."

He wasn't letting her move. "I know you're scared. I know your mind is racing at the fact that you and I had sex. Yesterday morning, you couldn't stand me, and I pretty much felt the same. You may not remember, but we called a truce. We had a great night. Maybe too much to drink, but I don't regret anything."

Aubrey looked up at him with discriminating eyes. She opened her mouth to speak, then had second thoughts. She was not ready for this conversation. Not now. Maybe not ever. They would just forget this ever happened.

Aubrey didn't know what to feel. Seth's departure was like the ending of a story she should've let go of years ago. She had accepted the pain. She was so used to pushing that pain down and burying it beneath her smile. The pain rested behind the busy distractions of her life, clinging to the illusion that moving forward meant leaving her past behind. Her night with Benson was forcing the truth, the weight of emotions swirling to the surface and wanting to break free. She would have to face all of it if they talked right now.

Twisting to free her wrist from Benson's grip, Aubrey announced, "I gotta go." She ran into his living room, snagged her purse, checked to make sure her phone was inside, grabbed her shoes and walked out the door barefoot, shutting it behind her. Knowing Benson would follow behind her, she jogged down the stairs and began walking toward the sidewalk. Not seeing her car in front of his house, she panicked. Did she have to go back inside? Within moments, Benson came out, dressed in gray sweats and a black t-shirt, keys in hand.

"Your car is at your restaurant. I'll drive you home."

"I'm not talking to you," Aubrey blurted. She didn't want to discuss anything. She needed time to process what this was.

"I know. We'll talk when you're ready. I'll call you a car in an hour to take you back to your restaurant."

Benson kept his word and didn't say a word to Aubrey on the drive to her house. A car did arrive within the hour to drive her to work. When she got to the restaurant, Starr furrowed her brow and tilted her head slightly, a flicker of confusion crossing her features. Her eyes narrowed as she searched Aubrey's face. "Boss lady? Are you alright?"

"I'm fine, Starr. Thanks for asking." Aubrey tried to make her voice sound cheery. She was thankful for the filled seats and the busyness of the kitchen. Maybe it would keep her mind off of last night.

"I got worried when I parked my car and there your car was, parked in the same spot as last night. Did you go out? Finally loosen up and have some fun?" Starr shimmied her shoulders and smiled ear to ear.

Aubrey couldn't help but laugh. It was a moment of levity amidst the storm of emotions she was trying to navigate. "I did have a few drinks last night." She had to give Starr something. Otherwise, she would be relentless with her questions.

Starr opened her mouth in disbelief. "Who did you have drinks with?

Was it the handsome man who owns the restaurant down the street?"

Aubrey rolled her eyes. She didn't want to admit to Starr she was with Benson. The memory of him made her cheeks flush.

"Are you blushing, boss lady? You *did* have drinks with him!" Starr clapped her hands.

"Calm down. I don't need everyone to know my business. Keep this to yourself, please."

"Did you kiss him?" Starr asked.

"Starr. Please." Aubrey shook her head. She could still feel his kisses on her lips, the faintest memory of their heat lingering on her skin.

"Go ahead, boss lady. Get yours." Starr chuckled, then went into the kitchen to pick up orders and deliver them to their tables.

Aubrey grabbed her purse and stepped out from behind the counter, casting a quick glance around the restaurant. The kitchen hummed with the familiar sounds of sizzling pans and chopping knives, but today, her attention was elsewhere. She removed her chef's coat and grabbed her sweater. Her fingers brushed the cold leather strap of her bag as she stepped into the brisk afternoon air. The drive to the accountant's office was a short one, but the weight of the decision ahead made the distance feel like miles.

As Aubrey exited her car and walked toward the building, her clogs squeaked against the pavement, the rhythm echoing in the quiet street as she lost herself in all she had going on. She hadn't intended for this—didn't plan to feel like she was carrying the world on her shoulders.

The thought of the books, the figures, the financial mess, and now Benson. It was consuming her. The accounting office came into view, a plain glass door with an understated sign. She inhaled deeply and pushed through.

"Hey, Christy." Aubrey waved, walked into her office, and sat down in one of the chairs in front of Christy's desk.

"Hi, Aubrey. How are things?" Christy asked as she tapped the keys on her laptop.

"Things have been pretty good. I got the three estimates you asked me to get." Aubrey reached into her tote bag and pulled out the manilla envelope, setting it in front of Christy.

"Let's get down to business, then." Christy opened the envelope, pulled out the stacks of paper clipped papers and began reviewing them.

"I'm really hoping we can make this work. I know we're working with a tight budget for the bakery build out. I have to find out if we can really get everything I want without cutting corners too much." Aubrey sat back in her chair, waiting for Christy to say something.

"Let's go through the estimates first and see where we stand. The biggest costs are typically the construction, equipment, and any design elements you might want. If you're looking to stay under budget, we might need to get a bit creative with those."

Aubrey reached into her tote bag again, this time pulling out a notepad. "I have a list of must-haves, but I need to prioritize to stay within budget. I really want the place to be inviting. I just don't want to be completely broke before I open."

Christy flipped through a few pages, then looked at Aubrey. "I think some of these labor costs are high. Do you know any of these contractors?"

"They come recommended. I hear some of them are really good. I don't want to risk cheap work. Maybe we can negotiate?" Aubrey held up two crossed fingers.

"Negotiations can be good. Even a small reduction in labor or materials might give you a little more breathing room. The cost of equipment can be very expensive. Have you thought about buying refurbished items?"

Aubrey sat up straight and smiled. "I already purchased my commercial ovens. They are so fabulous."

"And where did you get the money?"

Of course Christy would ask that. She was a money person. "I purchased them with some of my winnings from the Chef Supreme contest."

"Ahh." Christy nodded. "Well, with the uncertainty around construction and unexpected expenses, I recommend you keep a contingency of around ten percent of your total budget. We can find savings elsewhere and redirect those funds."

"So, do we go with this one?" Aubrey pointed to the estimate from the contractor her parents recommended.

"Maybe. I have a client who recently opened a restaurant. Before you make the final call, let me ask him for his contacts."

"Should I be doing anything in the meantime?" Aubrey really wanted to get started with the bakery.

Christy paused, then said, "We need to stay on top of the numbers."

"I think I may need to go with my dad's recommendation." Aubrey hated to admit it, but his decisions were always solid.

"Okay. Stay on top of the numbers. Get started. The sooner you make money, the better." Christy gave Aubrey a big smile.

Aubrey stood, gave Christy a hug, and opened her office door. Sitting in the waiting area was a tall, familiar figure. His khakis and button-up shirt made him stand out, even in the plain hallway. "Benson?"

Benson froze when her eyes narrowed in recognition.

"What are you doing here?" they both asked in unison.

Aubrey's stomach tightened. She hadn't expected this encounter. She stood in Christy's office doorway, smoothing her sweater, her mouth going dry. Her thoughts tangled, trying to make sense of the unexpected confrontation.

Benson stood and walked toward Aubrey. His voice was low but firm, carrying an edge that made Aubrey's heart skip a beat. "We need to talk," he said, his gaze intense, knowing their conversation was something that should happen immediately.

Aubrey ignored his request. "Thank you, Christy. I will work on our plan and get back to you soon, okay?"

Aubrey quickly walked over to the elevator and pushed the down button. The soft chime of the elevator doors opening felt like a reprieve. She stepped in, leaned against the back wall, her fingers drumming nervously on her purse. She let out a sigh of relief when the doors shut and the cabin moved toward the parking garage.

Chapter 21

Benson

"That was interesting." Christy eyed Benson. She may want an explanation for the exchange between him and Aubrey, but he wasn't offering one. He and Aubrey shared the best night of his life. What was next for them? Did he want to be with Aubrey? They had gotten to know one another at the bar, but he didn't really know her. They were culinary school classmates. Recently, they were so busy hating each other, they didn't get an opportunity to be civil or become friends. He wanted that to change. They could at least be friends.

"Benson? Do you hear me? How's your restaurant?" Christy asked, waving a hand in front of his face.

"What? Oh, I'm so sorry. I was in deep thought."

"Yeah, you were," Christy said with a soft laugh.

"The restaurant is good. I think we've done well in our first month. That's why I'm here. Can you tell me how things are going?" Benson wanted numbers. He wanted proof that he was on his way back to the top.

"Well." Christy typed on her keyboard, then waited a few moments until what Benson assumed was his account appeared on her screen. "Your opening was a complete success." She tapped on a few more keys before speaking. "Your aim was thirty thousand for the first month. I see a dip in sales not long after your opening. You didn't meet your goal of fifty thousand in sales. You had a minimum of fifty customers or table sales per day. On average, you made just under twelve hundred to fifteen hundred a day. Maybe an average of forty-five dollars per customer?"

"What do you think is causing my dip?"

"After a little research before our appointment, I found some reviews. Waitstaff was the common theme. Where did you get your servers?"

"I used the same national service I used in New York." Benson was perplexed. His servers in New York were top-notch.

"I would make a few changes with your staff. That will fix your problem, I think. Based on what I've read, you should've exceeded your goal for this period."

Benson sighed with concern. Piper wouldn't be happy, he was certain. By the time she catches the decline in sales, he will have hired new people. Without thinking, he asked, "How long has Aubrey been your client?"

Christy gave him a perplexed look. "She and I went to undergrad together. I've known her for a while. We recently started working together, though. My dad is her parents' accountant. So the water runs deep. Is that what you were wondering?"

"I was just curious." There were so many things Benson was curious about. Especially where Aubrey Carroll was concerned.

Sunrise and Shore sat just steps away from the beach, offering a perfect spot to watch the waves and enjoy a good breakfast or lunch. It was a charming mix of coastal simplicity and casual elegance. The weathered wood and pale blue shutters evoked a serene beach house vibe. Large windows framed the breathtaking ocean view. The doors were left open, letting in the salty breeze and the sound of seagulls. Wooden picnic tables dotted the outdoor patio, with colorful umbrellas providing shade from the sun. Inside, the walls were adorned with nautical-themed elements, shades of coral, teal, and sand. The open kitchen allowed the air to be filled with the aroma of eggs, bacon, and fresh grilled fish. Soft reggae music plays in the background, complementing the laid-back coastal feel.

Benson walked into Alan's restaurant eager to have a good hearty breakfast and chat with his closest friend.

"Grab a seat at the reserved table on the patio. You want the usual?" Alan asked when Benson walked toward him.

"Yep." Benson did as he was told.

"I'll join you in a second," Alan said, walking into his kitchen.

The gentle waves of the ocean lapped at the shore. The stretch of water was endless. This was what he needed to clear his head.

"Here you go." Alan sat down a plate of thick brown sugar crusted bacon, scrambled eggs, and breakfast potatoes with a side of sourdough toast.

"Aww man. This looks awesome. Thank you." Benson rubbed his hands together, ready to dig in.

A server set down a pitcher of freshly squeezed orange juice and a mug of hot coffee.

"Thanks, Josie. Let me know if you need me." Alan sat across from Benson with his own plate of a veggie and ham omelet. "So, what's good, man? It's been a minute."

"I don't even know where to start. So much has happened," Benson said as he sipped his orange juice, then took a bite of his eggs.

"Just start at the beginning," Alan suggested.

Benson took a bite of bacon, scooped up a mouthful of potatoes, and began chewing. "Aubrey and I spent the night together."

Alan choked on his food and had to take several sips of his water before he could respond. "What? You two spent the night together? When?"

"Look. Men don't usually talk about this, but I need to talk to someone. My head is spinning. She isn't just someone from one of the dating sites." Benson sipped his coffee.

"I get that. But I'm different." Alan took a bite of his fruit, then said, "Start from the beginning."

Benson started from making out in San Francisco to the time he first walked into Aubrey's restaurant. He told Alan about Nicole and Cameron, his dates meeting him at Aubrey's place, her being shocked at how great his restaurant looked, and his almost disastrous opening with the reporter. He mentioned the truce and how the night started with drinks.

"So, she woke up shocked and bolted," Alan summarized.

"Yep. And we haven't spoken since. She refuses to talk to me."

"You two have to talk. How are you feeling about all of this?"

Benson turned to look out at the water. The sudden breeze carried a saltiness of the ocean, mingling with the warm scent of breakfast pastries drifting from the restaurant. "I like her." He focused directly on Alan and nodded. "I really like her. She is focused, a successful business-woman. She's funny, hella fine. She has a good heart. Knowing she's near keeps me focused. She's kind of badass, in a good way. I like that."

"What happened to all the dates you went on?" Alan took the last bite of his omelet.

"They were just dates. I wasn't interested, really. I was just filling time. I had absolutely no chemistry with any of them. Just a meal and mediocre conversation." Benson took another sip of coffee.

"Well, my friend. You can't do anything if she won't talk to you. I say you come clean. Lay it all out and see what she says."

"That's easier said than done. I think she may have some history or past experiences that are against me."

"A man did her wrong?" Alan asked.

"Not sure. But I have a feeling." Benson wiped his mouth with the napkin and sat back in his chair.

"Just go into her restaurant and demand to see her. She's there every day. You're bound to run into her."

Benson sat for a moment, then said, "You're right. I'll do just that."

Chapter 22
Aubrey

"Where is she?" Aubrey could hear Benson ask Starr.

"Well, hello to you, too," Starr barked back. "She's not here. She went out to get more seasonings. We ran out."

Aubrey hid between the kitchen and the checkout area, hoping Benson couldn't see her eavesdropping on his conversation with Starr.

"Do you want to order something?" Starr asked in her sweetest tone. Someone could get a toothache with that tone.

"Can I get a cheeseburger? And how long ago did she leave?" Benson seemed even more eager than yesterday.

"You just missed her. She may be awhile, though. She mentioned something about running an errand for the wedding." Starr was good. She was quick on her feet.

"Can you tell her I stopped by? Again. I'll wait for my burger." Aubrey peeked around the corner to see Benson's arm folded across his chest.

Crouched down, walking like a duck, she moved into the kitchen to see her dad dropping floured chicken breasts into the fryer, a peculiar look on his face.

Bill opened his mouth to speak, but Aubrey placed a finger over her mouth to shush him before he could say a word.

Aubrey stood, watching Benson and Starr in a discreet spot in the kitchen, where she could see into the dining room without being noticed by him, quietly listening to their conversation.

"You can wait over there," Starr said, pointing to the space in front of the pastry bin.

"Can you throw in a piece of the lemon pound cake?" A smile formed on Benson's lips.

Starr let out a soft laugh, then said, "You like that cake, huh? You've ordered a piece like every day."

"Whatever." Benson's tone was laced with sarcasm, and this annoyed Aubrey.

How many times did Benson have to come into the restaurant before he understood she didn't want to talk to him? They were going on day three. Three days since their night together. The night they shared played a loop in her brain. She usually liked to be on the floor, greeting diners, helping Starr run the front of the restaurant. But since that night, Aubrey stayed in the kitchen or her office. Maybe today would be the day he gave up. She found herself drawn to his determination. There was something undeniably captivating about the way he moved, his focus unwavering as he pushed past any hesitation to make sure they spoke. The urgency in his voice, the need to connect, made her pulse quicken. She couldn't help but appreciate how serious he was, how he didn't want to waste any more time. His intensity, the way he cared so much—it was, in its own way, sexy. But she wasn't ready to talk.

Aubrey pinned her crossed arms across her chest, waiting for Benson to leave. She sensed her dad's presence behind her.

"Aubrey. What's going on? Are you hiding from that customer?" Bill asked.

She closed her eyes and pulled breath in from her nostrils, then said, "No, Dad. I'm not hiding. I just don't want to speak to Benson right now."

Bill tossed his daughter the side eye. "Who is Benson to you?"

"Shh. I don't want him to hear you or know I'm here."

Aubrey peeked up to see Benson carrying the white paper bag with his burger and piece of cake, in one hand, pushing the door open with the other with so much force it just missed hitting the window. Aubrey had to talk to him soon. She couldn't keep avoiding him. What was she going to say to him? He was her nemesis. They hated each other. Truce or not, they had to forget their night together.

"He's gone," Starr yelled.

Aubrey peeked around just to be sure. "Thank you."

"Aubrey? Who was that man? Is he bothering you?" Bill's tone was suddenly protective.

"Dad. His name is Benson. Benson Carter. He owns the restaurant a few doors down."

Bill nodded. "Your mother and I read about Stonewood and Ember. We went the other night. The food is very good."

Aubrey blinked rapidly in stunned disbelief. "You ate at his restaurant?"

"How well do you know him?"

Aubrey couldn't ignore her dad's intrusive question. "We went to culinary school together."

"He was in the contest with you? You both won, right?"

She nodded.

"Why was he insisting on speaking with you?" Bill's voice raised a notch. "Are you two dating?"

"No!" Aubrey wasn't lying. She and Benson were not dating.

Starr came from behind the counter and into the kitchen. "Benson's been in here every day asking for you since you two went for drinks. What's so urgent?" Now Starr stood facing Aubrey, her hands on her hips.

Aubrey gave her a stern, non-expressive stare, begging her to not say another word with her dad standing at her side.

Starr stared back. Then her eyes opened wide, a devilish grin appearing on her face. "Boss lady. You two slept together, huh?"

Now, Aubrey's eyes widened in shock as the truth sank in—she had been found out, right in front of her dad. She'd been running for days, but she would soon be pushed up against the wall. She wanted it to be with Benson standing right in front of her, not her dad.

Eyes pleading for Starr not to say another word in her dad's presence, she hissed, "Lower your voice."

Starr then grabbed her wrist and led Aubrey into her office. She shut the door, leaving Bill standing in the kitchen. She turned to Aubrey and said, "Spill."

Aubrey crossed her arms and frowned. She took a deep inhale, then exhaled, and spoke. "Yes, we spent the night together. No, I don't want a relationship. No, I don't want to talk about it. Obviously, he wants to talk, but I don't know what to say."

Starr clapped her hands, then said, "Don't be scared. If he didn't care, he wouldn't be hounding you, coming in here every day trying to talk to you."

Aubrey stood there for a moment. Starr had a point.

"I haven't really processed it all."

Starr let out a laugh. "Was it fun at least? Was it good?"

Aubrey's eyes got big as she shook her head. "Starr? I'm not having this conversation with you."

"No need. I have my answer. It's written all over your face. Go get that man, girl." Starr then walked out of Aubrey's office, leaving her with her thoughts. She had too much to think about. With her dad in her kitchen for the day, she had to sidestep the inevitable conversation she had to have with him.

"Aubrey?" Bill called as he rounded the corner, walking toward her office. "We need to talk."

Elbows on her desk, Aubrey lowered her head into her hands, bracing herself for the chat she had to have with her dad. With no time to prepare, she shared her truth. He heard what he heard. She couldn't deny anything.

"Benson and I are sorta friends. We've spent time together. He wants to talk about it, but I don't." Aubrey let out a breath and looked her father in the eye. If she wanted to be a true grown up, she had to own up to her behavior.

Bill nodded in thought before he spoke. "Do you like him? You haven't dated since Seth, right?"

"I have not dated since Seth. I don't have time to date, and I don't want a relationship. I don't want to be in a relationship. My time with Benson was a mistake." There. She said it. Now if she could muster up the courage to tell Benson the same thing. And mean it.

"For what it's worth, the little I know about Benson, I like. He has his own business and is not trying to join up with you and yours. He's ambitious."

Aubrey gave her dad a small smile. "Thanks, Dad. I'll keep that in mind."

The air was thick with the scent of freshly baked goods. At exactly three o'clock, Piper Ramsey walked into Aubrey's Favorites, tote bag swung over her right shoulder, dressed more casually than usual. Dark jeans, cranberry red leather loafers, and a crisp white collared blouse would be most people's business attire. Her mentor recognized well-made clothes like she recognized well-made food. High quality, well put together, and appealing to the eye. Aubrey slid out of the booth and walked to greet her with a handshake.

"Hello, dear. It's so good to see you," Piper greeted, reaching in for a hug and touch of Aubrey's left cheek.

"Hello. I'm happy you're here." Aubrey gestured her hand for Piper to sit across from her. "I've made some of the signature pastries I want to serve at the bakery. These are pastries customers can order with coffee. Or not."

"What you serve has to be appealing to the eye. You should stage these pastries in a way that's different from what your customers see in your restaurant. The stage should be different from any other bakery in the city. You want your bakery to stand out and be a fresh experience." Piper didn't waste any time getting down to business. After all, this is what these coaching sessions were for.

"Do you want to taste the pastries?" Butterflies swam in Aubrey's belly as Piper grinned and nodded. "Let's start with the croissants," Aubrey suggested.

Piper picked up the flaky, buttery pastry and took a bite. The sound of the crunch of her biting into the croissant rang loudly. She chewed thoughtfully, then looked at Aubrey, a slight smile tugging her lips. "The layers are perfect—thin, crisp, and light. But I think you can push the flavor a tiny bit more. The butter could come through more strongly. Maybe a bit more salt to balance the sweetness."

Aubrey nodded. "Try this fruit danish."

Piper picked it up, studying it for a moment before taking a bite. Her eyes narrowed as she chewed. Then she set it down slowly.

"Hmm," Piper considered. "The dough is tender. The fruit could be more balanced. It needs more sugar. It's a bit too tart. You need to bring the sweetness forward. The glaze gives a nice sheen, though."

Aubrey made a few notes in her notebook. "Try this lemon eclair."

"Your lemon pound cake is the best I've ever tasted. You know how to work with lemon." Piper took a bite, closed her eyes, and nodded.

"This," her eyes flickering over the pastry, "is your best yet. The filling is velvety and bright. The balance of lemon zest and cream is spot on. Everything in this eclair is in harmony."

Piper moved to the small tart, a rich chocolate ganache filled pastry. She took a bite.

"Now this is where you can challenge yourself. Play with flavors. A salted caramel or a touch of chili with chocolate, something unexpected. The goal is to set your pastries apart from others."

Aubrey took more notes. She then presented her raspberry scone.

Piper took a bite and nodded. "Pastries are as much about feeling as they are about technique. If you can capture a moment with each one, you'll have a bakery people can't resist."

Aubrey nodded, knowing she had a lot of work to do. "Thank you for your insight."

"I liked everything. However, I was critical because I understand your vision and what you are trying to do. You're wanting to be one of the best bakeries in the city. You can't serve less than." Piper then made her own notes on her tablet.

"Should I start over with new selections or perfect what you've tasted today?" Aubrey spent hours combing through her recipes and tried new ones to come up with this spread.

Piper used her pilot to point at various plates. "I would redo the croissant recipe. I would add more sugar to the tart. Maybe try a coffee ganache filled pastry."

Aubrey scribbled the ideas Piper shared in her notebook. When done, she looked to see Piper standing.

"Dear, I must go now. Let me know when you're ready for another session."

Aubrey stood and walked Piper outside. "It's always a pleasure. I learn so much from you."

Just as Aubrey reached out to shake Piper's hand, she detected his presence approaching her.

Benson's eyes furrowed, an expression of shock on his face. "Mom? How do you know Aubrey?"

"Mom?" Aubrey said, mouth agape. "Piper Ramsey is your mother?"

Chapter 23

Benson

Benson paced his office, waiting for his mother. His blood practically boiled with anger at the betrayal. Piper Ramsey, the woman who gave birth to him, was mentoring Aubrey. Thinking back to the morning she woke up in his bed, he recalled her words. She didn't want to be in a relationship. She didn't have time for a relationship. She didn't date. Those were Aubrey's words. All Piper's words. These were words spoken to him from the time he expressed wanting to date. His mother was the expert at drilling home her personal thoughts. She leaned in during conversations, her words dripping with conviction as she interrupted others to steer the topic back to her opinions. With every nod, she masked her impatience, waiting for the perfect moment to assert her views. What was thought to be your original ideas faded as her personal beliefs dominated, leaving little space for anyone else to voice their own.

"Benson, dear. Why are you upset?" Piper said as she walked into his office.

He didn't hear his mother come into his space. She dropped her bag on his couch and sat in the chair across from his desk.

Chest heaving up and down, Benson asked, "How long have you been working with Aubrey?"

"Well. You know I don't discuss my clients with you." Her sharp gaze rested on her son's jerky movements.

"You could have told me you had a client on my block. And of all people." Benson shook his head.

Piper was inquisitive about her son and Aubrey. "How do you two know each other?"

"We went to culinary school together." Benson was seeing red. How could this be his reality? Did Aubrey know that Piper Ramsey was his mother? He guessed not by the shocked look on her face as she registered that fact.

"And in culinary school, you became friends?" Piper asked.

"We were rivals. We competed in every rotation. She earned top scores, or I earned top scores. We were always close. We graduated top of our cohort." He looked at his mother, calculating a response.

"She's very talented." Piper examined her son. Benson already knew what was coming.

"I hope you two are still competitors, even though you don't cook the same type of food. You both have big ambitions."

Benson now sat in the chair behind his desk, his head resting in his hands.

"She's a pretty woman. Has a good head on her shoulders. She wants the same things you want. It could be easy for you, falling for her pretty face. I know how you are, son."

"We aren't dating. I learned my lesson in New York. You remind me almost every time we talk that relationships are a distraction and can detour the road to success." Benson thought about his so-called relationship with Deborah. She was his demise, between her occupation, social media presence, and her position on the board. He shook his head, trying to erase the memory of that night.

Benson looked straight into his mother's eyes, his gaze unwavering and intense. "Aubrey has a strong head on her shoulders. You've taught her well. She has no time for a relationship."

"So, she hasn't succumbed to your charms, then?" Piper sat back, calm and collected, yet Benson could see the whirlwind of thoughts and emotions darting behind her gaze.

"Were you going to visit me today? Or just get back in your car and drive away?" Benson needed to change the subject. His dating life wasn't his mother's business. He didn't know where he stood with Aubrey, despite his efforts.

"Of course. I wouldn't be so close and not at least stop in and say hello." Piper stood, straightened her blouse and leaned over to kiss Benson on his cheek. "Let's plan for dinner soon. I want to hear all about the success of this place."

He said nothing. She picked up her belongings and walked out of his office.

Benson glanced at his watch and realized that if he didn't leave now, he would be late picking up the newly printed menus with the new logo.

Benson pulled into the parking space in front of the basketball courts. He watched as Cameron focused intently, the basketball arcing through the air in a perfect line toward the hoop. Levi sat on the sidelines, eyes down, fingers working quickly to lace up his shoes, readying himself for his turn on the court.

He exited the car and announced his arrival. "Alright. Let's get this game going."

"Hey, man," Levi said, now standing, giving Benson a high five.

"You know you can't play," Cameron said, giving him a slap on the back.

Benson chuckled. "Yeah, you're right. But I can get a workout in by running up and down the court."

Cameron bounced the basketball as he, Benson, and Levi set up their three-man game of twenty-one. Cameron dribbled out from the baseline, calling, "Who's ready to get schooled?" A grin flashed across his face as he eyed Levi and Benson.

"Bring it on," Levi shot back, hands up, feet shuffling in anticipation.

Cameron made a quick move to the left, then faked right, driving toward the basket. Benson moved to block, but Cameron spun around him and went up for the shot. The ball rolled off his fingers, hitting the rim and spinning in. "That's two for me."

Benson shook his head. What did he look like playing against Cameron, a former college basketball star?

Levi grabbed the rebound, dribbling back to half-court. "Don't get too comfortable, hot shot," he said, signaling for Benson to go to the other side.

Cameron rolled his eyes, still catching his breath. "You're all talk, Levi."

Levi grinned as he crossed over, switching direction quickly and going for the layup. Benson tried to block him, but Levi spun past him, landing the shot. "Two to two," Levi announced with a quick wink.

Benson laughed, shaking his head. "Guess I've got to bring my A-game if I'm gonna beat you two show-offs." He picked up the ball and dribbled back, sizing them both up before making his next move.

Forty-five minutes later, Cameron boosted his win.

"I'm not sure if this win is legit. You played like you were in the NBA," Benson said, sipping his Gatorade.

"Yeah. I did." Cameron scanned the area. "Hey, you know I met Nicole in this park?"

"Oh, yeah? Were you two out for a run and ran into each other?"

Levi shook his head. "She actually fainted. Cameron was the EMT that responded to the call."

"Really? You hit on her when she came to?"

"Naw, man. We ran into each other a few times before we exchanged information. It was truly fate, she and I getting together." Cameron smiled, his eyes turning into hearts for his girl.

"Yeah, he's lucky I like him. Otherwise, he wouldn't be marrying my sister," Levi said, glaring at Cameron.

"You and your sister close?" Benson asked.

"Very," Cameron responded with a laugh.

"Besides Elle, my sister has my heart."

"Who's Elle?" Benson asked.

"The love of his life," Cameron said.

"Oh, the one you mentioned the other night?" Benson recalled.

"Yep. I'm not denying my feelings for her. We may not be together now, but I'll get her back," Levi said with conviction.

"You dating?" Cameron asked Benson.

He shrugged his shoulders. "There is someone I have my eyes on."

"Oh yeah? Bring her to the wedding," Cameron suggested.

Levi glared at Benson. "I think the one he's eying will be *in* the wedding."

Cameron shifted his gaze to Benson. "What? Did I miss something?"

Benson shook his head. "Levi doesn't know what he's talking about." He was not going to mention Aubrey, the night they shared, or his intentions. It was too early for all of that.

"Aubrey's a great girl. She saved me. Knocked sense into me. Otherwise, I was going to lose Nicole," Cameron admitted.

"Good to know," was all Benson could say.

Chapter 24

Aubrey

The time had finally come. Nicole and Cameron's wedding day. Aubrey sat, mentally bracing herself for the busy hours ahead. She wanted to double-check each menu item, making sure everything was perfect for her best friend's big day. The sous chefs needed to understand the hors d'oeuvres and how they should go out when the guests arrived at the venue. Her entire catering team gathered in the center of the kitchen as Aubrey ran through final instructions, like a conductor preparing an orchestra for the performance ahead.

By the end of the overview, each staff member understood their roles, from arranging the elegant reception tables to timing the courses with precision. With Starr taking point on all the day's activities, she would supervise the setup, casting an eye over every detail.

Her next task: the food. Double-checking the carefully curated menu, Aubrey reviewed each dish, making sure every plate would go out as planned. There was no room for error—especially with the couple's special requests. She inspected the freshly delivered items, tasting the hors d'oeuvres, sauces, and even the wedding cake to ensure the quality matched her high standards. Timing was crucial, and she coordinated with the wedding planner to make sure the food service flowed seamlessly with the day's events.

Aubrey checked her phone, hoping to hear from Starr. She was late. The day was passing quickly, and she didn't know how much longer she could remain in the kitchen before she had to be Nicole's maid of honor. Standing at the front of the kitchen, arms crossed, watching line cooks as they chopped vegetables, seasoned meats, and stacked plates for the first serving, her phone rang.

"Starr? Where are you? I can't stay in the kitchen all night," Aubrey said without greeting her with a hello.

"I can't be there." Starr's voice trembled, each word through clenched teeth as she fought to stay composed.

"Starr, what's wrong?" Aubrey didn't want to panic.

Starr sniffled and then said, "I fell down the stairs and sprained my ankle. I can't stand on my feet."

"Oh no, Starr. Are you going to be okay?"

"Yes, I have to stay off of it for two weeks, but I'll be okay. But..." Starr's voice filled with sadness. "The wedding. Who can you get to oversee everything?"

"Don't worry about that. You focus on getting better. We'll be fine." Aubrey hoped Starr didn't hear the panic in her voice. "Go on and rest. I'll call and check on you later, okay?"

"Okay. I'm so sorry, boss lady."

"Gotta run. Don't worry about us. We'll take care of things here."

Aubrey tapped her phone to end the call. She didn't know what she was going to do. Leaving the staff alone during the ceremony wasn't the best option but they could manage. Priority was to be in the kitchen before the reception started. She could run the kitchen but doing it alone could be disastrous. A guest list this size required at least one more person to supervise the team.

Aubrey stepped out of the kitchen and paced the hallway, willing an answer to come to her. She checked her watch and read the time. Two o'clock. She had an hour before she had to be in the bridal suite for pictures. Nicole could not find out the kitchen wasn't in complete control. She didn't want the bride to be worried. She could appoint one of her sous chefs to be in charge. But there was no room for any errors.

"No. No, no, no, no, no," she whispered. The idea shot through her mind like a bolt of lightning, fast and electrifying, sparking a flurry of thoughts before she could fully grasp it.

"Benson." Could she ask him to help? He was at the wedding, she was sure. With his help, there would be no mistakes. She needed someone by her side she trusted. Could she trust Benson? This was Nicole and Cameron's wedding. Everything had to be beyond perfect. But Aubrey hadn't talked to Benson since their night together. Would he help her?

Aubrey took in a deep breath, pulled out her phone and punched in Benson's number. After six or so rings, his voicemail picked up. She ended the call in frustration. She sent a text message.

Aubrey: Hey! I need a favor.

She stared at the phone, willing his response to appear on the thread. After a few seconds, the three dots began to bounce on her screen.

Benson: Who is this?

Aubrey sighed. This was not the time.

> **Aubrey**: You know who this is. It's Aubrey.

> **Benson**: Long time no hear from. A favor?

> **Aubrey**: Yes. Are you at the wedding venue?

> **Benson**: On my way

> **Aubrey**: Can you…

Just as Aubrey's fingers typed to ask him to meet her in the kitchen, Nicole's face appeared on the screen with an incoming call.

"Hello."

"Aubrey. Are you coming up here to get ready? I need you." Nicole's voice sounded nervous.

"Honey. Yes, I'm on my way." Aubrey ended the call. With only thirty minutes to get ready, she would find Benson later.

The sun hung low in the sky, casting a warm golden hue over the venue with wall to wall windows. Rows of white chairs, adorned with delicate floral arrangements, faced the front of the room bursting with white roses, peonies, and hydrangeas. Guests whispered excitedly among themselves, their smiles brightening the air with anticipation.

Cameron's mother, Patricia, sat beside her longtime friend, their hands clasped tightly in quiet solidarity. Piper Ramsey offered her unwavering support as her friend navigated the bittersweet emotions of missing her late husband on their son's wedding day. Amidst the unspoken sorrow, there was an undeniable sense of excitement and gratitude reflected in their silent exchange, a testament to their enduring friendship.

As the soft strains of a string quartet filled the space, the wedding party began their procession. Nicole's cousins and bridesmaids, clad in blush-pink dresses, walked gracefully down the aisle, arms entangled with the groomsmen, dressed in black tuxedos. Some whispered in the crowd, recognizing Cameron's college friend Terrell, a key player on the L.A. Lakers basketball team. Aubrey slowly strolled down the aisle. Her skin glowed, her smile sparkled with a joy she shared only for Cameron and Nicole. Cameron stood strong and looked so handsome. His best man leaned over to whisper something in his ear, then he nodded in agreement. The flower girl followed Aubrey. She was a tiny vision in white, scattering petals with a beaming smile, her innocence enchanting everyone present.

Then came the moment everyone had been waiting for. The music shifted, and Nicole appeared, like an angel, radiant in a fitted lace gown that glimmered with each step. Her hair, elegantly pinned back, was adorned with a delicate veil that caught the streams of sunlight that entered the room through the paneled glass, creating a halo effect. As she walked toward the altar, her father held her arm, his expression a mixture of pride and bittersweet nostalgia.

Cameron stood, his chest moving up and down with each heavy breath. His eyes lit up the moment they rested on Nicole. A smile broke across his face. It spoke volumes. He was transfixed. He took in his bride, who was about to become his wife.

Tara and Jim stood, their fingers intertwined, waiting to witness the union of Nicole and Cameron. Tears welled in their eyes, emotions overwhelming for a love so strong and undeniably meant to be. Happiness was an understatement of the depth of what they were feeling in that moment.

The crowd fell silent as the officiant signaled the beginning of the ceremony.

"You may be seated." He opened his bible, looked at Cameron, then Nicole, and nodded.

"Dearly beloved family and friends. We are gathered here today to witness the union of Nicole and Cameron in marriage. We're celebrating the deep love they share for one another and to honor their commitment to each other. Marriage is a sacred bond, a commitment to love and cherish one another…"

Nicole and Cameron were what marriage was supposed to be. Aubrey's own experience was filled with the ache of shattered promises and the empty space that replaced what should have been a forever. Still, there was a piece of her, though guarded, that wondered if love could someday feel real again. Witnessing Nicole and Cameron's relationship made her believe in it. She wanted to believe in it. She wanted to trust that somewhere out there was someone who wouldn't walk away, someone who could see her heart's worth and choose her without hesitation. Love far away, in the distance, but as she gazed out at the guests, she found Benson. Their eyes locked. Was he a possibility? For a split second, a glimmer of hope washed over her.

When it was time to say their vows, Aubrey inhaled and released a long breath. She could hear Nicole's voice tremble slightly as she promised to stand by Cameron through life's storms, while Cameron's deep, steady tone vowed to cherish her forever. Exchanging rings, they smiled at one another, the symbols of their love gleaming under the soft glow of the setting sun.

"I now pronounce you husband and wife," the officiant said. "You may kiss the bride."

Cameron slowly stepped to Nicole, cupped her face, mouthed he loved her, and pressed his lips to hers, giving her a soft, sensual kiss that gradually built to one of passion and foreverness. A cheer erupted from the guests, everyone on their feet, applauding the newly married couple.

As Mr. and Mrs. Davis walked down the aisle hand in hand, the air was filled with sweet congratulations. The celebration was just beginning, but their journey together had already taken flight.

Chapter 25

Aubrey

Before leaving the altar, Aubrey searched the now standing and applauding crowd for Benson. She and Cameron's friend Myles linked arms and followed behind Nicole and Cameron. Scanning the crowd for Benson is when she noticed Piper standing next to Cameron's mom, clapping for the couple. She spotted him, but he was not looking in her direction. She did her best to burn Benson with her gaze as she approached his seating area. There he stood in his black-on-black suit, looking effortlessly striking. The rich, dark fabric of his suit jacket hugged his broad shoulders, accentuating his strong frame. The intensity of his dark eyes made his features stand out with a refined allure. He cleaned up well. Their gazes met. She tilted her head toward the exit, praying he understood to meet her outside.

People flooded the exit, trying to get a glimpse of the bride and groom. Aubrey did her best to smile, nod and look as if she were fully committed to the next phase in the late evening's festivities. Where was Benson?

Unable to find him in the crowd, she was instantly alarmed. Did he leave? A tap on her shoulder broke her out of her panic.

Aubrey turned to find Benson now standing in front of her. "Oh, good. I need your help."

"Hello to you, too, Aubrey." He looked her over, taking in every detail from head to toe. "You look stunning, by the way," Benson said, then flashed all of his teeth.

In a whisper, Aubrey spoke. "No time for compliments. Starr sprained her ankle, and I need help in the kitchen."

Benson gave her a puzzled look. "Help. What kind of help?"

"With everything. I'll change after pictures and go straight to the kitchen. Can you help me?"

Aubrey's eyes tangled with his, pleading for him to say yes.

Benson stood in silence for several moments, looking at Aubrey. She huffed and shifted her weight from one foot to the other, then crossed her arms across her chest. She turned to find Piper staring in their direction. Her eyes narrowed as she studied them, trying to pinpoint the unspoken connection between the two of them.

Aubrey glanced in the other direction to see her parents approaching her and Benson.

"Oh, great," she said in a whisper. "Whatever they say and ask, just go with it."

Benson nodded.

"Hello, beautiful girl." Bill kissed his daughter on her cheek. "You look so beautiful."

"Yes, baby girl. You look stunning. It was a beautiful wedding, yes?" Tara said, turning her attention to Benson. "And who are you? I've seen you somewhere before."

"Mom? Dad? This is Benson Carter." Aubrey said a silent prayer for this interaction to go well. She had enough stress on her plate for one day.

"Hello, Mr. and Mrs. Carroll. It's a pleasure to meet you." Benson shook Bill and Tara's hands.

"You're the new chef in town. Your restaurant is a few doors down from Aubrey's Favorites. Your food is delicious, by the way. It's nice to see you and Aubrey know one another."

"Dear. They went to culinary school together. Isn't that right, Mr. Carter?" Bill's tone was overbearing.

"Yes. We go way back." Benson stood, working up a cocky smile.

"Mom? Dad? I have to cater the wedding. Catch up with you later?" Aubrey grabbed Benson's hand, pulling him out of earshot of her parents.

"We'll see you later, honey," Tara said, turning their attention to Nicole's parents.

For several moments, Aubrey and Benson stood in silence, her eyes fixed on him as she waited for his response.

"Are you going to help me?"

Benson's expression, like an exclamation point, said, "I will help you. IF, and only IF... we can talk later, after the reception."

Aubrey opened her mouth to speak, then shut it without saying a word. She then replied, "Fine. We can talk after the reception. Do you have a chef's coat?"

"I keep one in my car. I'll change and head over there in ten minutes."

Aubrey carefully arranged the delicate micro greens in a soft, verdant mound on the plate, ensuring each sprig stood just so. With a steady hand, she lifted a small spoonful of champagne vinaigrette, letting it drizzle in a gentle, golden stream over the greens, adding a glistening finish.

"Where do you want me to jump in?" Benson asked as the water ran over his soapy hands.

"The salad plates are going out in less than five minutes. Bread is on the table. Can you oversee the cooking of the steak? I think the guys got it, but I know that's your specialty." The compliment she just gave Benson sent a cold shiver up her spine.

"Sure thing. Then I'll jump in and help plate the entrées."

Benson was a professional chef that understood his assignment. Did she really need to give him directions? With his presence, the kitchen buzzed with a focused energy, chefs and servers weaving in a seamless dance as platters were carefully arranged and dishes plated to perfection. Stainless steel counters gleamed under the overhead lights, covered with pans of macaroni and cheese, collard greens, trays of tender braised meats, and bowls of creamy mashed potatoes. One by one, servers took plates dressed with steak, potatoes, macaroni and cheese, and sauteed collard greens, whisking them away to the dining room.

His presence was powerful. He was a calm, commanding force. He moved with purpose, his hands a blur of efficiency as he assumed the role of co-head chef. Aubrey couldn't help but glance at him in quiet admiration, her gaze lingering as he selflessly helped a staff member with plating the entrees. His unselfish contributions didn't just lighten her load. He was her backbone during stressful moments. Benson passed her to push the trays of dessert in her direction. It was his scent that always captured her attention. Today was no different. It was a magnetic pull so intense it made her heart skip a beat.

"Focus, Aubrey," she told herself.

As Aubrey whipped the cream for the peach cobbler, Benson called orders, his voice steady and calm, as assistants swiftly plated the mouth-watering food Nicole and Cameron requested. As the final dishes left the kitchen, they exchanged quick nods, a silent acknowledgment of teamwork and a job well done. Small plates of warm, bubbly peach cobbler topped with caramel whipped cream was last to go out. She scooped while he gently placed dollops of the cream on top of the delicious dessert. The meal matched the beauty of the celebration waiting beyond the kitchen doors. All the food went out without a hitch.

"Teamwork makes the dreamwork," Benson said as they both stood, spooning bites of the sweet treat that was left over.

"Girl. You know you can bake your ass off. This is outstanding. I thought your lemon pound cake was your best. This is running a close second." Benson scooped another bite of the cobbler in his mouth.

"Thank you, sir. I'll take the compliment." Aubrey leaned against the stainless steel counter. "I don't know what I would've done if you didn't step in and help me today."

"I'm glad I was here to help." Benson crossed his arms across his chest, glanced over to Aubrey, then said, "Let's go get a drink and talk. Like you promised."

Chapter 26

Benson

Benson and Aubrey sat across from one another at a small table in a bar near the wedding venue. Who was going to speak first? Aubrey furrowed her brow, her eyes darting between him and the floor as the silence stretched. Every time she opened her mouth, it appeared she wanted to say something, but the words seemed to stick in her throat, refusing to form. Her inability to say something only deepened his confusion, and the awkward silence between them hung heavy, like walls he couldn't break through.

Benson leaned forward, putting his elbows on the table, staring into Aubrey's eyes.

"The wedding was beautiful," he said.

"Yes, it was. I'm so happy for them. But I'm glad it's over. It was a lot of work." Aubrey slumped in her chair.

"You cater all the time. How was this a lot of work?"

"Maybe because it all was emotional. Nicole is like a sister to me. Seeing how Cameron loves her makes me love him like a brother. And I wanted the day to be perfect for them."

Benson hesitated before he asked his question. "Do you want to marry one day?"

Her face shifted, the weariness draining her features, leaving her pale and stiff, her eyes wide with an emotion he couldn't quite name.

Aubrey only shrugged her shoulders.

Then there was silence. Like he and Aubrey didn't have anything left to say to one another. "So, I guess I'll address the elephant in the room." He rubbed his lips together, then spoke. "I know you woke up the morning after... regretting the night, but I didn't and still don't." In that moment, he was losing time. The seconds were slipping away, waiting for her response.

"Benson. I don't know what to say. I don't even know what that night meant."

"Do we have to define it? Can we just say we had a good time, and maybe we can truly be friends?" Benson ignored his mother's words. He could have a relationship with the right person.

"We hate each other. Remember?" Aubrey gave him her devilish grin.

"We didn't hate each other that night." Benson chuckled. His throat suddenly parched. He waved his hand so the server could take their drink orders. "Do you want something to eat?"

"I sampled all night. I'm stuffed. Are you hungry?"

Benson sampled everything that went out. That's what chefs do. He was full, too. "Naw, I'm good."

The server pulled a pencil from behind her ear and pulled a small notepad out of her pocket. "Hey, you two. Can I take your order?"

"Two beers, please? Aubrey, is that okay?"

"Yes." She looked up at the server and nodded.

"No food?" The server looked at Benson, then Aubrey.

"No," they said in unison.

"We just catered a wedding. We're stuffed." Benson smiled up at the server.

"Oh, wow, you two are chefs? I bet you don't have to argue who'll make breakfast." She gave them a wink. "I'll be right back with those beers."

The server walked away. Benson turned to Aubrey. "She's hilarious."

"She thinks we're a couple." Aubrey widened her eyes as she spoke. "Do we look like a couple? I don't do the couple thing."

"Why is that?" Benson figured now was better than later. He wanted to get behind the mysterious Aubrey Carroll.

"The same reason you don't couple. Piper Ramsey is your mother. I'm sure the same speech she gives me is on a loop in your head. You heard it growing up, right? And why didn't you tell me she was your mother?"

Benson hesitated before answering. "If I tell people she's my mother, they won't take me seriously. I'm trying to make a name for myself."

"You may be right. I'm trying to figure out if you should've told me. Finding out the way I did caught me completely off guard. I was stunned."

The server arrived with their beers. Benson lifted his bottle and titled it toward Aubrey's. "Cheers." Their bottles clinked. They both took a gulp before setting their bottles on the table.

"How do you think I felt? She's my mother. Knowing how she feels about everything. I was just worried she'd figure out we had a little more than fun, rather than a friendly chat between business neighbors."

"Your mom is intuitive, but she isn't psychic." Aubrey took a sip of her beer.

"Is your mom happy that you're in L.A. and not in New York?"

Benson cast his eyes away, then grabbed his beer and took a big gulp. "I'm not sure. She doesn't always reveal how she really feels, other than giving me critique with her ridiculously high expectations."

"Why did you leave New York? Really?" Aubrey asked.

Benson's jaw tightened. He needed to tell her sooner than later, if he wanted any kind of chance with her. He first needed to understand where they stood.

Chapter 27

Aubrey

"New York was good. It was really good... until it wasn't."

Aubrey studied Benson, his head down, jawline tensing. She recognized a pattern. At the mention of New York, his shoulders tightened, and his easygoing smile faded. His jaw clenched just slightly, eyes flickering with a momentary tension that seemed to disrupt his usual calm. He generally stayed calm unless they were arguing. He took a slow, controlled breath, as if bracing himself against a tide of unwelcome memories.

"Benson. What happened in New York?" she asked again.

He looked up at Aubrey, studying her face for several moments. "I thought it was a good place to be in business. I soon learned it wasn't for me. So, I came back here. To Los Angeles."

Her brows knit together, and her lips parted slightly, a glint of confusion flickering in her eyes as she tried to piece together what she'd heard him say, compared to Nicole's story that printed in the Los Angeles Times. She tilted her head, waiting for seconds before asking, "What made New York bad? I think I read somewhere you were at the top of your game in New York. It's one of the best culinary meccas in the world."

"New York is definitely the ultimate hub of culinary excellence. It was exhilarating to be a part of that unique clique." He stopped talking. Aubrey waited for his next words. She wanted a deep explanation for why he uprooted himself to come to L.A.

"You know my dad is here, right? My mom, too, but my dad. We're close, and it was time for me to be here, close to him." Benson smiled at the finality of his words.

"Okay. I get it. I think." Aubrey didn't know what else to say.

"The elephant is still in the room. Can we talk about the other night? Please?" Benson reached across the table for Aubrey's hand, then thought better and rested it close to hers.

Aubrey let out a deep sigh. "I owe you an apology. I was wrong to run out like I did."

"Was it something I did?"

She shook her head. "No, you didn't do anything." She giggled. "You did everything right, actually." A rosy hue crept up her cheeks at the admission, a telltale sign of the emotions budding beneath her composed exterior. Her gaze shifted downward, a shy smile playing on her lips as the color deepened.

"Oh, yeah?" Benson straightened his back in arrogance. "We can have a repeat, you know."

A deep, rich laugh escaped Aubrey. She could barely keep a straight face. "You are too much, you know that?"

Aubrey and Benson reached for their beer bottles, taking a sip at the same time.

"I don't think our night together was a mistake. I don't regret it at all." Benson was staring into Aubrey's eyes with focus and determination, telling her just what he wanted and hat he was feeling.

"I don't do relationships. Like I said."

With his strong gaze on her, Benson asked, "Why? What are your fears, Aubrey Carroll?"

"I don't want to trust the wrong person. I don't want to open myself up only to get hurt. Again." There. She said it. Fear of trusting the wrong person had only been in her head until now. It was something even Nicole didn't know.

Benson spoke in a soft tone. "What happened?"

Aubrey took another swig of her beer and relented to tell Benson her story. If they were truly calling a truce and trying to become friends, she had to be honest. "I was stood up at the altar." Aubrey's hands were clasped tightly under the table, fingers intertwining and twisting as she fidgeted. Her hands were a silent giveaway of the tension simmering beneath her calm facade. "I was sitting in the dressing room, my makeup was done. I was ready to put on my dress. My dad entered the room. The truth was all on his face. Then he sent me a text message, saying he couldn't marry me."

"You were stood up on your wedding day? Like at the church and everything?"

Aubrey nodded. "My parents were against it from the beginning. They thought I was too young. They said I was taking a huge risk. I know now they didn't think he was good for me."

They sat in silence for a minute. "We were supposed to go to culinary school together. Open a restaurant, then another. But, at the last minute, I wasn't enough. He was very ambitious and greedy. He was an opportunist who prioritized himself over our relationship. He had a single-minded focus on wealth. He wanted part of what my parents built in their coffee shop chains. I made the mistake of trusting him—trusting we would spend the rest of our lives together."

Aubrey faced Benson. His brows drew together, casting a shadow over his eyes. A muscle flickered along his cheek as he clenched his teeth, a storm raging in his dark eyes.

"That was years ago, Benson. You don't have to be angry. It is what it is. But I'm not someone who dates. I don't have time. I don't want to date. I don't want to find love, only to lose it. Staying single is easier. Less heartache."

"So, is he the reason you are not open to a relationship? He was a jerk, Aubrey. He was emotionally detached, indecisive, and selfish. He was a coward."

"Now, when I look back, I believe he had unresolved issues. He had a problem with my parents."

"What's wrong with your parents?"

"My parents are really overprotective. They're obsessed with my safety. They're my business investors and early on, made it clear they would be involved in everything. I think he had a problem with that. His own financial ambitions were more important than our relationship and what I thought was love for one another. He was a deeply flawed person."

"His loss." Benson's eyes grew dark, now for a different reason. "His loss could be my gain, Aubrey."

"Are you serious? You can't be serious, Benson. We don't know each other. You don't have time for a relationship either. Running a restaurant takes up a lot of time. You can't have time to date. Besides, your mother would kill us both."

Their laughter echoed across the room. Covering her mouth, Aubrey said, "I don't mean to be loud, but the thought of your mom, it tickles me."

"I date casually because it's easy. And because of my mom." He chuckled. "In all seriousness, though. I think we have more in common than you think. I know we argue, but you can't deny our chemistry. Maybe our fights are our frustrations based on desire?"

"Do you desire me, Benson Carter?" Aubrey made eye contact, then smiled.

"What if I do?" He was so direct.

"What do you fear?"

Benson dropped his head, thinking about the question. "I think I have trust issues, too. I fear failure. Failure that will prove Piper correct."

"Can I get you two more beer?" the server asked.

"Sure," they said in unison.

Aubrey and Benson exited the elevator on the floor of her hotel room.

"My room is a mess. I had to hurry and dress before the wedding," she explained.

"You know I don't care about that."

"Well, just in case." Aubrey slid her key over the electronic lock, waiting to hear the click and green light to signal the door was open.

"After you, sir." Benson walked in. She followed and shut the door behind her.

Benson abruptly turned around, Aubrey only inches from him. He reached for her, pulling her close. His right hand cupped her face, then his index finger trailed across her check. "I want to stay, Aubrey."

"Good. I wouldn't suggest you come here if I didn't want you to stay." She kissed him, not wanting to hold back anymore. She pulled him closer, desperate to have him against her again.

Benson's arm came around Aubrey's waist, bringing her hips into his. She pulled at his shirt, needing the barrier between them gone. He dragged his mouth down her neck slowly, nipping at her skin. She let out a moan.

"Damn, I love that sound." Benson planted kisses behind her ear. She let out another moan. "That sound is going to be the death of me."

Aubrey lifted his shirt, feeling the soft skin beneath it. Both hands gripped his waist, trailing beneath his pants, caressing his upper ass. "Can we take these off?" Aubrey tugged on his pants.

"We can do more than that." Benson unbuckled his pants, stepping out of his shoes and socks.

Aubrey whimpered, pulling at his clothes.

"Undress me?" he requested.

"Only if you undress me," she compromised.

In silence, with only the dim light lit on the nightstand, Aubrey pulled Benson's shirt over his head, revealing his beautifully sculpted pecs, biceps, and tight abs. She lightly ran her fingers across his stomach, like gentle ripples spreading across a calm lake. She slid his pants down and over his feet, tossing them to the side then tugged at his fitted black boxer briefs, pushing them down, revealing his erect penis. Her hands moved to stroke his length. Her eyes grew dark with intent.

"You have a beautiful body, you know that?" Aubrey whispered.

"Thank you. Now my turn," Benson growled.

He removed her shirt, then her pants, and socks, leaving her in fleshed colored lace panties and bra.

Benson's head titled, slowly, his eyes trailing up and down Aubrey's body. Had she ever been looked at in that way? It was so hot.

A sound of need climbed out of Aubrey's throat.

Benson chuckled. "Come here."

Aubrey stepped to him. She looked up, her heart stuttering, remembering him all over her body.

"Would you be upset if I ripped that pretty lace set off of you, pushed you on the bed, and devoured you?"

"Is that a promise?" Aubrey grinned devilishly, turning to walk toward the bed, looking back at Benson. "Are you coming?"

Benson strolled to the edge of the bed, standing in front of Aubrey as she sat. She pulled his boxers down, licking her lips at the sight of him springing free. She closed her hand around his length, slowly stroking him up and down. He led out a groan.

"Lie down on the bed," she directed.

He stepped out of his boxers and laid on top of the bed, his back pressed to the mattress.

Aubrey crawled to him, spread his legs, and took him into her mouth. Her tongue encircled his tip. She licked the sides of his shaft, taking him in again, this time sucking, massaging his balls, slowly releasing him with a pop.

"Aubrey." Benson's voice was low and dark. He grabbed her, lifting her on top of him, unhooking her bra, watching as her breast jiggled free. His hands traveled to her panties. He linked his fingers around the rim and pulled. Aubrey straddled him, feeling his hardened length against her entrance.

He stroked her, feeling the moisture between her legs. She whimpered as his thumb rubbed circles around her clit. Her body went into a frenzy.

"Benson." His fingers began to move faster, deeper until her mouth parted, the cry ready to fall from her lips. Her body spasmed, then went limp on top of him.

"You okay?" he asked.

Aubrey couldn't speak. She could only grunt.

Benson, still hard, gently placed Aubrey to the side of him. He got off the bed, reached for his pants, pulled out his wallet, opened it, and grabbed a condom.

He rolled it on and laid on the bed. Aubrey straddled him, slowly lowering herself onto him. Benson lifted his hips and thrusted into her. She slowly gyrated her hips, riding him, until she felt her climax. Just as she was on the edge, he flipped her, not losing their connection.

He hammered into her with quick movements, causing Aubrey to arch her back into the feeling.

"Benson. I'm coming."

He reached down and kissed her hard, feeling her tense up beneath him.

"I'm coming, baby." He pulsed inside of her.

Within seconds, they fell together.

Neither spoke a word. Benson feathered kisses down her neck as their racing hearts slowed.

When her breathing was normal, Benson went to the bathroom to dispose of the condom and clean up. She followed, hugging him as he stood at the sink.

"What now?" she asked.

"We sleep. Then wake and do it again." He turned to her, brushed a kiss on her lips, and led her to the bed.

Chapter 28

Aubrey

Aubrey turned to face Benson, her naked body curling softly toward him as her eyes fluttered closed. Lying beside him, she could feel the warmth of his breath, steady and calm, brushing against her bare skin. Each gentle rise and fall of his chiseled chest became a quiet rhythm, anchoring her in the stillness of the early morning. She was familiar with her surroundings, a soft smile playing on her lips. A sense of peace spoke of a familiarity. She was grounded, as if every detail around her belonged exactly where it was meant to be, just as she did.

Benson wrapped his arm around Aubrey's waist and pulled her close. He kissed her check. "Good morning."

She blinked awake, her eyes slowly adjusting to the rays of sunlight shining through the bottom of the window curtains. He was watching her intently, his expression unreadable, as if he was waiting for her to open her eyes. Aubrey moved slightly, only to feel Benson's hold tighten.

"My lemon drop, I don't want you to go anywhere." He nuzzled his lips against her neck, planting soft kisses. His cool, soft lips thawed her hot skin.

Aubrey lifted her chin to give Benson more access to her. "Good morning to you." The warmth of their naked bodies was like a warm blanket on a cold winter night.

"You feel amazing next to me, but I need to take a shower," Aubrey announced.

"Can I join you?" Benson asked.

"If you wash my back, I'll wash yours." Aubrey laughed all the way into the bathroom.

Aubrey stepped into the shower first, adjusting the water's temperature, letting it run down her back. The hot stream warmed her body again with the loss of Benson's against her.

Benson watched her through the shower door. A mix of disbelief and satisfaction flooded her thoughts as she lazily shifted her gaze onto him and his luxurious nakedness. Her skin tingled with the memory of him. A small involuntary smile crept on her face. Being with Benson was undeniably good.

"What are you smiling at?" Benson asked, now in the shower, covering his body with soap suds.

Aubrey didn't answer his question. She stepped close to him and rubbed her body against his, allowing herself to be covered in soap. Benson lowered himself to kiss her. The kiss was slow and deep, his tongue dipping between the seams of her lips. She opened her mouth, allowing his tongue to play with hers. He slowly turned her body around, allowing the stream of water to rain over her.

Benson pumped the vanilla, white tea scented body wash into his palm and rubbed it between his hands, creating a lather he gently smeared over Aubrey's breasts. He made circular motions down to her stomach, then wrapped his hands around her ass, giving it a squeeze.

Aubrey took the soap from Benson, rubbing it between her hands.

She ran her fingers over his shoulders, chest, and around to his back, massaging his shoulders and down his spine.

In a swift move, Benson lifted Aubrey, prompting her to wrap her legs around his waist. He positioned her against the tiles, dropping kisses down her neck to her mouth.

"Can I?" he asked.

"Can you?" Aubrey looked into Benson's eyes. "Oh. Can you pull out?"

"Yes." He then positioned her to take him. He lifted her so she could lower herself onto him.

Her breath skipped, feeling all of him, full and tight. With the water falling down on their soapy bodies, Benson thrusted inside of her.

"God, you feel good, Aubrey," he whispered into the nape of her neck.

Aubrey moved with him, wanting to ride his wave. She wasn't sure how he managed to massage her clit while holding her up and smashing into her.

"Benson." Her head dropped, feeling her arousal increase. "That's it, baby," she moaned.

"I want you to release. Let go." As he whispered her name, she let go, letting out a cry.

"I'm pulling out," he announced. Just as he set Aubrey on her feet, he let go, sperm sprouting out onto the shower floor and down the drain.

Aubrey dressed in leggings and an oversized sweatshirt, only giving Benson a warm smile when she found his eyes on her. The gray sweatpants he wore hung loose and low on his hips. If he would only put a shirt on. Shirtless, his sex appeal was almost too much to stand. If she stared another second, they would end up back in bed.

The quiet of the room was suddenly punctuated by a low, rumbling growl from her stomach, breaking the stillness like a thunderclap. Cheeks flushing with embarrassment, she was reminded that it had been too long since her last meal. "Are you hungry? I can order room service?"

"I would love to have breakfast with you." Benson smiled.

Over pancakes, eggs, bacon, fruit, coffee and several glasses of water, Aubrey and Benson spoke freely about their work. She learned he worked under some of the best chefs in New York, learning all the best tricks of the trade. She shared her experiences with her parents' Brewed Awakening chain before she took the leap to open Aubrey's Favorites.

"So, your parents are your investors?" Benson asked, popping a grape into his mouth.

"Yes, they're my investors. But it's the control that is the motivating factor." This was the first time she voiced her recent revelations about her parents and their overprotectiveness.

"What do you mean?"

"I was a baby when my sister died. Avery was only six years old." Aubrey took in a deep breath before speaking again. "She and my parents were leaving a store in a bad part of the city. Without notice, two cars pulled up. The guys got out and began shooting at one another. My parents tried to pull Avery and take cover. I guess her instinct was to run. She ran into the street and was hit by a car." Aubrey looked up to see Benson still and staring at her.

"I'm so sorry, Aubrey." He reached over to grab her hand. He gave it a squeeze.

"I grew up under their close, watchful eyes. I wasn't allowed to have what I would consider a normal childhood. I literally grew up in the coffee shop. When I got to high school, I wasn't allowed to attend games, dances, or even date. College was my first taste of freedom. That's where I met Seth."

"Seth? The moron who left you?"

Aubrey nodded. "He was my first… everything. I think now, my naïveté was the reason I didn't see the signs. He was selfish, he tried to be controlling, and was only thinking of his own gain. I didn't see he was a lot like my overbearing parents."

Benson sat silent for a second, then said, "I get what you were thinking, but he wasn't a decent person. Don't beat yourself up about his unresolved emotions or unwillingness to be truthful."

Aubrey smiled. "Thank you for that. But my parents still worry about so many things where I'm concerned. Me being in San Francisco was a flex. I lied and said I was only going to be across town at a conference."

Benson chuckled. "Really? Wow."

"After culinary school, I went to them about opening Aubrey's Favorites. The plan was for me to expand their already successful coffee shop franchise. They agreed only to help if my restaurant followed their financial template. Essentially, they've been in control of everything up until recently."

"What happened recently?" Benson asked, a mouth full of bacon.

"I bought the space next door. You know, the one you wanted?" Aubrey giggled. She took a sip of her coffee. "That was the first risk I've taken on my own. I made a decision without their consultation and now, they refuse to help me build out the bakery."

"Do you have enough to build it out and open? We did win a big chunk from the competition."

Aubrey moved the eggs around her plate with a fork. "I bought some top of the line commercial ovens, which was probably not the best decision. I've got three estimates. I'm working with Christy to draw up the best-case scenario."

"Let my guys give you an estimate. They did an amazing job with my place, as you know, and believe it or not, they came in with the best prices of all the contractors I spoke to." He drank half of his water bottle before speaking again. "Why don't we check out your space when we leave here? That is, if you don't mind. I want to help if I can."

"Don't go all boyfriend on me, Benson. You know I don't want a relationship."

"You've made that very clear. We're friends. With benefits." He winked at her, stood, and reached to kiss her on her cheek.

"This is it." Aubrey walked to the middle of the space and slowly turned to admire the space that would soon be her bakery.

"So, this should have been my space," Benson teased.

"Well. I outbid you. I won," Aubrey teased back. She walked to him and stood toe to toe. She lifted her head to stare into his eyes.

He bent down to whisper in her ear. "I think I won." He then planted a trail of soft kisses behind her ear and down the side of her neck. Aubrey closed her eyes and inhaled all the air she could, shivering at the sensual touch of his lips on her skin.

Aubrey took a small step back. When their lips were only a whisper apart, she could still feel her whole body tremble. She got on her tiptoes and pressed a soft, sensual kiss on his lips.

"Girl, if you keep this up, the folks outside will get an x-rated show." Benson chuckled, then stepped a few feet away from her.

"I'm going for warmth and charm," Aubrey said, attempting to shift the sexual friction lingering in the air.

"I'm listening," Benson said as she gestured for him to see her vision.

"I'm thinking the walls will be painted a soft inviting sage green, contrasted against white subway tiles behind the counter. The exposed brick will give the space a slightly rustic edge. We'll polish the wood beams." Aubrey pointed to the beams that ran along the ceiling. "It will add a touch of modernity, don't you think?"

"I do. I can see pendant lights hanging above each small table that you will add to the space." Benson suggested.

"The large windows let in natural light, which will be welcoming for the early morning crowd. I'm thinking the main counter can be made from reclaimed wood. We can display an array of pastries and desserts on slate and glass."

Benson rested a finger on his cheek. "I recently ran across a photo of a space that had rows of mismatched chairs surrounding tables made of smooth, light oak. You could have a small barista station at one end."

Aubrey's eyes sparkled. "I've always wanted chalkboards to list the day's specials. My handwriting isn't elegant at all, but maybe Starr can try."

"Based on these ideas, the most expensive parts will be the labor for the tile, wood polishing, and kitchen build out. You can find furniture. Do you like to go antiquing?" Benson asked with a raised eyebrow.

"I love to go antiquing, but who has the time? I think Nicole knows a vendor who can help with that."

"Nicole is very resourceful. She's helped me a lot," Benson admitted.

"Oh? With what?"

Aubrey studied Benson as his expression shifted, catching him off-guard, like a child found with their hand in the cookie jar.

"She's an excellent writer. I believe my restaurant stays full because of her reviews."

Aubrey nodded. "She is good."

Benson walked toward Aubrey. Did he sense her sudden wave of sadness?

He came from behind and wrapped his arms around her shoulders and kissed her cheek. "What's wrong?"

Aubrey sighed. "I'm not sure I have the finances to build the bakery. My parents are refusing to help me. They are really upset that I overspent with the purpose of this space."

"They really do have a hold on you." He rested his chin on her shoulder. "Do you have any ideas?"

"I can begin with the portion of the Chef Supreme winning. I already spent a chunk on the ovens."

"Speaking of Chef Supreme, have you received any emails with offers and proposals because of that contest?"

"I have. But nothing substantial. You?"

"Same."

Aubrey turned to face Benson. "We should really figure out a way to capitalize on that win."

"I agree. We can always ask Piper her thoughts."

Aubrey let out a soft laugh. "How would that look? Us coming to her for ideas. As a pair."

Shrugging, Benson said, "She would know just by looking at our faces."

"It would be that obvious?"

"Yep."

Aubrey took Benson's hand and began walking toward the door. "We aren't in a relationship."

Mouth gaping open, Benson said, "We're not? Friends with benefits is a kind of relationship."

Flashing the "OK" sign, Aubrey said, "Yes. We are."

Chapter 29

Benson

Whenever Benson and Aubrey were together, he found himself looking at her, eyes trailing her every move. He couldn't get enough of her. When she laughed, it pulled something out of him he didn't know he had. When she wasn't around, his mind drifted back to her—scanning his phone for her latest reply, thinking of her smile while he stirred a pot in his restaurant kitchen. During those quiet afternoons, they'd sit side by side over coffee or sharing a quick bite in her bustling restaurant. His text messages were sent just to get a laugh or a quick reply from her. They made him smile every time.

At the end of a long shift, it was common for them to unwind over drinks, catching up on everything and nothing. Benson showered her with thoughtful gifts, each one a subtle reminder she was always on his mind. A t-shirt emblazoned with *Boss Lady* across the chest brought a huge grin to her beautiful face. He had pens engraved with *Chef Supreme* to add a winning touch to their chef coats, hopefully making her feel celebrated. He could feel her warming to him, easing into his presence. They started sharing lazy rare weekends off, testing new recipes, critiquing cooking competitions with the intensity of the chefs themselves. One night, neither could bring themselves to hang up, their voices lingering until sleep quietly claimed them both.

Benson and Aubrey got into an unspoken rhythm, each day blending into the next, and it was hitting him harder than he was prepared for. She hadn't put a label on it, hadn't hinted at anything more, but he knew it was something. It was getting hard to keep her a secret. For "friends with benefits," it was going too far, wasn't it? Because he was falling—no question about that.

Benson positioned his office fan to blow directly on him as he worked. Why his air conditioning wasn't working in his space on this hot July day was beyond him. Taking the last bite of his burger, he closed the current work orders tab and opened his email tab. Aubrey's Favorites made the best burger in town. He could make a good burger himself, but ordering from her restaurant gave him an excuse to see her. Today, he stood at the kitchen entry waiting for his order. Pulling him into her office, Aubrey wrapped her arms around him in a warm embrace, feeling the tension of the day melt away. Their lips met in a kiss that sparked something electric between them, a kiss so intoxicating it almost urged him to lock the door behind them. In that moment, the playful energy felt deliciously reckless, hinting at the possibility of taking her right on her deck. Friends with benefits could do that. Aubrey with benefits made his body temperature rise. He turned his fan up a notch, with the sudden need for more cool air to put out the heat he felt for her.

The email from Bold Brew Espresso Co. sat on top of Benson's received emails, marked high priority. He clicked it open, and it read,

From: Richard.Douglas@BoldBrewEspressoCo@co
To: Benson@BensonCarter.com
Dear Mr. Carter,

I hope this message finds you well. My name is Richard Douglas, CEO of Bold Brew Espresso Co., a brand dedicated to delivering the finest coffee experience to our customers. We have been following your work and believe that your passion for quality and excellence aligns perfectly with our values. Congratulations, by the way, on your win in the Chef Supreme competition.

We would be thrilled to explore the possibility of having you endorse our coffee company. Your influence and reputation in the industry would greatly help us reach a broader audience and elevate our brand.

We would love to schedule a meeting at your earliest convenience to discuss this collaboration further. Please let us know your availability, and we will do our best to accommodate your schedule.

Thank you for considering this opportunity. We look forward to the possibility of working together!
Warm regards,
Richard Douglas

Without hesitation, Benson replied to Mr. Douglas' request and provided him with a few dates and times he was available to meet and that he was happy to host him at his restaurant. Based on the letter, it was safe to say, the coffee company hadn't learned of the incident in New York. The Bold Brew Espresso Co. was one of the biggest coffee suppliers to all the mid to high range restaurants. They monopolized the entertainment industry by supplying to all the movie companies, set locations, and concert venues. This offer was not to be taken lightly. Did Aubrey get the same email? A surge of excitement bubbled inside of him, the kind that made his heart race. He wanted nothing more than to run and share the news of this opportunity with her. After all, they talked almost every day. She had quickly become one of his closest friends. However, she was the only close friend that had the pleasure of seeing him naked. But if she didn't get the email, how would the news make her feel? Ultimately, he chose against sharing the news until after their meeting.

The executives from Bold Brew Espresso Co. sent a car to pick Benson up from his home. He arrived ten minutes prior to his scheduled meeting and was asked to wait in a room. The space was sleek and modern; glass walls framed a view of the city below. He sat at the head of the polished conference table, his fingers tapping on the surface as he waited for the management team to arrive. He straightened his dark gray suit jacket. The faintest tension was visible in the set of his jaw. He spent days preparing for this meeting. He glanced at the clock, his nerves creeping in.

When the door swung open, the team filed in. Three executives were dressed in sharply tailored suits, their confident strides matching the intensity in their eyes.

"Hello. I'm Richard Douglas." He stretched his hand out to shake Benson's hand. "Thank you for meeting with us today."

Benson nodded. "Thank you for making the time. I'm eager to hear what you have in mind."

After a round of introductions, everyone took their seats. Mr. Douglas slid a folder across to Benson containing slides with numbers. "As you know, we've been looking for a high profile culinary brand to partner with, someone with the potential to expand beyond what's already been achieved in your restaurant. We think your name and your unique style, along with the title of Chef Supreme, could be a perfect fit."

Mr. Douglas clicked the remote he held in his hand. A large screen lit up with statistics, projected images of his dishes, his restaurant decor, and a few video clips from the contest. "Since the opening of your restaurant, your social media presence has grown. We'd like you to expand into exclusive branding, and ask you to exclusively promote and serve our coffee in your restaurant. We envision commercials, public appearances, and the like. We like your image and how the camera loves you."

Benson nodded, considering the numbers they had laid in front of him. It was at that moment Aubrey crossed his mind. "You know, I wasn't the only Chef Supreme crowned in San Francisco."

Mr. Douglas nodded. "Yes, you paired with another chef. Aubrey Carroll, is that right?"

"Yes. Her restaurant is a few doors down from mine. Excuse me if I seem too forward, but did you reach out to her? She will be opening a bakery next door to her restaurant. I'm sure she will be selling coffee to accompany her baked goods."

"Oh." Mr. Douglas considered this news. "What are you suggesting, Mr. Carter?"

"We work well together. I do believe I wouldn't have won without her. Would you consider a dual endorsement deal?" Benson briefly gazed at each executive.

Mr. Douglas rubbed his chin. "I will admit, Mr. Carter. We didn't consider that. It could actually be a solid consideration."

Benson smiled, nodded his head, and clapped his hands together. He said, "Then let's get to work."

Chapter 30

Aubrey

Aubrey and Benson were minutes from signing a high six-figure endorsement deal with Bold Brew Espresso Co. Even her parents couldn't deny this was a good business decision.

The terms of the endorsement outlined for the agreed amount, Aubrey and Benson would exclusively promote Bold Brew Espresso Co. and their products. Their three-year contract would pay them quarterly. In return, they would have opportunities for collaboration on creative concepts for marketing campaigns. This could involve photo shoots, videos, or even product development input. Promotion and marketing would include social media posts, advertisement, and public appearances. At the end of the three years, both parties could decide to renew the deal based on the success of the collaboration.

The camera crew set up lights and angles as Aubrey and Benson sat close, hands intertwined over a steaming cup of coffee.

"Benson, don't hold my hand. We can't let people think we're a couple. We aren't a couple." Aubrey released his hand like it was on fire. She didn't want people to be confused about who they were. On this day and during this shoot, they had to be about business.

"Right." Benson rolled his eyes. "You can fool yourself if you want to," he said with a chuckle.

Aubrey glared at him, trying her best to hold a stern expression, only to break by laughing at herself.

The director shouted instructions to pose while taking a sip from their coffee mugs. Aubrey lifted the mug to her lips, casting Benson a warm smile, and he looked at her, eyes crinkling and mirroring her gesture with his own cup. Flash after flash captured the easy intimacy between them—the stolen glances, the way he brushed a strand of hair from her cheek, their heads leaning together as they studied each other's expressions between takes.

The director approached them before preparing them for the next set of photos. "The camera loves the two of you. I'm not sure if I'm shooting the product or your love story."

"We aren't a couple," Aubrey said abruptly.

"Well, you could've fooled me. These photos are going to sell our coffee and ship you two at the same time." The director raised his camera and gave them a wink.

In another shot, Benson playfully dipped a spoon into her coffee, teasingly offering her a taste, while she laughed and rolled her eyes, leaning into him. The crew moved around them, capturing the chemistry that practically danced in the air. The final shot had them leaning into each other with matching grins, coffee cups in hand, as if caught mid-conversation, comfortable and wrapped in each other's presence, the perfect picture of effortless connection and warmth.

"I gotta say," a member of the ad team approached Aubrey, "we are changing our slogan for your ads. Brewing Moments Together! Not sure if you're selling coffee or a love connection. Either way, we're all in."

Aubrey was seated in a booth in Benson's restaurant, waiting for him to join her for a review of the plans for her bakery. Sipping her lemonade, nibbling on a cheese biscuit, a woman's voice caught her attention.

"Hi. I'm looking for Benson Carter. Is he here?" The brunette, dressed in a midnight blue tube dress, high ponytail, and five-inch heels, stood knowingly, her posture calm but expectant, as if she anticipated her question would be answered and that Benson's greeting would follow without hesitation.

"Is he expecting you?" his hostess asked.

The woman smiled, placed a hand on her hip, and replied, "Yes. He is."

Aubrey turned her body and crossed her arms across her chest, waiting for the show. A flicker of jealousy tightened in her chest as the woman approached Benson as he walked out from the kitchen onto the dining floor.

He walked past the woman, heading toward Aubrey, when she grabbed his elbow.

"Hey, Benson. I stopped by to say..."

Aubrey couldn't hear the conversation over the blood boiling in her ears. Her glare was on Benson, watching his every move. Why was she feeling jealous? They weren't a couple. She had no right to him. So what, they spent a lot of time together? They spent a lot of nights together.

"Thank you for stopping by. I have a meeting right now. Maybe we can talk later," Benson told the woman.

"Hey, beautiful," he greeted Aubrey with a warm smile.

"Hey, yourself. Player," Aubrey clipped.

"Player? What are you talking about, Aubrey?" Benson appeared irritated at her title for him.

Aubrey leaned in and said in a low tone, "Look. The commercials and print ads are bringing a lot of attention to us. But we aren't committed, so you can do what you want."

Benson let out a low laugh. "Babe. Are you referring to the random that stopped me just now? I don't know her."

"She looked very comfortable approaching you."

"Aubrey, are you jealous? You're so cute." Benson flashed his signature smile.

"Oh please. Am I jealous? You wish." Aubrey could feel her face flush.

"Just say it. Claim me right now and make us official," Benson dared.

Aubrey sat, her fingers tapping nervously on the table, her mind racing through every scenario. His words resounded in her mind, tempting her to step into something real, something more than what they had. But fear lingered, like a shadow over her thoughts. What if she opened herself up again, only to be hurt? What if it didn't work? She couldn't shake the feeling that jumping into this would be a leap of faith she wasn't ready to take. The safety of her comfortable routine seemed so much easier, but she couldn't ignore the pull toward him.

Aubrey forced a smile. "Well, aren't you forward? Am I worth your commitment?"

Making a kissy face, Benson said, "Oh, you're worth it. I'll spend a lifetime making you realize you believe it. That you should be mine."

This conversation was getting to be too much for her. She couldn't think about a commitment. Not right now. "Let's just look at these plans, please?" Aubrey pleaded.

"Anything for you."

Aubrey was at the counter, typing Jim and Tara's order into her computer system, when Nicole approached her.

"Can you please explain this?" Nicole flashed a magazine in front of Aubrey. "Hey, Tara. Jim." She gave them quick hugs and turned back to Aubrey.

"Hello to you, my married friend. How are you?" Aubrey let out a gurgled laugh.

"How is married life?" Tara asked Nicole.

Nicole turned her focus to Tara and Jim. "It's amazing. I'm sure you two can attest to that. And how are you two together, in the middle of the day, in uniform?"

"Sometimes our paths cross and we coordinate our lunch time to spend it together. Our schedules are busy and stressful. I need to see my girl to make it through the day." Jim pulled Tara in for a kiss on her cheek.

"I know you enjoy your food and spending time together." Nicole gave Tara and Jim a genuine smile, then turned a sharp gaze back to Aubrey. "Explain this, please?"

"It was good to see you both. I need to have a conversation with

Nicole. Your order will be ready shortly. I'll see you soon?" Aubrey came from around the counter to give her favorite law enforcement couple a hug.

"Of course," Tara said.

Aubrey motioned Nicole to follow her to her office.

"Let me see that." Aubrey snatched the magazine from Nicole. In front of her was one of the ads for Bold Brew Espresso Co. "Oh, that. It's nothing."

"It doesn't look like nothing to me. Are you two together?" Nicole stood expectantly.

"The directors said they got a glimpse of chemistry between me and Benson, so we went with it." Aubrey didn't know how much longer she could keep her secret from her best friend.

"Brewing Moments Together. It looks like you two have been brewing alright." Nicole sat in the chair across from Aubrey's desk.

"This endorsement deal is funding my bakery build out. I had to go with it." Aubrey looked at her friend, silently pleading with her to believe her words.

Nicole sat back in her chair and crossed her arms across her chest. "Bullshit. You forget I know you, Aubrey Carroll."

Aubrey looked down, ready to surrender her truth.

"Okay, okay." With a sigh, Aubrey came clean, telling Nicole everything.

"So, if I'm hearing you, you first kissed in San Francisco. That explains Benson's comment about San Francisco when I met him. Then, you got together one night after work. Benson wanted to talk about it, but you said no and ran, basically."

Aubrey nodded.

"Then, you needed his help at the wedding and he only agreed if you agreed to talk to him about that night."

"Yeah."

"You talk and spend another night together. And since then, you've been in a relationship, unbeknownst to anyone."

Aubrey shook her head repeatedly. "We're not in a relationship."

Nicole laughed out loud. "We are too old for friends with benefits, Aubrey. Face it. You're in a relationship with Benson."

Aubrey sat, looking at her friend. "Maybe I am, but if I put a label on it, I run the risk of getting hurt. Right now, I could walk away at any time."

Nicole frowned. "You can walk away at any time, but can you really walk away from Benson and not feel a thing?"

It was the way his eyes lit up when he spoke to her, something that made her heart flutter. Aubrey told herself it was just convenience, the late-night talks, the spontaneous coffee breaks, and the cute gifts he gave her. But now, when he smiled at her, there was a shift—an intensity that made her second-guess everything she'd convinced herself of. Benson wasn't what she'd planned. He was crossing into territory she hadn't mapped out. She had been fine keeping things casual, just two people enjoying each other's company, no strings. But now, a different kind of tension lingered between them. It was in the small touches, the lingering looks, and the way he seemed to anticipate her every need before she could even ask.

"He's a good guy. I still am not sure what brought him back to L.A., but based on knowing who his mother is, the pressure she puts on me, I can only imagine what she does to her son. I think something happened in New York. He's out for blood, to redeem himself. He has done so much for me. I want to do the same for him."

Nicole nodded. "You don't have to defend him to me. I know he's a good guy. I can imagine New York was hard."

But Aubrey was scared. Scared of giving in to something she didn't know she could handle. Scared of letting herself want him, because that meant trusting him—and trusting someone was a gamble she wasn't sure she could afford anymore. So, she pushed the feeling down, burying it beneath her mask, as if pretending it wasn't there would make it disappear. Deep down, she sensed the trouble closing in on her.

"No. I can't walk away." Aubrey had to fess up to someone. Why not let it be the one person she could truly trust? "I really like him, Nicole. I think our initial interactions were chemistry we both were denying. When I met Benson, I had just broken up with Seth."

"And you haven't been with anyone since Seth. Aubrey, Benson is not Seth. You two have so much in common. You two could really be great together." Nicole reached over to Aubrey, grabbed her hand, and gave it a squeeze. "You spoke the truth and supported me through my grief and realizing my love for Cameron. Let me do the same for you. Don't give Seth the power he holds over you. He doesn't deserve it. Benson is a man who wants to be with you."

The idea of Benson loving Aubrey made her feel lightheaded. "He always jokes that I can just say the word and he will be mine."

Nicole's eyes brightened. "I don't think he's joking, Aubrey."

Aubrey spoke in a low whisper. "And that is exactly what scares me."

Nicole squeezed her hand, then said, "Surrender, Aubrey."

Chapter 31

Aubrey

The morning air was crisp as Aubrey and Benson wandered through the bustling farmer's market. It was filled with vibrant colors and fresh smells.

"What do you think about me grilling these heirloom carrots?" Their vibrant hues caught in the sunlight.

"Those carrots will be amazing with a cut of beef. Add some potatoes." Aubrey had an innate talent for combining food and flavors.

"I like these ripe strawberries. They will pair nicely in a pastry recipe I'm working on, a seasonal cake I want to sell in the bakery." Aubrey held one to her nose, the scent of the fruit was sweet, and tangy.

Benson leaned in, nibbled on her ear, then whispered, "I can think of a few things we can do with those strawberries."

Aubrey's cheeks flamed thinking about him... strawberries. "Oh yeah? I'll pick up a few extra baskets."

He flashed her a seductive grin, then moved to jarred sauces.

The market was a haven for them. For the rest of the morning, they picked fresh ingredients to add for the day's menu specials. Their bond between food and each other was stronger than ever.

Benson carried a handful of bags through the front door of Aubrey's Favorites with her trailing behind with a bag full of fresh peaches.

"Starr? Can you help Benson put these things in the refrigerator, and…" Aubrey's sentence faltered at the sight of Seth sitting in the booth to the far right of the restaurant. He lifted his arm to give her a gentle wave and revealed a tentative smile.

Aubrey's expression turned from joy to anger. The emotion seared her cheeks a fiery red. She walked toward him, stopping short at the edge of the table. "What the hell are you doing here?"

Seth cleared his throat. "Hello, Aubrey. It's been a while."

Aubrey had no words for the man that stood her up. He left her at the altar. Now, he sat in *her* restaurant years later, saying hello like they had recently seen or spoken to each other.

"Well, look who finally decided to show up. It took you… years. Did you get lost in your own mess?" Aubrey's nostrils were flaring.

"I came to see you. I was hoping we could maybe go somewhere and talk." Seth now stood. He now wore his hair in a man bun, tapered on the sides. It fit his handsome face. His trendy look of baggy jeans, Jordans, and a designer hoodie looked good on him. But Aubrey knew the exterior didn't match the interior. He was not a good guy. Nothing could convince her otherwise.

Aubrey took a step back. "It's nice of you to drop by. A little too late, though, don't you think?"

"I know it's been a long time. And I can't make up for lost time. What I can do is apologize and ask for us to at least try to be friends?" Seth's gaze was pleading.

Aubrey inhaled a deep breath. She wanted to make sure her words were clear and hit the target. "Did you run out of excuses, or are you just here to make things even more complicated? You left me at the altar. I didn't hear from you until today, and you expect me to give you my time and space to talk? Why you thought this was a good idea is beyond me."

Seth rubbed the back of his neck. "You're doing well. You have your restaurant, opening a new bakery. You have that amazing endorsement deal. I thought we could talk shop. I have a food truck that's doing well. It would be amazing to see how we could partner..."

"You came here to talk about business? You want a piece of my success." Aubrey was fuming now. "Believe it or not, I know you, Seth. You are an opportunist. You want what's best for you. You wanted my parents' success. You hoped you could gain a piece of their pie while using me for your own personal gain. You never loved me. And I thank God you left me before I made the biggest mistake of my life."

"What's going on here?" Benson asked, looking at Aubrey, then Seth, and back at Aubrey.

"We don't need your help. You can go back into the kitchen," Seth barked.

Benson chuckled under his breath, took a step closer to Seth, and said, "I'm not the help. And if you know so much about Aubrey's business, you should recognize me. I'm the other half of the endorsement deal. Now, I'm asking you again, what's going on? You here to collect what you think is yours? You here to cause confusion and heartache for my girl?"

"Benson. I can handle this." Aubrey stepped between the two men.

"I know you can, Aubrey. But I don't think this fool is going to take your word for it."

Starr appeared, tugging at Aubrey's sleeve. "Come on. You don't have to stand here and talk to him. He lost his chance to explain."

"I don't want to see you in any of my restaurants, ever. Thank you for your visit. You just confirmed all the things I learned about you. My parents were right. You are not worth my time or my heart. Thank you for the closure." Starr pulled Aubrey into a hug and walked her into the back.

"Wait, Starr. I don't want Benson and Seth to get into it." Aubrey stood where they couldn't see her.

"You can leave now, Seth." Aubrey could see Benson's jaw tighten, his fists clenched at his side.

"I'll go now, but I'll be back," Seth promised.

"I don't think so. You missed out on an opportunity of a lifetime. Aubrey is pure gold, and I'm determined to cherish and honor her for it. As a matter of fact, I should shake your hand. If it wasn't for you, I wouldn't have the pleasure of winning her heart. You can go. And if I see you around, I won't be so nice." Benson's glare threw dangers into Seth.

Aubrey put her head into her hands. She bit her lip to contain her tears. She didn't know if the tears for finally letting go of Seth, for good, or for Benson, who was winning her heart.

Chapter 32

Benson

Benson sat across from his dad, savoring the flavors of their Mexican lunch. The aroma of fresh flour tortillas came from the corner of the restaurant, a woman pressing the dough and preparing them for consumption on the spot. Hints of grilled meats and spices tickled his nose.

"Do you want another margarita?" he asked, taking his final sip of his second frosty glass of the sweet and tangy blended icy concoction.

"No, son, two is enough for me." David covered his half filled glass, then lowered his hands, grabbing his index finger, twisting the gold ring. "I'll finish this one, though." He took a chip and dipped it into the flavorful salsa bowl, then took a bite. "So, tell me, son, how are things going?"

"Pretty good, Dad." Benson's eyes sparkled, thinking about his restaurant and Aubrey. "Can I ask you something? Well, I have two questions."

"You can ask me anything, son."

"Why do you always twist that ring on your finger? I've seen you do that for as long as I can remember."

David's smile slipped off of his face. "What's your second question?"

"I know you and Mom are divorced and have been for a long time, but were you ever in love with her? And how did you know?"

David sat back in his chair and lowered his head, obviously thinking about Benon's questions. "Do you think you might be in love?"

Aubrey made Benson fearless. She had a way of looking at him that made him feel exposed, like she could see past the walls he had built around his heart. There was something in her gaze—soft, but intense—that stirred feelings in him he'd never known before. It wasn't just the way she smiled or the way she laughed, but the way she made him want to be better, to open up in a way that was both terrifying and exhilarating. He was sure Piper would be against his feelings.

No other woman had ever made him feel like this, not with the ease that she did. He'd always prided himself on his control, on never letting anyone get too close, too deep. But with her, it was different. When she was near, his pulse quickened in a way he couldn't explain. The tightness in his chest when she wasn't around was a reminder that he had started to care—maybe more than he should.

Her touch had a warmth to it that was unlike anything he had experienced. It wasn't just physical attraction—it was something deeper. It was the way her presence seemed to fill a space that had been empty for so long, making him feel seen in a way he didn't think he could ever be. He didn't know if he was ready for it, but he couldn't deny that every part of him wanted to explore whatever this was, even if it meant giving up the control he had so carefully guarded.

For the first time in his life, he wondered if there was more to love than just passion—with her, it was possible to feel both the thrill and the comfort that came with being truly known.

The idea of loving Aubrey lit up within him. "Maybe."

David gulped down a steady breath before talking. "Your mother was a different person when we met. We were young. She was just beginning her culinary career. I was working in a food distribution warehouse, trying to learn all I could to open my own. That's how your mom and I met, you know. She came into the warehouse wanting to set up an account. I asked her out, and that was it. Even though our schedules were busy, we were together." A soft smile played on David's lips. "We were married six months later."

"That's how you met. But how did you know she was the one?" This was all familiar to Benson. His dad's experience at that warehouse gave him the knowledge to open his own chain of food distribution warehouses, specializing in meats.

"Your mother was charming. She had a magnetic personality. She was confident, ambitious, and she had a good heart. She was a looker. She walked into a room and commanded all eyes to be on her. These were the things that attracted me to her. We wanted the same things. We understood each other. We respected each other. I liked being around her. We had chemistry, an emotional connection. She knew me for who I was and all my potential. And I know she knew I saw her. We had mutual support for each other as people and of our ambitions. We trusted one another with our secrets, our feelings, and what we could become. I was giddy every time I was around her. I didn't want to be around other women. She was it for me." David tipped his margarita glass back, letting a big gulp of the tangy blended drink slide over his tongue.

"What changed? I was so young when you two divorced. I don't remember much." Benson was staring at his dad, intent on absorbing every word he spoke.

"There's so much you don't know, son. But I think you should know the whole truth. You're grown and can handle it." David inhaled a deep breath, then exhaled, eyes on his only child. "You were so young when it all hit the fan. Before I opened my first warehouse, I had an accident. I fell off of a ladder, injuring my back. When you're in constant pain, you find unconventional ways to get relief. I developed a pretty bad drug habit."

"A drug habit? This is the first I'm hearing of this. Why didn't you tell me?" Benson was shocked. As much as his mother spoke poorly of his dad, she never revealed this.

"No parent ever wants to tell his son he used to be a drug addict. Your mother hid it from you. She didn't let me see you much in those days. We didn't spend a lot of time together. I only came around when I knew you were at school or at a friend's house. I was embarrassed. By the time my habit got really bad, your mother was on her rapid climb to culinary royalty. I think what broke her was the amount of money I spent to fund my habit."

"I don't know what to say." Benson's eyes widened, brows knitting together as he leaned forward, replaying the words his dad just spoke, trying to make sense of them. The words were almost too unbelievable to be real. "Wait. Is that why you were in and out?"

As a kid, he often noticed strange things about his father's behavior, like how he would sometimes disappear for hours. There were late-night phone calls that always ended abruptly, and he would catch fleeting glimpses of his father's mood swings, from jittery excitement to dark silence. He couldn't quite put the pieces together then, but now, looking back as an adult, he could clearly see the signs: the erratic behavior, the isolation, and the constant need for secrecy. He never understood what was happening, only that something wasn't right. Now, he could name it for what it was: addiction.

David nodded. He waited a few moments, then spoke. "Your mother threatened me with never seeing you or her again if I didn't get clean. It was as if an ice bucket was dumped on my head. I woke up and went right into rehab."

"How was that? Rehab, I mean?"

"One of the hardest things I ever had to do. I wanted to save my family. I loved you and your mother too much to lose you."

"How long were you in rehab?"

"I was away for ninety days. I continued an outpatient program for a year after that."

"And you still go to the meetings. Your meetings are on Tuesdays nights, huh?" Benson recalled so many times he would try to reach his dad on Tuesdays, his less hectic day of the week, unable to connect with him. "Is this what led to your divorce?"

"By the time I got out, I realized my destruction. Your mother filed for bankruptcy. She almost lost her business. During the whole time I was in rehab, I had no contact with your mother. I focused on healing and sobriety. I bought this gold ring as a reminder of my struggles. I never take it off. I twirl it to soothe my thoughts. I've been sober for over twenty years now, but sometimes you get these notions, you know?"

"Dad. I had no idea. I'm glad you have coping mechanisms to help you. But what happened when you got out of rehab?" Benson could see his father's nostrils flare with a hint of emotion.

David drew in a lungful of air. "I went straight to the house. It was the early afternoon. You were still in school. It was on a Monday. I knew your mom would be home because Mondays were her days to relax and..."

"And what, dad?"

David twirled his ring and sighed. "I found your mother with another man."

A heavy weight immediately settled in Benson's chest, pulling him down as the words echoed in his mind. He was momentarily breathless.

"Breathe, son. Take some breaths." David motioned to the glass of water. "Take a sip of water, please."

Benson downed the entire glass. "So, she cheated on you?"

"Yes. She had been with this man for some time. He was a business associate. It was easy to cover it up. They worked together. I wasn't in my right mind. It was easy to get away with it."

Benson's thoughts collided like a wind storm swirling around in a dizzying haze. He grappled for clarity amid the sudden chaos of this truth. "A business associate? Is this why she preaches to not get involved with people I work with? Why is she so insistent that relationships are a distraction?"

"I know your mother is extremely hard on you. It seemed to get worse the older you became. I think your mother has loved you out of fear. Fear of you making her mistakes."

"Hell, she didn't want history to repeat itself. My mother is a hypocrite." Benson's jaw tensed, knowing now of his mother's lies, each one like a fresh cut he hadn't allowed himself to feel until now. The way she'd weave stories to cover up the truth replayed in his mind like a broken record. He'd spent so long convincing himself that denying himself was part of the big picture. That it didn't matter in the big scheme of success, but now, with each recollection, the weight of her deceit pressed harder on his chest. He could now see the cracks in her words, the way she twisted reality to fit her own needs. And it stung deeper than he cared to admit.

"Whoa, son. Your mother and I may not be the best friends, but I won't let you bad mouth her. You have to understand the circumstances. What happened, what she did, was inexcusable, but I understand it. She is the love of my life. I still, to this day, love her. She is the mother of my son. You."

"Why are you protecting her, Dad? She cheated on you. She ruined our family. She wasn't there for you when you needed her most. She's been deflecting her behavior and pushing her crazy notions on me." Benson's head throbbed like a relentless drum, each pulse sending a sound wave of the turmoil within him. Yet, amidst all the noise, a flicker of understanding began emerging from this conversation. Insight cut through the fog, illuminating a path ahead, offering a sense of direction he desperately needed.

Chapter 33

Aubrey

The kitchen was alive with energy as the clock began ticking down for Los Angeles' version of a Chef Supreme cooking competition. With the success of their endorsement deal, The Recipe to Table Network reached out to Aubrey and Benson with an idea to crown one Chef Supreme. Both chefs being in Los Angeles put a unique spin on things. Only one chef would be crowned, but both would take home a hunk of cash.

Aubrey glanced over to Benson's station, then mouthed, "I'm going to beat you."

"You wish. I'm Chef Supreme," he mouthed.

Aubrey and Benson were armed with an array of the fresh ingredients to prepare their winning entrées. He was to make his pork chops, grilled broccolini, butternut squash and chocolate souffle for dessert. She was making her collard green spring rolls, fried chicken, sauteed green beans and macaroni and cheese with her lemon pound cake. Who would outdo the other with their culinary skills and be crowned Chef Supreme? It was up to the judges.

Both of them had a lot at stake. This win would be another proof to Aubrey's parents she could stand on her own two feet. Benson needed to get in good graces with his mother. Her competitiveness kicked in with fierce determination. There was no way she was going to lose this one.

Benson worked with precision, his eyes focused as he skillfully cut the pork into chops, just like his dad taught him. His station was immaculate, each ingredient carefully measured and placed as he prepared his entrée. He moved quickly, his hands a blur as he expertly seasoned and plated with a top tiered chef's touch.

Aubrey, working across from him, was a whirlwind of creativity. She quickly mixed her macaroni and cheese together, added them to individual serving ceramic dishes, and put it into the oven to bake. She seasoned her chicken pieces and got them into the fryer, then quickly cut her collard greens, stirring in the flavorful seasonings. Her gaze lingered to Benson, heart strings pulling at the thought of losing to him. He needed this win more than she did. Even though she wanted to show her parents she could stand on her own two feet, Benson had more to prove. She grabbed the sugar and scooped a few heaping scoops into her pot of collard greens. She finished with a flourish, adding glaze to her lemon pound cake.

The judges observed closely. Benson's pork chops were perfectly cooked, the butternut squash adding beautiful color to the plate. Aubrey's fried chicken was a revelation and famous in its own right. The chicken was tender, melt-in-your-mouth perfection, with a depth of flavor that lingered long after the bite.

As the timer buzzed, both chefs stood back. Benson winked at Aubrey, then turned his attention to the judges, waiting for the verdict. The competition was like a regular day to her. She and Benson had experience being in the kitchen together, whether working as a team or in competition. It was clear that both dishes were a reflection of their makers' talents—each a true contender in their own right.

The judges took their first bites of Benson's plate.

The first judge spoke. "The pork chop is perfectly seared, the crust crispy and golden, while the inside remains tender and juicy. I'm savoring the rich, smoky seasoning that enhances the meat without overpowering it.

Another judge tasted the butternut squash. "Its natural sweetness is intensified by a subtle hint of cinnamon and nutmeg. The texture is smooth, almost buttery, complementing the savory depth of the pork chop. The broccolini adds a bright contrast—its slight bitterness balanced by a delicate char and a drizzle of olive oil. The crisp-tender stalks offered just the right amount of crunch, bringing a fresh, earthy note to the plate."

The third judge rounded out their thoughts. "Each bite was a harmony of textures and flavors, the entrée coming together in a way that showcased Chef Benson's expertise and attention to detail."

The judges exchanged looks of approval, nodding as they took in the complexity and precision of the meal.

The three of them moved to Aubrey's plate. One judge took a bite of his piece of the fried chicken, crispy and golden. He nodded in approval.

"The macaroni and cheese is creamy, flavorful. It melts in your mouth, really," one chef confessed.

But it was the tasting of the collard greens that Aubrey was certain would do her in.

"Collard greens are normally rich and earthy. However, these greens are drenched in a syrupy sweetness that clashes with their natural bitterness. The usual smoky, tangy notes are absent, replaced by a cloying flavor that makes the dish feel more like a dessert than a vegetable side."

The judges collaborated in conversation, one preparing to announce L.A.'s Chef Supreme.

"And our winner, Los Angeles' Chef Supreme: Benson Carter."

Chapter 34

Aubrey

Aubrey eased her car into her parking space, the engine's hum fading into the silence of the morning as she turned the key. She lingered in the stillness, staring out the windshield, lost in a whirlwind of thoughts that buzzed in her mind like summer bees flitting from flower to flower, each idea vibrant and lively, yet elusive, making it difficult to settle on just one. Images of Benson, her restaurant, the sting of her parent's refusal to lend financial support, and the excitement mixed with anxiety about the bakery's opening mentally floated, circling like a Ferris wheel at a carnival. Business was better than it ever was with her endorsement. The money from the endorsement deal funded the build out of her bakery. In just a few weeks the bakery would be opening and it had her heart racing, a mix of excitement and nerves churning in her stomach. The pressure was mounting, knowing the two people she wanted to impress most were her parents. She was standing on her two feet, out of their protective hold. She wanted them to be proud and move on from the devastation of her sister's death all those years ago.

Benson was quickly capturing Aubrey's heart. Their connection was authentic, something they both initially ignored, but now, it was undeniable. They shared so many real, unguarded moments of attraction, emotion, and feeling. She felt heard, supported, and encouraged around him. Seth didn't hear her. He only focused on what he wanted and made it seem like a joint goal. He was, in many ways, threatened by her parents and their success, likely feeling he couldn't provide or live up to their unspoken expectations.

Benson encourages her to dream bigger, to push beyond what she believed to be possible. With each conversation, her trust for him grew, creating a connection that was both thrilling and secure. Maybe it was time for them to have that talk. The one she long sensed he was ready to have. Could she see herself in a real relationship with Benson? She was falling for him. Maybe she already fell for his charms, his winning smile, and for his beautiful heart.

Aubrey stepped through the front door, the jingle of her keys in hand as she took in the stillness of the empty restaurant. But there, at one of the tables usually filled with lively patrons, sat a man, calmly scrolling on his phone, as if he belonged. They weren't due open for another hour. She approached him with a mix of surprise and suspicion, her voice firm but polite.

"Can I help you?"

"Hello. My name is Steven Niles, from the New York Daily News."

With him now standing, Aubrey accepted his outstretched hand and shook it.

"I'm Aubrey Carroll."

"Your manager, Starr, let me in. I hope you don't mind. I'm doing a story on restaurants, their successes and failures. This establishment is new to me. I've seen you, though, on the Bold Brew Espresso Co. commercials and print ads."

"Please, Mr. Niles. Sit. Can I get you anything?" Aubrey stood, tote bag still on her shoulder.

"Starr offered coffee and a slice of your lemon pound cake. The best I've ever tasted. I'm fine now, thank you."

Aubrey glanced at the empty crumb filled plate and coffee mug sitting at the corner of the table. "Do you want to ask me some questions?"

"Please. Can we sit?" Mr. Niles held out his hand, motioning Aubrey to join him.

Just as she sat, Starr entered the room. "Oh, boss lady. You're here. Good. Do you need me?" Starr glanced at her, then to Mr. Niles, brow raising in curiosity.

"We're good. Thank you. I'm sure Mr. Niles will only be a short while."

"Yes." He pulled out a notepad and pen from his messenger bag next to him. "How long have you had this restaurant, Ms. Carroll?"

"I've had this restaurant for about five years."

"Did you always know you wanted to open a restaurant?" Mr. Niles wrote something on his notepad.

"Yes. My family owns a string of coffee shops. It was there I learned a few things about the business. I wanted to try to see if I could succeed with my own business." Maybe she shared too much. It was an interview about restaurants, though. People liked the origin of where the idea of a restaurant came from.

"Where did you learn to cook?"

"I learned a few tricks of the trade from my father, but I'm professionally trained. I went to culinary school." Looking at Mr. Niles, she notices a mixture of curiosity and hesitation in his expression. With each question, his eyebrows lifted slightly, eyes squinting as if anxiously waiting for her to stop talking so he can ask the next question.

"I read an article that stated you'll be opening a bakery next door. I'm guessing the lemon pound cake will be the star?"

Aubrey chuckled. "Yes, but like I said, I'm professionally trained. I'm a good cook. Pastry is a specialty."

"The restaurant, Stonewood and Ember, a few doors down. Have you been? I know you and Mr. Carter went to culinary school together. You both won Chef Supreme and have the endorsement deal with Bold Brew Espresso Co."

Aubrey sat for a few seconds, staring into Mr. Niles' eyes. "What did you really come here for, Mr. Niles? Are you interviewing me, or are you here to ask questions about Benson Carter?"

Mr. Niles tapped his notepad with his pen. "How well do you know Mr. Carter?"

"You already know we met in culinary school. Now we are business neighbors. We go back a few years." Her lips pressed into a thin line as he continued questioning.

"Did you ever visit his restaurant in New York? It was the talk of the city."

"I don't travel much." She couldn't muster any other words to this question. Aubrey didn't like where this conversation was going. "I did hear his restaurant in New York was popular."

Mr. Niles made a note on the paper in front of him. Without looking at Aubrey, he asked, "Do you know why it closed?"

"I don't keep up with much news. I'm sure you're going to tell me, though." She gave him a curt smile and sat back in her chair.

"I'm hoping you can help me. Ms. Carroll. I would like to interview Mr. Carter, but he isn't responding to my requests."

"So, you thought you could come here with hopes I can help you? I have a business to run, Mr. Niles. I'm sure whatever business you have with Mr. Carter, you can resolve on your own without me." Aubrey stood, ready to end the conversation.

"Please, Ms. Carroll. I don't mean to upset you. Mr. Carter's fanbase in New York wants a follow up to his abrupt closing of his restaurant." He gave her a pleading look.

Aubrey sat back down. "You have five minutes, Mr. Niles." She wasn't sure what compelled her to sit down and hear him out, but she did.

"The story is, Mr. Carter abruptly closed his overly popular restaurant over a bit of a scandal." He looked at Aubrey to see her nod to continue. "He was up for a prestigious award. It was revealed he was dating a board member. Nepotism is the last thing you want to be accused of when you're trying to build your career. We've been told Mr. Carter ended the relationship immediately, but the woman felt rejected. She proceeded to go on her locally syndicated talk show and social media to slander Mr. Carter's name and restaurant. With her large following, his business fell into a hole. New York audiences take their food and loyalty to a chef and restaurant seriously. Patrons began to question his ability as a chef."

Aubrey's face went ghost white. She quickly put her head down, not to alert Mr. Niles this was news to her. She covered her mouth, raised her head, and gave him another nod.

"My connections confirmed that Piper Ramsey, his mother, tried to erase the incident, but a few stones were left unturned. The woman sold her story, but Ms. Carter paid for that story to die."

Aubrey coughed into her hand, trying to maintain her composure. This news was raw and unintended for her to know. Benson told her only his place was open, then it wasn't. He basically lied to her. Omitting the truth is lying. Piper wasn't obligated to tell her anything. She barely found out Piper was Benson's mother. His mother wouldn't share something so personal about her son. Was she kidding herself? Thinking she was falling for him. Love almost escaped her lips. They were done. Their relationship was over before it started. She was just beginning to trust, and now she hears this. Lying was a non-negotiable offense in her book. How can you have a relationship with someone who hides things from you? He had countless opportunities to share his truth. He chose not to. Was she not important to him? Were they not really friends? Friends share everything. She'd been honest with him. He owed her the truth.

"Mr. Niles, I can't help you. You are going to have to go. With all due respect, please don't come into my place of business under false pretenses. If you want a story, you have to get it from Mr. Carter. Now if you'll excuse me. I have to get ready to open my restaurant."

Aubrey stood. "Starr?" she yelled. "Can you lock the door behind Mr. Niles? Thank you." And with those last words, she hurried into her office, shut the door, and pulled out her phone. She pulled up his contact information and pushed the call button.

Straight to voicemail.

Aubrey was seeing red. The minute she was ready to let her guard down, trusting the warmth of him and what she thought he represented, the truth hit her like a tidal wave. It wasn't something she expected, not in the slightest. She had believed the smile, the soft words, the promises that had been whispered in the quiet of late-night conversations. But now, as the truth unfolded before her eyes, it was as if the ground beneath her was crumbling away. Every piece of the puzzle that was assumed to be complete now had glaring holes in it. Her heart sank as the reality set in, leaving her with nothing but the sharp sting of betrayal and the bitter taste of regret. How had she been so blind?

Aubrey opened the text thread between her and Benson.

Aubrey: I had a visit today from Mr. Niles.

Aubrey: From the New York Daily News

Aubrey: He was happy to share the story of why you are now in L.A.

Aubrey: An award? Going viral? Wow!

Aubrey: You were a superstar.

Aubrey: New York was sorry to see you go.

Aubrey: Now, you're here. Trying to find redemption?

Aubrey: I should have known you were too good to be true. LIAR!

Chapter 35

Benson

People poured in the door, waiting for a table at Stonewood and Ember. Waiters darted between tables with plates balanced effortlessly on their arms, weaving through the maze of chairs, offering welcoming smiles even as they rushed back to the kitchen for the next order.

Benson stood in the open kitchen, calling out orders over the hiss and crackle of sauté pans. The scent of rosemary, garlic, and seared steak wafted through the air, mingling with the delicate notes of truffle from the pasta special and the sweetness of freshly baked bread. Plates slid onto the pass, expertly arranged, each dish a small masterpiece in color and texture. His voice rose above the clamor, keeping the team in sync, his eyes scanning each plate before giving it the nod of approval.

Amidst the bustle, Benson had an open view of the entire restaurant. He watched his new manager discreetly check on tables, her eyes darting from guest to guest to make sure everyone was enjoying their night. With his new manager's help, he was able to assemble a team of highly skilled, enthusiastic hospitality professionals who had restaurant experience. Service became swift and attentive. Positive reviews rolled in, praising the food and the friendly waitstaff.

Noticing the patrons at her station, the manager walked to them. "Can I help you?" Her smile ready, her presence reassuring.

"Yes, we have a reserved table? I'm Nicole Graham-Davis. My party and I are here and ready to be seated." Nicole flashed her media badge.

"Yes, Mrs. Graham-Davis. Follow me." The manager led the party of six to the table near the back, closest to the kitchen. "The chef will be with you shortly, to take your orders personally."

Benson approached the table seating his closest friends in L.A. "Hey, family. How are you? Are you ready to have some good food?"

Cameron stood to give Benson a slap of the hands and a hug. "I hear this is the spot. I'm happy to finally be able to see and enjoy it."

"Good to see you, man. Levi. I see you." Benson eyed the young lady seated next to him. Levi had good taste in women.

There was another couple in their party Benson didn't know.

"Benson, let me introduce you to Jim and Tara Stone. They're friends of ours. I told them about this place, and we are so happy they left their badges at home and could join us."

"It's nice to meet you," they said in unison, holding out their hands to greet him.

Benson doubled his smile. "The pleasure is all mine. I hope you enjoy your meal. I know you're in good company."

As Benson stood making small talk, Starr walked by on her way to the restroom. She paused, recognizing the group at the table.

"Hello, y'all." Starr held up her hand, the light catching her beautiful shiny engagement ring, and flashed it to them all with a proud smile. "I'm engaged!"

"Oh my goodness, Starr. Congratulations!" Nicole stood to give her a congratulatory hug. "When did this happen?"

"Tonight! We just had dinner. Jamaal dropped to one knee and asked me to be his wife."

Squeals of joy went around the table.

"Does Aubrey know yet?" Benson asked.

Starr hugged herself, grinning ear to ear. "Not yet. We're done eating now. Jamaal and I are going to tell her together."

A tremor rippled through his chest. Aubrey. He would give anything to be enjoying a good meal with her. The sensation was so subtle, yet undeniable, catching him off guard. Her face surfaced in his mind, bringing him a mixture of longing and nerves he couldn't ignore. He had to see her tonight.

"What'll you guys have? Or better yet, do you trust me?"

"We trust you," Levi said.

"Let me bring out some of my favorites. A medley of the best on my menu." Benson nodded. The group returned the gesture.

Benson sent a bottle of his best wine to their table. Twenty minutes later, a server arrived with a tray of assorted foods.

"Compliments of Chef Benson." The server set the platters of smoked meats, potatoes, an assortment of grilled vegetables, and his famous cheese biscuits onto the table.

"Thank you," they all said in unison.

Nicole pulled out her phone to snap a picture of the spread. "This all looks delicious."

Benson appeared as soon as she took the photo. "I hope you enjoy everything."

Benson plopped into his office chair and sighed. Business was good, but tonight, he was more tired than usual. There was no time to catch his breath. He slid open his desk drawer, fingers brushing past papers and pens until they landed on his phone. With a quick familiar motion, he pulled it out, the screen lighting up as he held it to his hand. Three missed calls and eight text messages from Aubrey. Without reading the text messages, he dialed her number. No answer. He tried again. This time, it went straight to voicemail. He opened his text messages to read the messages from Aubrey.

His heart wanted to beat out of his chest, reading her words. Mr. Niles. New York. "Liar," Benson said aloud. Aubrey thought he lied to her. He didn't exactly tell her the complete story, but he didn't lie.

Benson had to get to Aubrey. He checked his watch. It was after midnight. She wasn't at her restaurant at this hour. She couldn't be. He took a steadying breath, gripping his phone tighter. He needed to talk to her, to get everything out in the open. The tangled mess of New York, the weight of his mother's expectations, and most of all, his feelings for her—all of it had to be said. He'd been avoiding everything for too long, but deep down, he couldn't hold back anymore. He needed to tell her how much she meant to him, to finally admit out loud that he loved her.

The wail of sirens cut through his office walls, sharp and urgent, jolting him from his thoughts. He froze, ears straining as the sound grew louder, closer, like it was right outside his door. Benson bolted from his office, footsteps pounding through the empty dining room and out the front door, skidding to a halt at the curb. A cloud of thick gray smoke billowed ahead, swirling up toward the night sky. His heart hammered as the flames got dangerously close, stretching toward Aubrey's restaurant. He stood frozen, dread filling every inch of him.

"The bakery," he yelled. Some nights Aubrey tested recipes in the new space. Benson broke into a sprint, racing toward the building, his mind spinning with fear and determination. But before he could get any closer, a firm hand grabbed his arm, stopping him dead in his tracks.

"You can't go any further." The firefighter's eyes were stern beneath the helmet, shaking his head.

Benson was winded and out of breath. "Someone may be in there. Aubrey Carroll. She's the owner. She may have been working when the fire started."

The firefighter lifted his walkie and pushed the side button, then said, "Check the building for a woman. She would have been working when the fire broke out."

Benson's wide eyes scanned the scene, desperately searching for any sign of hope. His chest rose and fell in rapid succession, breaths shallow and shaky. He stood, rooted in place, heart pounding as he waited for someone, anyone, to tell him what was happening.

"It's too early to tell if anyone was in the building. If there was some-one, we'll search for remains when the fire is out," blared through the firefighter's walkie.

"What?" Benson held his head in his hands and said a silent prayer. Aubrey had to be safe. He refused to believe she was in the fire. He padded his pockets, thinking his phone was near when he realized he left it in his office.

Benson turned and jogged back to his restaurant. His phone lay on top of his desk. He lifted it to find no call or messages. He pulled up Aubrey's number and pushed to dial her. It went straight to voicemail. He tried again with the same result. He then called Cameron.

"Hello?" Cameron's voice was groggy, as if half asleep.

"Man, where's Aubrey? There's a fire. I can't find her," Benson said in a panic.

The sound of shuffling came through the phone, Cameron likely sitting up. "A fire. Where?"

"Her bakery's on fire. I can't find her. They said they would have to search for the remains." In a shaky voice, Benson then said, "Can you ask Nicole if she's heard from her?"

"Hold on." Cameron must have put Benson on mute. He didn't hear anything.

A few seconds later, he came back to the line. "She's at her parents' house."

"She's not answering her phone. I need to talk to her." Benson then took a sigh. She was alive.

"If you have a message for her, I can share it," Nicole said. "I'm not sure she wants to speak with you right now, Benson. I'm just being honest. You two have some things to discuss. You'll want to give her some time."

"I've got to see her. I know we need to talk." Benson didn't know how long he could wait. But if there was one thing he knew about Aubrey was that you couldn't push her. He had to be satisfied with the fact that she was safe with her parents.

"Can you just tell her I'm here when she's ready? Tell her I'll tell her everything."

"Sure. Hold on." Nicole must've given the phone to Cameron.

"Man. You have to be patient," Cameron said with a yawn.

"I know. Listen. Can you do me a favor and let me know the damage to her place?"

"I'm sure she's been notified by now. But let me give you some advice. Stay away. Let her come to you. Go home," Cameron said sternly.

"Sure thing, man. Good night." Benson ended the call. Cameron and Nicole were right. Her bakery was likely a total loss. She wasn't speaking to him. This was all an overwhelming tangle of confusion, untold truths, and emotion. All he could do was wait to tell Aubrey everything.

Chapter 36

Benson

Four days later

Benson was in his car, driving to Aubrey's house. He'd waited long enough. She was going to talk to him, one way or another. Starr spilled it. Now that she was engaged, Starr was more talkative than usual. She said Aubrey was at home and she'd been running the restaurant since the fire. One thing he could say about Starr, she was skilled in how to keep the business running with no mishaps.

Benson was around the corner, gathering his thoughts, when his phone rang.

"Cameron. What you got for me?"

With a chuckle, Cameron said, "Well, hello to you, too."

"Sorry, man. How you doin'? What's up?"

Cameron sighed, then said, "The bakery isn't a total loss. The kitchen was the source of the fire. The ovens, to be exact. Insurance should cover most of the cost. She will likely be able to begin rebuilding in about two weeks."

"That's not too bad. Okay." Benson was relieved by this news.

"Where you headed? Levi and I are hoopin' later. You want to join us?" Cameron asked.

"Maybe. I'll give you a call in a bit. I'm on my way to Aubrey's," Benson admitted.

"Is that a good idea? Did she call you?"

"Nope. I need to talk to her. I know her. I know I'm risking it. But I need to come clean." Benson couldn't deny his feelings any longer.

"Nicole told me what happened. Or at least how Aubrey heard it. Is that all true?" Cameron was Benson's close friend. Almost as close as he and Alan were.

"Yeah. I won't deny it. I didn't check her out. I didn't think I needed to. She was New York's favorite foodie. She had the followers and a big audience to prove it. I didn't know she sat on the board and was part of the deciding committee that would determine if I got that award. The biggest mistake of my life." As soon as Benson said that, he had to come clean. "Well, one of the biggest mistakes."

"What's the biggest?" Cameron asked.

"Lying to Aubrey. Well, not telling her the whole truth," Benson admitted.

"You care about her, huh?"

"Cameron, man. I do. I'm losing my mind not being able to talk to her—to tell her everything." He wasn't ashamed to admit it now. He could lose Aubrey.

"Take it from me. I was a complete idiot when Nicole and I were dating. You would've thought my lips were sealed shut, my communication skills were nonexistent." This was the first Benson was hearing about Cameron and Nicole's challenges. They seemed so perfect. "If it weren't for Aubrey, I don't know if Nicole and I would have made it. I don't know what I would do without my baby."

Benson smiled. "Man, you two are perfect. Couple goals. For real."

Cameron was silent for a second. "Good luck, man. You're gonna need it."

"Thanks. I appreciate it." Benson ended the call.

Benson leaned against the door frame, waiting for Aubrey to answer. He could see her shadow through the window. The curtain moved to the side ever so slightly, then back again. Seconds later, she opened the door.

When he finally laid eyes on her, the toll of the fire was written all over her face. Her dark-circled eyes were bloodshot. Dressed in baggy sweatpants and an oversized shirt, hair in a messy bun on top of her head, she looked like someone who'd been carrying the weight of a thousand thoughts. She still radiated beauty. He hoped she wasn't hurt over him. He was here for her, and he was going to prove it. She didn't say a word as she opened the door wider, stepping aside to let him in, her silence speaking louder than anything she could have said.

They stood in silence, her arms crossed over her chest. Benson stood, hands at his side, itching to touch her, pull her in and hold her tight. Aubrey spoke first.

"Where were you, Benson?"

Benson stepped closer, only for Aubrey to step back. "I've been trying to reach you. The night of the fire, I thought you were in the building." He cleared his throat, then continued, "Nicole said you were with your parents, and it was best for me to give you some space."

Aubrey looked down at her bare feet, then looked up at Benson, glaring into him like she could strike him down with her stare. "You lied to me. New York? Why did I have to hear about it from a reporter?"

Benson had to think fast. He wasn't ready for the questions. She knew the story, so he had to say something. "When I came back to L.A., I thought I could put New York behind me. I didn't think the story would follow me."

"You said you wanted to be friends. In San Francisco. You could've told me the truth then, when I asked." Benson could see the pain in Aubrey's eyes.

"We were new friends. We hated each other in culinary school. Remember? We had just reconnected. I was vulnerable. I wasn't going to share such a big part of my life with anyone. Not yet."

"The first night we shared? What about then?" Her lips were tight, nostrils beginning to flare.

"We were tipsy. I was just as shocked as you were, us waking up together. That was not the best time to tell you I fumbled my culinary career because of bad decisions." Benson had to maintain his composure. He was fighting for his life.

"What about the night of the wedding? The next morning, and all the times after that?" Aubrey's voice trembled. "I trusted you, Benson. You know my history, and I told you trust was huge for me. You didn't trust me with that huge piece of your life."

Benson took a few steps to close the distance between them. He reached for her, pulling her into him. Aubrey was hesitant. He got closer, feeling the warmth of her. Just as he was going to put his arms around her, she shoved him away.

A single tear slipped down her cheek, tracing a silent path across her skin. She didn't brush it away, her gaze steady but vulnerable. "I need you to go."

In a low whisper, Benson let out all of what he came to say. "Yes, we dated. I had no idea she sat on the board that would potentially award me my highest honor, being a new chef. As soon as I found out, I told her we couldn't see each other anymore. She used her local celebrity status to destroy me. Her posts went viral. She talked about me on her show. It wasn't good. Benson chuckled, then looked down at Aubrey. Their eyes met. The hurt reflected in her eyes twisted in his gut like a sharp kitchen knife, churning his insides with a wave of nausea. All the unspoken words, every moment of doubt, and the pain was condensed into that one look.

Benson sighed. "My restaurant tanked, like, within forty-eight hours. My name was worthless." He rubbed the back of his neck. "I had to disappear."

Aubrey stared into his eyes. Benson felt bare and exposed. She slowly turned to walk into her living room and sat on the edge of her couch. "You could've told me this sooner."

"I have fear, too. I'm in deep, Aubrey. I waited for the right time to come to tell you. To tell you everything. But…"

"But the right time never came. Right?" She put her head into her hands. After a few seconds, she wiped the tears away and stood. "Benson, you need to go."

Benson knew better than to try to push or get closer to her. "Aubrey. I came to tell you the truth. I came to talk about plans for your bakery and the rebuild."

"I need some space. I was ready to let my guard down, Benson." She fended off a laugh. "I even added sugar to my greens instead of salt, so you could win Chef Supreme. I'm the better chef. With Piper being your mom, I figured you could use a win." She gave him a forced smile. "I was ready to think about a relationship with you, Benson. I don't know now." Aubrey walked to the door, opened it, and looked down at the floor.

Benson stood, threw his head back and took in a deep breath. He walked to Aubrey, stared into her eyes, cupped her face, and softly kissed her lips. "You are the better chef. I didn't miss you adding way too much sugar to your pot of greens. I don't miss much, Aubrey. And I can handle Piper Ramsey. She doesn't scare me. I know I've missed telling you the whole truth. I hope it doesn't cost me, you. Whether you believe me or not, I wanted to tell you I love you."

He released her and slowly walked out. He didn't turn around, didn't look back. He walked to his car, turned the key to start the engine, then slowly pulled away from the curb, onto the street, and headed nowhere.

Chapter 37

Aubrey

Aubrey could still feel the lingering warmth of Benson's soft lips gently pressed on hers, the memory leaving her breath catching in her chest. His whispered "I love you" echoed in her mind, each word stirring emotions that settled deep within her. The ache of missing him was now woven into every heartbeat. Even though she missed him, she took a steady breath and brushed the thoughts of him aside. She couldn't afford to get lost in her love life, or what remained of it. She straightened her shoulders, setting her focus on the tasks ahead. There was work to do. She had to pull herself together.

With determination tightening her resolve, she pushed open her restaurant doors, the familiar scent of pound cake and fried chicken grounding her. Aubrey called her staff together for an impromptu meeting.

"Thank you for being patient and holding everything together in my short absence. As you know, the bakery was to open in a few weeks. The fire has only set us back. We will push forward, rebuild, and open, stronger and better." Aubrey smiled at her staff, holding back the tears.

She had to maintain her strength.

"Boss lady." Starr looked at each one of their team, then at Aubrey. "I think I can speak for all of us. We're happy to have you back. We will do whatever we can to rebuild."

All heads nodded in agreement with Starr's sentiment.

"You know I love you all. Now, let's get to work." Aubrey clasped her hands together and followed the group into the kitchen, each resuming preparation for the lunch crowd.

Aubrey walked into her office, and there they were. A grand bouquet of red roses dominating her desk. The vibrant blooms spilling over in lush waves of crimson. The room was filled with their rich, intoxicating scent. Her heart fluttered as she took in the unexpected sight. They couldn't be from anyone other than Benson. The tips of her fingers grazed the rose petals. She pulled the card from its holder.

I'll spend the rest of my life showing you my truth and loving you.

Her fingers brushed over the words as she read them again, feeling the weight and promise behind each letter. Benson's words were more than a declaration. His words read like a vow, and they left her breathless.

Aubrey wiped a tear from her cheek and then grabbed a tissue to blow her nose when Starr walked into her office.

Eyes turning as big as saucers, she said, "Boss lady! Are those from Benson?"

Aubrey nodded. "Yes."

"Those are from a grown ass man. This bouquet makes my little roses from Jamaal look like we're in middle school." Starr twirled her hair, popping her gum.

"They are beautiful. But we have work to do." Aubrey stood to move the vase to the side table.

"Y'all love each other, huh?"

Aubrey grabbed her chest. "What are you talking about, Starr?"

"I don't say much, but I see everything. You two think you've been hiding your relationship, but I know the signs. You two are good together. I don't know why you fight it. Be happy."

Starr was right. She had been fighting it. She was ready to commit. Then Mr. Niles showed up. Aubrey looked at Starr. She studied her for a moment. She was young, a hard worker, and had a great future ahead of her. She seemed to live with no fear.

"Starr? How do you know so much about love?"

"Boss lady. I read romance books. I have Jamaal. You and Benson are rivals. The classic enemies to lovers, not wanting to admit your true feelings. You two could have a happily ever after, you know."

"Bye, Starr. I need to get some work done before the dinner rush."

Aubrey shuffled through the stack of mail that had accumulated in the short few days she was gone. The large envelope lay squarely in the center of the pile, its edges slightly crinkled as if it had been handled with care. It seemed to pulse with anticipation, holding the answers she dreaded but needed. The cause of the fire was sealed within, waiting to be uncovered. She reached out, her fingers hesitating just above it, knowing that in one swift motion, everything could change. She reached inside her drawer and pulled out the letter opener. With one quick slit across the top of the envelope, its contents awaited reading.

Subject: Claim # 19500413 - Fire Damage at 1920 Main Street

Dear Ms. Carroll,

Following a thorough investigation of the recent fire at 1920 Main Street, our findings indicate that the fire originated from the commercial ovens in the kitchen area. A malfunction in the stove's electrical components appears to have caused the ignition, leading to the fire damage sustained.

Please note that this finding will be used to evaluate coverage under your policy. Our claims team will reach out shortly to discuss the next steps in processing your claim.

Aubrey sat back in her chair. The commercial ovens? The expensive splurge she had to have was the cause of the fire in her bakery? A sinking feeling settled in her chest as she realized the weight of what she'd done. It was one of the few business decisions she made on her own, and in an instant, devastation was the outcome. Her parents laid out their expectations and conditions, and she defied them in every way. First, the property purchase. She squandered a huge sum on the ovens. They denied financial help to build out her bakery. She'd found her own way and money to open the bakery. Now she had to clean up and rebuild because of a poor decision. The reality of her business estrangement from her parents was a stark and cold path she had chosen to follow on her own.

Aubrey paced her office, her mind swirling with the endless tasks ahead. Realizing she needed guidance, someone who could help her clear the fog and help her take her next steps, she found herself reaching for her phone, pulling up her dad's contact information.

"No," she said firmly. Aubrey always went to her dad. He couldn't rescue her. Not this time. She wasn't used to asking for help from anyone other than her dad. He denied her once. She had to do this on her own.

Aubrey grabbed her keys and tote bag. "Starr. You're in charge."

"Where are you going?" Starr finished wiping the counter. "Oh, go get your man, girl," she said, pumping her fists.

Aubrey didn't look back. She just waved her hand and walked to her car.

Chapter 38

Benson

Benson looked up, startled by the knock on his door. On his day off, the last thing he expected was someone visiting him. Setting down his ice tea, he rose slowly, wondering who it could be.

Opening the door, he was met with her familiar face, slightly flushed, eyes filled with a mix of determination and hesitation. Aubrey shifted her weight, clearly as uncertain as he was.

"I... I hope this isn't a bad time," she began, glancing past him as if she hadn't quite expected him to be home.

Benson leaned against the doorframe. "You know it's my day off, right?"

Aubrey managed a sheepish grin. "That's actually why I'm here."

"Come in." Benson stepped aside to watch her walk in. He was ecstatic to see Aubrey. He had to play it cool, though. He poured his heart out with the few words he wrote on the card attached to the flowers. It was her turn to talk.

Aubrey set her tote bag on the edge of the couch, standing with her arms folded across her chest. "I need your help."

Benson sat down and took a sip of his ice tea. He turned the television off and gave Aubrey his full attention. "Help with what?"

"The fire was caused by the commercial ovens. I want to rebuild in time for the original opening day." She now sat at the edge of the couch, facing him.

"Did you already get the insurance money? How do you plan to do that?" Benson rubbed his chin, waiting for her response.

"No. That won't come for weeks. The end of the quarter is coming up. An endorsement check. I figured I could use that. I just don't know if it will cover the repairs."

"So, you want me to front the difference?" Benson looked at her with an inquisitive expression.

"No. I don't want your money. I want you to help me with a plan." She was now sitting with her legs crossed, hands resting in her lap.

They sat in silence. Benson stood. "Do you want something to drink?"

Aubrey shook her head. "You aren't going to answer my question?"

"I thought the fact that I'm always willing to help you was an obvious answer," he replied, smirking. "Guess I just needed to let that sink in for you."

"Careful. I wouldn't want that ego of yours to drown."

"You have such a smart mouth for someone who came over here asking for help," Benson said, moving in on Aubrey.

She sat, pouting on the couch and appearing to ignore his proximity.

Benson sat next to Aubrey, leaned over to her and whispered, "I'll help you on one condition."

"You and your conditions."

Aubrey shivered at Benson's closeness. "I'll help you only if you let me kiss you." He could see her cheeks flush pink. She was so sexy.

Aubrey tilted her head, giving Benson more access to her neck.

"You know I love you, right?" Benson began planting soft kisses behind her ear, down her neck, on her cheek. His lips were grazing the side of her mouth when he said, "I do just about anything for the woman I love. You, Aubrey, are that woman, my love."

Aubrey turned, grabbed his face, and kissed him. Their kiss was rushed, urgent.

Benson laid Aubrey on the couch, not breaking their embrace.

"I need you. Now," Aubrey barked.

They didn't bother to remove their tops. He rushed into his room, got a condom, and returned to the couch, pants at his ankles. Aubrey dropped her pants to her ankles and welcomed Benson between her legs.

He pressed his mouth onto hers, not slowing his kiss as he put on the condom. He nudged Aubrey's entrance. Blocked by her underwear, he slid them to the side and thrusted inside of her.

"Yes. Yes. Yes," Aubrey cried.

Benson's movements were strong. He pumped into her with intensity and purpose.

"Aubrey. Baby. You forgive me? Please forgive me," he begged.

"I forgive you." She moaned.

Aubrey went rigid, trembling with orgasm. Benson followed her, collapsing on top of her, out of breath, smiling into her neck.

"I love you, girl."

Aubrey lay nestled in Benson's bed, her breathing soft and steady. She lay there with a blend of wonder and longing. Last night, she'd come to him in a whirlwind of frustration. She didn't have a plan. Being an independent woman, a pillar of strength, she let her guard down, showing vulnerability. In the hazy glow of the early morning sun, reality set in. If he truly wanted to win her heart, he now had to give her the space she needed, to let her come to terms with all they'd shared and all he hoped for. He loved her deeply, and he would prove it—not by holding on too tightly, but by trusting that she would love him when she was ready.

After their call earlier in the day, Cameron's text message to Benson confirmed the estimation of what it would cost to rebuild Aubrey's bakery. It was steep. He told Aubrey he would help her. He wasn't about to go back on his word.

It was before eight in the morning. Benson sat in his office, leaned back in his chair, hands holding the back of his head. The numbers played over and over in his mind, each one adding up to be the cost of a lifetime. The bakery had been Aubrey's dream, her passion, and watching it reduced to rubble was like watching her heart break. He wanted nothing more than to help her rebuild, to see her smile behind the counter of Aubrey's Sweets, but how could he manage it without her catching on? Every idea he came up with led back to one problem—she'd never accept his help. His mind raced with possibilities, desperate to find a way to quietly step in, to put her dream back together piece by piece, all while staying hidden in the background.

"Christy!" Benson said as he slammed his hand on top of his desk. He grabbed his phone, pulled up her contact information, and pressed the button to dial her number.

After five rings, Christy answered his call. "Hello?"

"Good morning, Christy. This is Benson Carter. Do you have time on your calendar to see me today?" Benson could not wait another day. Aubrey had to get her bakery rebuilt.

"Benson? You had to call my cell phone to ask me that? You could've waited until I got in my office. Hold on."

He waited the few seconds it took for Christy to get back to his call.

"I can see you today at ten. Does that work?"

"Yes. Thank you. I'll see you then. Oh. Christy? Are there any standard approaches or legal considerations to keep in mind when providing financial support for a business anonymously?"

"We'll talk about it when you're in my office." She ended the call.

Benson sat outside Christy's office at 9:50 a.m. He took out his phone, a soft smile tugging at his lips as he pulled up the photo he'd snapped early that morning. Aubrey looked peaceful, tangled in his sheets, her hair spilling across the pillow like it belonged there. The sunlight had filtered through the window, casting a gentle glow over her features, and he couldn't resist capturing that moment. Now, looking at it, the heat spread through his chest, realizing just how much this woman meant to him.

"Hello, Mr. Carter." Christy walked past him and opened her office door. "Please come in."

Benson followed her into her office and closed the door. "Thanks again for seeing me this morning."

"I'm sure this is really important. Otherwise, you wouldn't have called me before I even got out of bed." Christy sat behind her desk and motioned for Benson to sit in one of the chairs opposite her.

"It is important. Well, it's important to me." He clasped his hands together and rested them on his lap.

Christy pulled her laptop out of her tote bag, plugged in her power cord that laid across her desk, opened the lid and typed in her password. "What can I do for you?"

Benson leaned forward, glancing around as if ensuring privacy. "Okay, here's the thing. I need to make sure Aubrey can rebuild her bakery. Has she called you? I know you know about the fire and the cost of rebuilding. I want to cover the costs, but I don't want her to know it's from me."

Christy nodded, intrigued. "Got it. But I thought you and Aubrey were rivals. That's what I heard, anyway. What changed?" She looked at Benson, tilted her head, and studied him. "You're in love with her?"

Benson's eyes got wide. Did his heart eyes at the mention of Aubrey's name give him away? "If you must know, yes, I do love her. But when I come to see you, we only discuss business, not my love life."

"No judgment here, Benson. It's about time my friend finds happiness. I have to hear how you made that happen. But let's get down to business. Funding her rebuild can be done, but we'll need to be careful to structure it right. Are you comfortable giving me some guidelines on how much you're looking to spend? And do you want this structured as a donation, loan, or something else?" Christy busied herself punching keys on her laptop while she waited for Benson's response.

He paused thoughtfully. "I've been thinking about that. Let's call it a donation for now. The bakery is her dream. I can't stand the idea of her giving it up. Money shouldn't be the reason she has to walk away from something she built from scratch."

Christy considered the options. "Alright. We'll need to route it in a way that doesn't raise questions for her, especially if it'll be a lump sum. I suggest setting up a new, separate account with restricted access. I can manage the transfers from there to her business."

Benson nodded approvingly. "Perfect. I'll set up the account and give you access. Can you make it look like it's from a grant or maybe a small business relief fund? That way, if she asks, it looks like legitimate support. I'll tell her the truth when the time is right."

"That's actually a smart angle. I can have the funds routed directly to her business account, labeled as support for 'local small business recovery.' She'll see it in her statements, but there will be no identifying details that lead back to you."

Relief spread across Benson's expression. "Exactly what I was hoping for. I'll send you the account details. Once everything is set, we can start with a larger sum to cover construction, and then maybe smaller amounts for equipment or other expenses."

"Got it. I'll keep track of every dollar and make sure it's all documented cleanly. When are you hoping to get this moving?"

Benson smiled. "Yesterday. But really, as soon as possible. Let's set it up, and I'll leave the rest in your capable hands."

"Consider it done. I'll handle everything and keep you updated. She'll never know it came from you. I just have one question though. Where are you getting this money from? Your restaurant is doing really well. But I don't see this kind of money sitting in that account."

Benson nodded gratefully. "Piper Ramsey is not the only one that has made smart business investments." He gave Christy a devilish smile.

"Thanks, Christy. This means more to me than you know."

Chapter 39

Aubrey

Aubrey was used to spending the spare time she had with Benson. She needed time—time to think about her bakery, her restaurant, and her feelings. Her mind was a constant whirlwind, never settling for long. Thoughts of her restaurant consumed her days. Menus to refine, staff to manage, and the never-ending quest to perfect new additions to her daily specials. Late at night, her imagination wandered to the bakery she would soon open. She could almost smell the freshly baked goods and envision the cozy, bustling space filled with customers enjoying her creations. The details spun in her head—recipes, layouts, branding—each idea building her excitement and anxiety.

As if drawn by a force that Aubrey couldn't resist, her thoughts shifted to Benson. She replayed their conversations, analyzed every glance and word, and wondered what it might feel like to intertwine her chaotic life with his. Could he handle her ambition, her endless drive? He was just like her. More importantly, could she make room for him in a world already bursting at the seams with dreams and responsibilities? She couldn't stop herself from dreaming. Of success, of love, the love of

Benson Carter, and of somehow making it all work.

With only three days before Aubrey's Sweets grand opening, she sat alone, feeling the weight of it all, the years of her parents' watchful eyes, always hovering, ready to shield her from unseen threats. They'd always been there, relentless in their protection, guiding her every step as if any stray path would lead to disaster. It stemmed from a love marked by tragedy. Avery. A sister she'd never met, only being a baby when Avery's life was taken. A shadow whose absence left her parents clinging tightly to what remained. Their one precious daughter. She could only imagine the hole Avery's absence left in their hearts, but sometimes, it felt like her life was built around a void she'd never be able to fill.

As Aubrey considered Benson, something shifted. He was so different from the sheltered walls of her life—open, steady, warm. A breath of fresh air in a room that had long felt stifling. She'd been drawn to him cautiously, her own fears making her hesitant, but now she found herself longing for that trust he so patiently offered. Despite her parents' voice echoing in her mind, warning her to be careful, to stay guarded, although her heart was softening. He was good—more than good.

Benson was finally worthy of her trust. The fear of disappointing her parents was there, yes, but her desire for her own life, her own love, outweighed it. And in the quiet of this realization, a release came over her, letting go of the chains of worry that weren't hers to carry. For the first time, she allowed herself to feel the freedom of her own choice, to be vulnerable, and to be truly seen by Benson. She was ready to believe, to love, and to build a life not just within her parents' grasp, but in her own open hands.

Aubrey sat in her bigger office inside her bakery. Organizing her notes, preparing for the press that would be covering her opening, she sensed his presence. It made her heart flutter with excitement. Benson entered her office, clean shaven, dressed in a charcoal suit, crisp white shirt, and black leather dress shoes. She hadn't seen him in a few days.

Aubrey smiled. "To what do I owe this honor? You look delicious."

Benson laughed. "Down girl. We can save that for later." He set a small box on her desk, then sat down in front of her.

Aubrey's eyes got big, panic settling in at the sight of the Tiffany box.

"Don't worry. It's not what you think. One day, though." Benson winked.

"What's this? It's for me?" Aubrey stared at it for a few seconds before looking up at him.

"I know I've been absent for the last several days. I wanted to give you your space. I wanted you to get ready for this big day." Benson rubbed a hand over his mouth. "If nothing else, we are friends. Best friends."

Aubrey nodded. "Best friends with benefits?"

Benson chuckled. "Whether you realize it, we've been fooling no one. You're my best friend. I want you in my life. Today and forever. I don't want to pressure you, but I want to officially let you know my heart belongs to you."

Aubrey rested her head in her hands. Benson was confessing again. She couldn't let him hang out without saying anything. "Can I open the gift?"

He nodded.

"It feels like Christmas." Aubrey untied the white bow. She lifted the lid to see a soft cotton pouch setting on a white pillow. Opening the pouch, she pulled out a locket. "What's inside?"

"Just open it, girl." Benson sat patiently waiting.

Aubrey held the opened box in her hand. "I need to come clean." She inhaled a stuttering breath. "I've been attracted to you since the first day you walked into class. There you stood, behind your station, so handsome. I picked fights because I thought I couldn't have you. I've been in denial about how I feel about you." A tear rolled down her cheek.

Benson stood, leaning to wipe the wetness from her face.

Aubrey gave Benson a warm smile. "I want to open the locket." Her fingers trembled as she struggled to open the locket. Once opened, one side was her baby picture. The baby picture next to her appeared to be her sister. "Is this me and Avery?"

Benson nodded. "I went to your parents. Nicole helped, of course. Your parents and I had a long chat. They gave me the baby pictures. I thought it was important for you to have her close as you venture out on your own, in business and life."

"You went to see my parents?" Aubrey didn't know how to digest his actions. He was there, dressed in a suit, giving her a heartfelt gift.

"I did. We had a good conversation." Benson smiled and chuckled under his breath before continuing. "You are the light of their lives. You are their greatest joy. They admitted being strong protectors, guiding you in business and life. They're ready to let go, Aubrey."

"Let go? What does that mean?" Aubrey didn't understand what her parents revealed to Benson.

"They're ready to entrust you to run your restaurants the way you see fit. They want to see you build this new chapter in your life, at your side, and not as forceful hands that make decisions for you. They're ready to see you soar." Benson nodded.

"I don't know what to say." Aubrey wiped her tears from her face. "Why didn't they share this with me?"

"They will." Benson waited for Aubrey to process his words.

Several moments passed without a spoken word.

"I have a confession to make, Benson." Aubrey unloaded a cleansing breath.

She went misty eyed, then blurted, "I love you. Over and over again, I love you, Benson Carter."

Benson stood and rounded her desk to take Aubrey into his arms. "How long have you been holding that in?"

Aubrey rushed Benson, wrapping her arms around his neck, kissing him lightly at first. He deepened the kiss. She savored the taste and smell of him. Benson pulled away.

"I've been holding that for a longer time than I care to admit. I was in denial." A weight lifted off of Aubrey's chest.

Benson lifted Aubrey's chin, giving her a soft-as-silk gaze. "I have to be honest, Aubrey."

"About what? Everything is all out in the open, right?"

"The locket isn't my grand gesture."

"Your grand gesture? What do you mean? I think this locket says it all." Aubrey reached for it and put it on, gripping it before letting it hang around her neck.

"I'm the anonymous donor," Benson admitted.

Aubrey looked up at him, her eyes searching for his meaning. "What do you mean?"

"I donated the money to rebuild your bakery." Benson stepped back, gazing into her eyes.

Aubrey put her head down, processing his words. He was the anonymous donor, clearing the path for her to rebuild in time to keep her opening date. Her instinct was to be angry. She told him she didn't want his money, but she loved him.

"Is this what you do for love?" She grabbed his hand, kissed his palm.

"I didn't want to lie to you. It's just the beginning." He pulled her into a tight hug, then kissed her on her forehead.

Chapter 40

Benson

Benson stood in Aubrey's Sweets kitchen, now in a chef's coat, ready to work. "Where do you want me?" he asked the star of the day.

"That's a loaded question." Aubrey winked. "Can you chop apples for the mini tarts?"

"Anything for you." Hearts were drawn in his eyes.

In the kitchen, the air was thick with anticipation. Aubrey, Benson, and the sous chefs worked in harmony, their movements fluid as they fell into a familiar rhythm. Cookies went into the oven, croissants came out of the oven, and glaze went on top of lemon pound cake and fruit tarts. She sprinkled flour on the counter, then reached for the rolling pin as he added a dash of cinnamon to a bowl of apples. Their teamwork was effortless, each anticipating the other's next step.

They exchanged quick glances and soft nods, their unspoken communication a testament to their years of experience in the kitchen and their newfound love for one another. When she needed an extra pair of hands to pipe cream into eclairs, he was there, steady and quick, filling each one with the perfect amount. He smiled at the sight of the delicate pastries as she placed them carefully onto a cooling rack, the perfect symmetry making them almost too beautiful to eat.

"Isn't this a sight?" Starr entered the kitchen with empty cake plates waiting to be topped with different designs of wedding and special occasion cakes.

"Hello to you, too, Starr," Benson said, filling pie pans with sugar-coated apples.

"I knew y'all would get it together. My new favorite couple. Besides me and Jamaal, of course." Starr went to the refrigerator to gather the prepared mini cakes.

Benson bent down to whisper to Aubrey, "Is she serious?"

Audrey let out a laugh. "Very much so."

"You are now the new power couple. You both have successful restaurants. I know you will open more. I want to learn how you run your show, Benson. Can I moonlight Stonewood and Ember?"

"Starr!" Aubrey commanded. "You can't leave me."

"I just want to be part of the empire." Starr winked and then focused on the cakes.

The energy in the bakery shifted as the doors swung open and the scent of freshly brewed coffee mixed with the sweet aroma of pastries. The soft clink of the bell above the door was almost drowned out by the steady hum of conversation. Guests trickled in, some grabbing a quick espresso before heading out, others finding cozy corners to settle in with a pastry and a warm drink. The display case, now filled with golden croissants, delicate macarons, and an assortment of pastries, drew eager eyes and hungry hands.

In the corner, a bridal party burst through the door, their excitement palpable as they chattered amongst themselves, their dresses and tuxedos a blur of color. They gravitated toward the cake display, their eyes wide as they took in the selection of cakes and pastries laid out in elegant tiers. One woman, wearing a white dress with a veil still pinned in her hair, stepped forward, her eyes lighting up as she gazed at the cakes.

"I think we found our wedding cake," she said with a grin, turning to her friends. "Can we sample some flavors?"

Aubrey stepped forward. "Are you getting married today? Right now?"

The presumed bride smiled. "Yep. We were on our way to the chapel by the beach. Social media blasted this place. It was on our route. We figured, why not stop and pick up a cake."

"Well, welcome to Aubrey's Sweets. I'm Aubrey." She held out her hand and greeted the soon to be wife. "We'll get some samples of the cakes we have made and you can pick one, okay?"

The team sprang into action. One by one, the baker and pastry chefs pulled small tasting portions from the back, offering slices of vanilla bean, chocolate ganache, and red velvet, each topped with intricate buttercream roses. The bridal party eagerly took bites, discussing flavors and textures, occasionally offering loud exclamations of approval.

After what seemed like endless deliberation, the bride-to-be nodded decisively. "We'll take the red velvet one. To go. Also, can we place an order for an anniversary cake for a party in six months?"

Starr guided the group to the corner while she placed their order. When the cake was boxed up and ready for transport, she said, "Congratulations! Come back and see us soon."

As they left, a wave of new customers flowed in, and the bakery hummed with the energy of a business taking flight. Conversations filled the air, laughter mixed with the clink of silverware, and the place buzzed with electricity. It was a perfect blend of hard work and the promise of new beginnings.

The bustling bakery surrounded Benson and Aubrey, as they greeted customers, hand in hand. They shared a smile, enjoying the simple joy of working together side by side.

"What if we put one of our pictures on the wall? You know, one of the Bold Brew Espresso Co. photos?" Benson suggested.

"Funny. Cute, even, but no."

Then, the door opened, the bell above it chimed. Aubrey and Benson looked up to welcome their newly arrived guests, only to realize it was her parents.

Aubrey reached to give her parents an embrace. "Mom. Dad. It's so good to see you."

"Hello, dear," Tori said, gathering her daughter into a hug.

Bill kissed Aubrey on her cheek. "Hello, Aubrey." He reached for Benson's hand and shook it. "It's nice to see you again, young man."

Aubrey's expression was an acknowledgement, and she asked, "I heard about your conversation. Do you care to share with me your resolutions?"

"Benson came to the house the other day. We had lunch. He wanted to meet us and discuss..." Bill gave Benson a wink. "Business. We discussed business and future plans."

Aubrey's attention focused on Benson, her brows rising in a slow arch. "You discussed business and future plans with my parents? I thought you said you discussed my newly found independence?"

The chime of the doorbell rang. Benson didn't need to look up to know who had entered—he could feel the shift in the air. Piper Ramsey.

Her heels clicked sharply on the floor as she stepped in, and the usual warmth in her eyes was nowhere to be found. She scanned the room, her gaze landing on them. The moment it did, her expression faltered. A deep frown creased her forehead, and her eyes narrowed. She didn't even bother to acknowledge the other customers, her focus locked solely on him and Aubrey.

The room seemed to quiet as she took a few slow steps forward. There was no mistaking the intensity of her glare.

Benson could feel it, even from where he stood. A weight, cold and sharp, settled over him as his mother's disapproval seemed to hang in the air like a cloud. He squeezed Aubrey's hand slightly, a small, reassuring gesture, but even he couldn't shake the uneasy knot forming in his stomach.

"Mom," he said, his voice steady but laced with tension. "It's good to see you. The place looks great, yes?"

Her lips tightened, and for a moment, she said nothing. The silence was thick, but it wasn't long before her voice broke it, dripping with thinly veiled judgment. "I didn't expect to see... *this*," she said, her gaze flicking between them, lingering far too long.

Benson's heart sank. He didn't need to ask what she meant. He had always known her feelings about his choices. But seeing her stand there, in the bakery full of customers, casting such an icy glare at the one person who made him feel truly alive—it stung.

Just then, David walked through the door. He headed straight toward Benson and Aubrey.

"Son. It's good to see you. Thank you for inviting me." David turned to greet Piper. "Piper."

Piper ignored David's greeting. She considered her son, then Aubrey, narrowing her scrutiny at them.

Benson knew Piper was initially there to support Aubrey's bakery, but with the new development, she wasn't here to celebrate. She was here to question them and dismiss their relationship.

The bakery symbolized new beginnings. However, it suddenly felt smaller, colder. Deep down, what he and Aubrey had was real. Despite the weight of her obvious disapproval, he wasn't backing down. Neither was she. They had come this far.

Gulping down a steady breath, Benson held Aubrey's hand a little tighter. "We're happy. I hope you can accept that."

"Aubrey, dear. Can we use your office to talk? My son and I?" Piper asked.

Aubrey nodded, giving Benson's hand a squeeze.

"I'm going, too." David looked at Piper, daring her to object.

Benson led Piper and David into Aubrey's office and closed the door behind them. He crossed his arms across his chest, ready for a fight.

"I don't need to tell you how I feel about you and Aubrey. You are now a couple, yes?" Piper's stare was frightening. Benson was ready today. He had the love of a good woman on his side and the truth.

"Yes, Mother. Aubrey and I are a couple."

"Son, that's wonderful," David said. "Congratulations. She's a wonderful girl."

"Do you realize what you're doing?" Piper asked.

Benson nodded. "I know exactly what I'm doing."

"You do know I know you used your money to help her rebuild this place after the fire." Piper continued her stare at her son.

"I didn't forget you're on my account in name only. I'd bet money you've been keeping tabs on every cent I've spent since you've been on the account. That's fine. Aubrey knows I financed her bakery renovations. We have no more secrets." Benson now sat in Aubrey's chair. "Speaking of secrets, I believe you have some of your own. Come clean, mother."

Piper turned to David, then back to her son. "I don't know what you're talking about."

"No? Are you sure about that?" Benson glared right back, staring his mother directly in her eyes.

Piper stood in silence.

"Well. For my father's sake, I'll get to the point. I know about his past. I know about your affair with your business associate, and I know why you've been a hypocrite all these years. You just don't want to see anyone happy. To know you spread your venom to Aubrey and who knows who else. Well, it didn't work. Truth always prevails, Piper Ramsey," Benson spit.

"Benson, don't be rude." David stood, twirling his ring.

"No disrespect intended. But I'm speaking a language only she understands. Aubrey and I are together and happy. Together, we can accomplish anything we set our minds to. We'll be happy in business and in love. Now if you will excuse me. I'm going back out there to support my girl." Benson stood, gave his mother a glance over, patted his father on the shoulder and opened the door.

"Benson. Wait," Piper pleaded.

He stopped, not facing his mother.

"I'm sorry. I truly am. I pushed my struggles onto you and did my best to prevent you from making my mistakes," Piper confessed.

"What were your mistakes, Mom?" Benson's question was pointed directly at her truth he wanted to come out.

"New York was like history repeating itself." Piper looked at David. He nodded for her to go on with silent permission.

"When your father got out of rehab, he caught me in a compromising position, in our bed, with another man. He was a business associate. He was a vendor. He owned the company that supplied all of my restaurants' wine and alcohol. Your father had been away. His drug habit had taken its toll on our relationship. Our marriage was over. I backed out of it all at a time your father needed my support." Piper's head was down. She sniffled, then rested her head in her hands.

Benson handed her a tissue.

"I only want the best for you. I have to face my issues. I know I was wrong to push my expectations onto you. I hope over time, you can forgive me. I hope Aubrey can forgive me." Piper stood with her head down.

"Mom, I can't speak for Aubrey, but I'm gonna need some time."

"For what it's worth, Aubrey is a lovely girl. If I had to pick a partner for you, it would be her. I'm truly happy for you both. Truly." With that, Piper left the office.

Benson followed her. She whispered something to Aubrey, hugged her, and left.

Benson hurried to Aubrey. "Are you okay?"

Aubrey looked up at Benson. "Yes. I'm fine. I'm sure I have never truly been given a compliment by your mother. But she just congratulated me and asked me to be sure to take care of you."

Benson offered a crooked smile. "Is that right?"

"She loves you, you know."

"Yeah."

Chapter 41

Aubrey

The light outside had dimmed, the sun dipping below the horizon, casting long shadows across the bakery shop floor. The evening had settled in, and the rhythmic clatter of plates and silverware had ceased. Aubrey and Benson began tidying up. He wiped down the counters while she stacked trays and wrapped up ingredients for tomorrow's prep. The kitchen was now calm, the hum of the refrigerator and the occasional drip from the espresso machine the only sounds breaking the silence. The tasks were small, but each one was significant, a part of the puzzle they were solving together.

Aubrey caught Benson's eye, a silent exchange passing between them—a shared understanding of what they built and what was still to come. They had faced challenges, and yet here they were, standing side by side, stronger for it.

They stepped outside into the cool evening air, the door of the bakery gently closing behind them. The stillness of the night surrounded them, drawing them closer together. Their hands brushed, and then intertwined, effortlessly.

"Are you hungry?" Benson asked.

Aubrey's stomach rumbled, thinking of food. "Starving. I had way too much sugar today." She laid her head against Benson's arm.

"Let's pick up some food and go to my place. Make some plans?"

Aubrey lifted her head to look up at Benson. "What kind of plans?"

With wide eyes and a tilted head, Benson fixed her with a look that screamed, "Seriously?"

"You're absolutely adorable when you're completely oblivious to the obvious." He kissed her on her forehead. "Don't you think after a day like today, we don't have things to talk about? Our future. Our future plans together."

Aubrey nodded. "Good point."

"You know I love you, right?"

Aubrey didn't know where Benson was going with his words. "Yes. I love you, too."

"Do you ever think about marriage?"

Marriage? Aubrey hadn't thought about marriage sense... Well, it had been a long while. But the more time she spent with Benson, the more she could see them having a life together. "To be honest, before you? No." She looked up at Benson, searching for a spark of disapproval.

Benson was searching in her eyes. Searching for what, she didn't know. "I've never thought about spending my life with anyone until you."

Aubrey's eyes softened as tears filled them. "I feel the same way, too." Her heart was full when she was around Benson.

"Good to know, babe. Good to know."

After dinner, Aubrey and Benson sat side by side on his couch.

Benson sat up and flashed a look at Aubrey, eyeing her from head to toe. "You look cute in my boxers and t-shirt."

Aubrey smiled. "Your gray sweatpants are a winner in my book. The way they hang on your hips does something to me."

"Oh, yeah?" Benson stood and grabbed Aubrey's hand.

Aubrey yawned. "I'm exhausted."

She sensed he had other plans for them, but sleep was calling her name.

"Before you fall asleep on me, can I kiss you?" Benson asked.

"Please." A flutter of anticipation came over Aubrey at the idea of him asking for a kiss. She had kissed Benson countless times. Feeling his soft lips on hers was a meeting of their souls. She cherished each one.

Benson kissed the side of Aubrey's face. He then kissed each cheek before landing on her lips. This kiss was different. It was sensual, passionate, and it made a promise.

"Wow. What was that for?" Aubrey asked, her eyes sparkling with a distant, dreamy glow.

"Just making a point." Benson smiled, then pulled Aubrey up from the coach and walked her into his bedroom. "Tonight, I just want to hold you. I want to sleep with you under me. I want to wake up knowing you're mine."

Aubrey gave him a sleepy smile. "That sounds amazing."

Benson pulled the covers back, inviting Aubrey in. He covered her, then got in beside her. He spooned her, snuggling as close as he could get without smothering her. They stayed that way until morning.

It was Aubrey's phone alarm that woke her and Benson. She dashed into the bathroom, her movements hurried. When she got out of the shower, she went into the kitchen to see Benson brewing coffee, the rich scent filling the air. A quick glance at the clock made her panic.

Aubrey grinned like a child waiting to open gifts at Christmas. "I have two businesses to run now."

"Yes, you do. You know I'll help." Benson poured the hot liquid into two mugs, handing one to Aubrey. "I was thinking. You have staff to open both stores, right?"

Aubrey sipped her coffee. "Yes, I do. Why?"

"We didn't get to discuss our future together. I know how I want our future to be, though." Benson added sugar to his coffee, stirred, then took a sip.

She held her mug, warming her hands on the hot cup. "I'm here. I'm not going anywhere. We're each other's future, right?"

Benson looked at Aubrey, smiling. "Do you trust me?"

"Yes, I trust you." Aubrey's answer would have been different a few weeks ago.

"Call Starr. Get her to run the show until dinner."

"Ugh? What are you planning?" Aubrey was confused, not knowing what was up Benson's sleeve.

"Are we together?" he asked, knowing the answer. He closed the distance between them and pulled Aubrey into an embrace. He brushed his fingertips along her exposed arms.

"You know we are." Benson's touch was electrifying. "You keep caressing me, and we'll spend the day in bed." She giggled. "What's up?"

"Go home. Change into something white. I'm taking you to celebrate. Meet me back here in two hours." Benson nodded, coaching Aubrey to do the same.

"Okay."

Two hours later, hair freshly curled, dressed in a pair of white fitted pants, strappy gold heels and a white sweater, Aubrey pulled up to see a town car in front of Benson's house. She looked up to see him dressed in a pair of white jeans ripped at the knees and a white cashmere sweater. He stepped out, locked his door, and jogged down the stairs.

"Let's go." He gestured for her to go to the waiting car. He stopped in his tracks, really looking at Aubrey. "You look beautiful. You know that?"

"Thanks. You look good, too."

Seated next to Benson, Aubrey tapped him on the shoulder. "What's going on?"

"It's a surprise. Can I blindfold you?" Benson held up a silk scarf.

"Blindfold me? Are we going to make out in the car?" Aubrey's eyebrows danced at the suggestion.

"Although, that sounds like too much fun, no. You have to trust me." Benson held up a colorful printed scarf.

"This is a sign of complete trust. I hope you don't ruin it."

Benson carefully covered Aubrey's eyes. "I'm not going to ruin it. Now. Sit back, and I'll take the blindfold off when we arrive at our destination."

After roughly twenty minutes, the car stopped.

"Where are we?" Aubrey asked.

Benson removed the scarf. In front of Aubrey was an airplane. A much smaller airplane than the commercial ones she normally flew.

"Come on." Benson grabbed Aubrey's hand and helped her exit the car. He gave her hand a squeeze and intertwined their fingers. He began a slow stroll on the tarmac, headed toward the waiting aircraft.

Aubrey's voice came out low and unsteady. "Benson. Where're we going?"

Benson pulled his phone out of his pocket, scrolled through his contacts, and landed on a name. He pushed the call button and handed the phone to Aubrey.

Aubrey heard a voice on the other end. "Dad? Is that you?"

"Yes, baby. Your mother is here with me. We wanted to say a few things before Benson takes you on a little trip."

Aubrey pulled the phone from her ear, looked at the phone, then at Benson. He nodded. Her hands began to tremble. "Dad?"

"Your mother and I wanted to say you are the light of our lives. Watching you grow into the incredible woman you are today has been our greatest joy. We've been your protectors, your guide, but now it's time for us to let go. We trust you to build your own future without so much of our input. You know business and how to make it successful. You now know your heart. We are so proud of you and want you to be happy for the rest of your life."

Tears were streaming down Aubrey's face. "Dad? Why are you telling me all of this?"

"Benson is a great man, and we think you will be happy with him. We know you will be happy with him."

Benson removed his phone from Aubrey's hands. "Thank you, Mr. Carroll. I'll take it from here."

Aubrey's dad said something, but she couldn't hear.

"Yes, sir. Okay." Benson ended the call.

He stopped and turned to face Aubrey. He inhaled, then exhaled. "Aubrey. From the first day I met you, I knew there was something special about you." He nodded. "Yes, that first day of culinary school. It took a long separation and a career crumbling disaster to bring us together. And I never want to let you go. You're the love of my life. I want to make you my partner, in life and business."

Tears streamed relentlessly down Aubrey's face. Benson pulled her close, wiping her tears with his thumbs. He kissed her wet cheeks, then looked into her eyes. "I will never leave you. You're worth all of my time, all of my heart. I love you. Will you marry me?"

Benson's unexpected question left Aubrey in stunned silence. She should have known what was happening after her phone call with her dad. Her mind was reeling. They hadn't discussed marriage. A wedding was certainly never on her agenda.

Emotions surged, and tears blurred her vision. "Benson. I'm scared."

His eyes glistened, filling with unshed tears. "Baby, I know. I'm scared too. But together, we can do this. I'm nothing without you."

Aubrey nodded repeatedly, her movement now steady and unwavering. "Yes." Just as she reached to give her fiancé a kiss, the sound of familiar voices came from the direction of the plane.

"Come on, girl. We're waiting. Let's get you married!" Nicole yelled, Cameron at her side.

Epilogue

Levi

One week later

The restaurant, perched on the edge of the coast, offering breathtaking views of the ocean, was the perfect backdrop for the special occasion. Levi stood and gave each guest seated around the table a sweeping glance. All were on him. Nicole and Cameron, Jim and Tara, his date, and the newly married couple.

"I'd like to make a toast. To Aubrey and Benson. I've never witnessed two people who seemed to despise each other so intently, only to end up falling deeply in love. You both are special people. You deserve happiness and success. May your love be as deep as the ocean behind us. Cheers to a lifetime of laughter, partnership, and unending love."

Everyone raised their champagne glasses and congratulated the newly married couple.

"Cheers!"

Applause came from around the table. Levi picked up a spoon and lightly tapped it on the water glass in front of him, signaling for Aubrey and Benson to share a kiss. Benson grabbed Aubrey's face and kissed her on the mouth.

Levi applauded the pair, then sat next to his date, stretching his arm across her chair.

"They're a lovely couple," she whispered.

"Yes, they are." Levi took another sip of his champagne, trying to shake his lingering memories of the one who still clung to his heart. He shook his head, turned to his date, then said, "Wanna get out of here?"

Levi was positioning to say his goodbyes, when the loud ringing of a phone broke his exit.

"That's my phone. I'm sorry." Benson stood. "I'm going to take this call outside. It's my business phone. We don't want to miss out on business."

Not wanting to be rude, Levi sat back in his chair and waited for Benson to return to the group to say a proper goodbye.

"Aubrey. So you guys just hopped on a plane, flew to Las Vegas, got married, then went back home to serve dinner at your restaurants?" Tara asked.

"It's kind of crazy. I know. When we landed, we went to the courthouse, got our marriage license, then went to a jeweler to pick out our rings." Aubrey raised her hand to flash her huge diamond solitaire and diamond band.

"How did Benson plan all of this spur of the moment?" Jim wondered out loud.

"I helped. He called me in the wee hours of the morning, asking me to make an appointment at the chapel and the jeweler. The man has a lot of connections." Nicole laughed.

"My friend at the firehouse flew by private jet a few weeks ago. I got his contact and luckily, a pilot was available," Cameron added.

"Did you guys take pictures?" Levi asked.

Nicole reached into her bag to pull out her phone. She tapped on the screen and displayed a picture of Benson and Aubrey, standing at the altar, hand in hand. "See. I even have a video."

Everyone left their seats to gather around her to watch Aubrey and Benson exchange their vows.

Ten minutes later, Benson reappeared.

"Who was that?" Aubrey asked.

Benson looked at Levi, then at Aubrey. "That was Elle Cunningham. She's requesting I cater her engagement party. It's in one month."

Levi's face turned stark pale, a fleeting expression that betrayed his usual composure. The instant her name was mentioned, his heart ached, a sharp pang that reminded him of everything he lost. Everything they lost. His love for Elle was endless, as fresh as the first spark, yet timeless. Forever. Any trace of ease dissolved, leaving him looking as though he'd been struck by a speeding truck.

His jaw tightened, eyes darting away from the table for a split second. He couldn't escape the weight of what was coming. His entire demeanor shifted—stiffened. A deep breath escaped him, one he probably didn't realize he'd been holding, and his expression turned distant, as though steeling himself away from reality. Elle's engagement party. Was she really marrying that dude?

Nicole got up from her chair and walked over to where her brother was sitting.

"Come inside." She grabbed his hand, pulled him up from his seat and led him to the room just inside from their table, out of the sight of others.

Levi's face remained stoic, a mask of stern disbelief barely containing the simmering anger beneath. His jaw clenched, and his eyes crinkled to slits. The shock of this news seized him. Each muscle in his face seemed locked in place, unwilling to reveal anything more than an intense, simmering fury that coiled just beneath the surface.

"I need you to relax," Nicole urged her brother.

His nostrils flared. "Her engagement party? She's really getting married?"

"Levi. You have to let her go," Nicole pleaded.

"No. I will *not* let her go. She's supposed to marry *me*. Not some clown her father arranged for her to marry." Levi's breathing became labored.

"Levi! I need you to calm down." Nicole rubbed his back in an attempt to soothe her brother's disappointment.

Levi released little painted breaths. "If it's the last thing I do, I'll stop that wedding and get my girl back. You have my word."

Acknowledgments

This book is a tribute to my own love of cooking and time spent watching countless cooking shows. I enjoyed writing this book and I hope you enjoyed reading it. Thank you. I appreciate you more than you know.

I want to acknowlege some special people. Without their love and support, this book would not be.

To my hubby... you are my rock and my biggest fan. Without your warm hugs and encouraging words, I wouldn't be able to do what I love to do and that is to write.

To my children, Mason and Maleyni... you are my rays of sunshine. I love you to infinity and beyond.

To my mother, Patricia. Always my cheerleader. I love you.

To my siblings, Afkara and Ray... all about business and love. You inspire me every day.

To my sister/cousin, Carolyn... you bring laughter and inspiration into my world.

To my dear friend and fellow author, Linda B. Martins. Girl! Where would I be without your unwavering encouragement, honest critique, and endless support. I appreciate you so much.

To Cathy Fong, Jade Mason, Leondria Brown, Sarah Cortes, and Tristen Gartrell—the best beta team a writer can ask for. You turned my words into reality. You're amazing.

To artist and friend, Danica Cordell... your talent is incredible. I look forward to our future collaborations.

To Jessica Barna... thank you for holding me accountable and guiding me along this author journey.

Thank you, Sarah Wentworth, for your professionalism and expertise.

To my father and grandfather, radiating down on me from above. You both not only taught me how to cook but also sparked my deep love for great food. Your memories continue to inspire me, my ideas, and my happily ever afters.

About the Author

Kat Neil is a contemporary romance writer who's been devouring happily ever afters for years.

She now crafts swoon-worthy love stories with characters you'll root for on every page. When she's not spinning tales of love, you'll find her buried in a romance novel, indulging in some retail therapy, or binge-watching cooking shows.

She's a devoted wife and mother of two amazing children.

Sign up for Kat Neil's newsletter and get a bonus scene from the In the Name of Love Series: https://katneil.com/newsletter

Follow Kat Neil on Instagram, Threads, and Bluesky: @katneilauthor

Find more information about books by Kat Neil at KatNeil.com and LinkTr.ee/katneil

Titles by Kat Neil

In the Name of Love Series:

Love on Patrol

Love to the Rescue

For the Love of Cooking

Reunited in Love (Coming September 2025)